The President's hesitation gave Price the answer she needed. Her face paled and she threw a glance in McCarter's direction.

"This can't happen," she whispered, her normal composure shattered. "And if it happens, *we* get dragged in?"

"Israel is our friend. We have an unspoken alliance we couldn't just ignore, because it's a given Iran would get support from the one country that will jump at the chance to strengthen its hold in the Mideast."

Price cleared her throat. "You mean, China?"

"Cutting all connections with Israel and stepping back would allow China to gain the advantage in the region. Like it or not, we can't allow that to happen."

"Oil."

"One of the factors I can't deny, or ignore," the President said. "A future scenario of China becoming a fixture in the region would be cutting off oil supplies for us and a good portion of the free world. One thing the U.S. military needs is oil. Without it…we become an endangered species."

DON PENDLETON'S

STONY

AMERICA'S ULTRA-COVERT INTELLIGENCE AGENCY

MAN

NUCLEAR INTENT

A GOLD EAGLE BOOK FROM

WORLDWIDE®

TORONTO • NEW YORK • LONDON
AMSTERDAM • PARIS • SYDNEY • HAMBURG
STOCKHOLM • ATHENS • TOKYO • MILAN
MADRID • WARSAW • BUDAPEST • AUCKLAND

Recycling programs
for this product may
not exist in your area.

First edition April 2013

ISBN-13: 978-0-373-80438-2

NUCLEAR INTENT

Special thanks and acknowledgment to
Mike Linaker for his contribution to this work.

Printed in U.S.A.

NUCLEAR INTENT

CHAPTER ONE

Somalia

The *Boa Vista,* a seagoing motor vessel, was anchored in calm water off the Somalian coast. While that might have been a risky prospect for most people, Raul Inigo had no such problems. He stood at the rail and watched a seaplane land, and waited for one of his speedboats to pick up a visitor.

Inigo had a long-standing arrangement with the local warlord that enabled him to sail the pirate-infested waters with impunity. Not only did the warlord receive regular cash bounties, but Inigo also provided the man's boat crews with ordnance and hard-to-obtain goods. Easy pickings for the pirates. A sanctuary for Inigo. While he was within the jurisdiction of Somalian territory he was sure not to be bothered. It was an arrangement that suited both parties.

The man who stepped on board, wearing a pale, light-weight suit, his shirt open at the neck, was in his mid-forties. He took off the Panama hat as he walked beneath the protection of the aft deck canopy, revealing thick dark hair and a strong-boned face. His eyes were hidden behind sunglasses he took off the moment he followed Inigo into the shaded main cabin.

"Good to see you again, Edgar," Inigo said, taking the man's solid handshake.

Edgar Bergstrom inclined his head. He was a tall, fit-looking man. He sat on one of the soft leather couches, dropping his hat beside him. The expansive cabin was cool from the circulating air.

"Yes. Almost a year since you completed that matter for me in Singapore."

Bergstrom's accent was American, a quiet Midwestern drawl. He never raised his voice, even in a crisis, and he had experienced a number of those.

"Drink?"

Bergstrom nodded. He watched as Inigo went to the wet bar and poured generous amounts of whiskey into thick tumblers. Inigo handed one to his visitor, then sat on a facing couch. They sampled the whiskey, enjoying the mellow taste.

"Obviously I didn't come all this way just to sample your drinks cabinet," Bergstrom said. "I have a proposition. To be exact, two propositions. Though they are both linked. They require your input and the expertise of your organization."

"And discretion?"

Bergstrom smiled. "That goes without saying. This operation is way beyond my normal remit."

"I never thought the CIA had a remit."

"You would be surprised," Bergstrom said. "But even CIA black ops doesn't really figure in this. We don't have the logistical capability."

Inigo leaned forward. "Now you have me interested."

Bergstrom reached into his jacket and took out a slim memory stick. "This will give you everything you'll need to initiate the operation. Names. Locations. Contacts. First phase is to eliminate the person identified. He has data that could hamper the main deal."

Inigo took the stick. He stood and crossed to a high-end laptop that rested on a flat surface, then fired it up and slipped the stick into one of the USB ports. A tap on the keyboard and the file opened. Bergstrom joined him as images filled the screen.

"High-priority target. Jean-Paul Alexis. Field agent who has data he shouldn't be in possession of. He's French. Works for the Central Directorate of Interior Intelligence."

"This CDII agent has learned about your operation?" Inigo said. "And you want him dead?"

"Simply put, yes. He's found some information he shouldn't have."

"If he gets anyone to listen to him, the operation could be compromised?"

"That's the way it could go."

"So, how do you know he hasn't already passed this information on?"

"Because I'm still walking around free and clear. I'm not that vain I believe I could walk away untouched from something like this. Alexis won't know who he can depend on, so he's been moving around, waiting until he can make contact with the one man he *can* trust. A longtime friend who has worked with him before—a CIA agent named Harry Jerome. I want you to handle this because I don't have any of my own people close enough."

"Where is this man Alexis now?"

"Sofia. Bulgaria. Jerome has been on station there for some time. Do you have anyone close?"

"That's no problem," Inigo said. "I can have a team there very quickly. In a few hours."

"Alexis will most likely have the data on him when he goes to meet Jerome. He will want to hand it to him. I need that information. Or know it has been suppressed."

"So, Alexis dead, the data retrieved. And the American?"

"Jerome? Take no chances. He has to die, as well."

Inigo studied the images on his screen. "These are recent photographs."

"Yes. Inigo, I have to keep this under close watch. If there's any suspicion the CIA is involved in any capacity…"

"I understand. Edgar, you should know by now I keep anything between us just that—between us. It does not leave the *Boa Vista*. This is a business deal. If I was a religious man I would be breaking the confessional."

"That's what I like about you, Inigo. You never question why, you don't pass judgment."

Inigo smiled. "Once I start taking sides my business is going to shrivel up and die. Why would I do anything to risk that?"

"And if I said I'm about to start a war?"

Inigo thought for a moment. "I'd most likely have to double my fee."

Bergstrom nodded. "Then we can move on to the next phase."

"Give me a few minutes to speak to my people and kick-start this first operation. I'll have a team on the move within the hour. Go and take a walk around the deck. Relax, Edgar. It's all in hand."

When Bergstrom had stepped from the cabin Inigo picked up the sat phone from the table at his side and tapped a speed-dial number. When it was answered he spoke quickly to the man on the other end.

"I'm sending the mission brief to your laptop. It has everything you need to move. Get a team on it. This has to be done quickly. Time's important. Call when you have something to report."

Inigo crossed to the laptop. He worked the keyboard, sending the contents of Bergstrom's data stick. Once the data had been sent, he withdrew the stick and made his way out of the cabin and rejoined Bergstrom.

"This is where it might get tricky," Bergstrom said. He took out a folded paper and handed it to Inigo.

"An interesting shopping list," Inigo said after reading what was written down.

"A can-do list?"

"Of course. Are we working to a fixed date?"

"Flexible. What makes you ask?"

"Only because the main item may take time to obtain."

"I expected that." Bergstrom turned to lean on the deck rail. He pointed toward the shoreline. "Can you really trust those Somalians? I mean, with their track record."

"They do what they have to in order to survive. I pay them to move around these waters in safety. We trade, too. Money and weapons. Other merchandise. They are businessmen. So, if I can cover some of their needs it becomes an easy option for both parties. I also have a base on Somalian soil."

Bergstrom looked at his empty tumbler. "Thirsty work, these negotiations," he said.

They walked back to the cabin. Once they had refreshed their tumblers Bergstrom broached the subject of finance.

"Understand, Inigo, money is no problem here. I have backing from a number of sources who want this plan to succeed. Funds are already in place. You need up-front finance, just say the word."

"I will work on a figure once I have located the items. As to up-front payments, that will not be needed. I don't expect anything until I deliver. It has always been our way. I see no reason to change that. I pay for everything up front and then present you with the bill at the end."

"I knew you would be the one. This could open new

sources to you, Inigo. The opportunity to make even more money."

Inigo's face broke into a smile. "Edgar, let's hope there will be enough people left alive capable of offering deals if your plan works."

CHAPTER TWO

Sofia, Bulgaria

Jerome had been at the rendezvous for over half an hour. His contact was late and Jerome was starting to become concerned because Jean-Paul Alexis was never late. The French intelligence agent was as dependable as a Swiss watch. Alexis had asked for the meeting, implying he had something important for Jerome. Alexis, who worked for the Central Directorate of Interior Intelligence, or CDII, wasn't one for wasting time on trivial matters. Jerome's concern manifested itself in a nervous bout of checking and rechecking the shadowed street, a fine, cold rain making the uneven surface glisten. Traffic was light in this quiet area of the city. It wasn't exactly the back end of Sofia, but it was far enough away from the main tourist routes that even foot traffic was never heavy. This particular section of the city housed many Turkish immigrants. Behind Jerome the small café, owned and run by a Turkish family, was host to no more than a half dozen locals. The rain had kept most customers away. Jerome finished his third cigarette of the evening and ground the stub underfoot before turning to go back inside. Despite his thick topcoat he was chilled. He decided to indulge in another coffee. There wasn't much else he could do. He would give Alexis another half hour, then quit the rendezvous. There was no way he could make contact with Alexis. The man did not like the way cell phones could be back-traced and always arranged their meets via landline calls to Jerome's field office, always from a public phone so Jerome couldn't call him back.

In the past it had always worked. This time was different. There had been an underlying urgency in Alexis's voice. None of his usual banter. Whatever lay behind the hastily arranged meet had taken away Alexis's light spirit.

Jerome pushed open the door and stepped back inside the low-ceilinged café. The mingled smells of tobacco and roasting coffee beans hit him. Smoke hung at ceiling level, some from the ever-present Turkish cigarettes, more from the meat kebabs being cooked in the small kitchen behind the bar.

"Would you like coffee?" the café owner asked in Turkish.

The American CIA field agent nodded.

The man behind the counter smiled beneath his thick mustache, nodding as he turned to make the coffee. Jerome watched as the man took one of the brass coffeepots, added sugar and ground coffee. After adding cold water and being stirred, he placed the coffeepot on the stove and brought it to a frothing boil three times before pouring the thick, rich brew into a small cup. Jerome let it settle for a minute before he picked up the cup and took a sip. Turkish coffee was never gulped down but was always sipped and the cup not drained unless the drinker wanted a mouthful of gritty coffee grounds. Jerome had learned that lesson the hard way with his first experience. Now he drank slowly, savoring the strong brew. He was acquiring the taste.

"Excellent," Jerome said.

The owner nodded, glancing across Jerome's shoulder. His amiable expression vanished and Jerome turned.

And saw Alexis stumbling to his knees on the other side of the café window. As Alexis fell forward his hand came up to brace himself against the window.

He left a glistening, bloody handprint on the glass as he toppled sideways.

Jerome put down his coffee cup and ran to the café door. He yanked it open and stepped outside, reaching for the Beretta autopistol he carried on his hip, fumbling his topcoat open to get to it.

At the far end of the street a dark SUV began to move forward. Its lights were off. Jerome didn't notice it immediately. His attention was on Alexis, his open jacket exposing a mass of glistening red where someone had used a knife to slash open his lower body. Jerome had never seen so much blood at one time. It was pulsing out of the gaping wound, spilling down to the sidewalk. It was only when the SUV's powerful motor revved that Jerome looked up and saw the vehicle moving toward him.

"Don't worry about me," Alexis whispered. "Take this and go before they catch you. You have a traitor in your Agency. Trust no one."

His left hand jammed something into the pocket of Jerome's topcoat.

"Go," Alexis said again. "They'll kill you, too."

"I can't leave you…." Jerome said.

"I'm already dead," Alexis said. "No point in both of us ending up like that. Now get out of here."

The SUV's tires squealed as power was increased and the heavy vehicle surged forward. A dark figure leaned out of the rear passenger window.

And started to fire on Jerome and Alexis.

Slugs whined off the sidewalk.

Jerome brought his Beretta into play. He put two 9 mm slugs into the shooter, his aim perfect. The shooter fell back inside the SUV. There was no hesitation from the driver. He flat-footed the gas pedal, swerving the big vehicle onto the sidewalk, and aimed it directly at Jerome and Alexis.

"Go," Alexis screamed, bloody hands pushing at Jerome.

Conflicted, Jerome couldn't save his friend without placing himself in direct line with the roaring approach of the SUV. He had seconds left as he realized there was no way he could pull Alexis clear. He made a supreme effort and threw himself across the sidewalk, into the street, landing awkwardly. He sensed the dark bulk of the SUV as it sped by, heard the brief, inhuman squeal as Alexis was crushed beneath the wide tires.

The SUV turned off the sidewalk, rubber skidding as the driver stamped on the brake and brought the vehicle to a jolting stop yards along the street.

Jerome had pushed upright, swinging around as he sensed the SUV coming to a halt.

The front passenger door was pushed open and a second shooter emerged, bringing a stubby SMG into view.

Damn you, Jerome mouthed, and two-handed his Beretta, sighting in even as the new shooter hit the street. He triggered the 9 mm pistol, placing three fast shots into the shooter. The impact slammed the guy back against the open door, his finger jerking the SMG's trigger, sending a stream of slugs skyward.

Even as the shooter started going down Jerome switched his aim and fired in through the rear window, angling his shots in the general direction of the driver's hunched dark shape. Glass shattered and the driver jerked as one of Jerome's shots found its target. The SUV jumped forward then stalled, the sound of the engine dying.

Keeping his Beretta online Jerome moved to where Alexis lay. One swift glance told Jerome there was nothing that could be done for the man. Alexis lay in a pool of blood and viscera, bones and organs exposed.

Jerome could hear the babble of voices as the occupants of the café came outside. The sound of their voices faded as he crossed to the SUV to check out the passengers. Jerome moved from man to man, his face taking on an expression of shock. Two were dead. One was the driver. Jerome's slugs had hit him in the side of the neck, opening a main artery. Blood had pumped from the ragged wound, soaking the target's body and pooling on the seat and floor. The man Jerome had shot first was slumped over in his seat, chest bloody. When Jerome touched the side of his neck he felt a weak, ragged pulse.

Jerome turned away. He holstered his pistol, starting to reach for his cell, then thought better of it. He recalled what Alexis had said.

You have a traitor in your Agency. Trust no one.

He turned away, moving out of the light and into the darkness of an alley. He remembered the object Alexis had slipped into his pocket and took it out. A slim silver flash drive.

The French agent had died delivering it. Jerome knew he needed to get to his hotel to check it out. He also realized he might not have a great deal of time. If Alexis had been spotted, so might he. He had no idea who the enemy was right now, but he did realize they were intent on getting their hands on whatever information Alexis had passed along.

At the end of the alley Jerome emerged on a main street and searched for a taxi. It took him five minutes before he spotted one. He told the driver where he wanted to go, then sank back in the worn seat.

He became aware he had blood on his topcoat. Alexis's blood. He slipped it off before the driver noticed, folding it in his lap. He could feel some blood on his left hand and wiped it away in the folds of his coat. When the taxi stopped outside his hotel Jerome pushed money into the driver's hand and climbed out. He turned and went inside, collected his key and made his way to his room.

He threw down his topcoat and shrugged out of his suit jacket. In the bathroom he washed his hands, seeing the pale swirls of bloodied water vanish down the drain. In the mirror his image stared back at him. He looked pale, hair plastered to his skull. He figured he had a right. He had seen his colleague die and had been forced to kill two men. Not an everyday occurrence in his life. CIA notwithstanding, Harry Jerome was not a seasoned assassin.

Back in the room, toweling his hands and face, he looked around for his laptop. He placed it on the unit and attached the cable connection that gave him access to the internet. He powered up and slipped the flash drive into one of the USB slots. The drive accepted the data stick. Jerome clicked into it and opened the single file. He watched as the screen filled with text and photographic images. He scanned the data, scrolling down the screen.

"Oh, fuck," he breathed quietly.

He sat back, mind racing with the implications of Alexis's data. His next question was what to do with it.

Alexis had told him not to trust anyone. That there was a traitor within the ranks of the CIA. Having seen the names on the screen and one in particular, Jerome realized Alexis had been right. And if there was one bad apple in the barrel there might be more.

So, where did he go?

He answered his own question. He had to go to the one man he knew without a shadow of doubt would be safe.

The man he had known for years. The CIA agent who had taken him on as a new recruit to the Agency.

Senior Agent Chuck Baker.

There was no way Baker would betray his CIA position of trust or enter into complicity against his country.

Jerome and Baker had been a working team for a number of years. Partners, Jerome and Baker had each other's back and trust both off and on duty.

Jerome keyed in Baker's private email address. Not his Agency address. Anything that went through the CIA servers could be viewed by prying eyes. Jerome figured if the conspiracy reached into the Agency, the connection between Alexis and Jerome would be on a watch list. Sending the contents of the flash drive to Langley would be akin to taking out an advertising spot on national television.

He wrote a brief message to Baker, bringing him up to date about the Sofia incident, and asked him to check the file he was attaching, telling him to keep it to himself. Baker would understand why once he read the contents. He attached the file, hesitated, then sent the message. The sending bar seemed to take forever to fill. In the end the email program informed him the message and attachment had been delivered.

Jerome slipped the flash drive from the port and held it in his hand, staring at it, unsure what to do. Now that he had sent the contents to Baker, the slim silver stick might be considered superfluous. Jerome had difficulty accepting that. What he wanted right now was for Baker to respond, letting him know he had received the file. Until he had confirmation Jerome decided he needed to keep the flash drive in his possession.

The door to his room crashed open, swinging wide. Three armed men pushed into the room. One turned to close the door and stand guard over it. The remaining pair closed in on Jerome.

The CIA agent reached for the Beretta holstered on

his hip. A futile gesture, he knew, but he had to react to the threat.

One of the men raised the suppressed autopistol in his hand and fired. The slug struck Jerome's right arm, high up, shattering the bone and blowing out a chunk of raw flesh. Jerome gasped from the impact. The next two slugs reduced his kneecaps to bloody mush. Jerome collapsed in sheer agony. The shooter leaned over and took his weapon away. He crouched, shaking his head slowly.

"That was not a smart thing to do," he said. His accent was Eastern European. His dark hair was cut close to his skull. "Oh, what is this?"

He reached out and took the flash drive from Jerome's left hand. He showed it to his partner.

"What Alexis passed to him?"

"Mmm, could be."

The second guy spotted the open laptop. He checked it out.

"He just sent an email to someone called Baker. And an attachment."

"This gets better and better. Agent Jerome, you are not making clever moves. I think now you have answered our question." He held up the flash drive. "Alexis gave you this and you have sent the contents to a man called Baker. It all adds up to becoming a bad day for you."

He stood, dropped the flash drive into a pocket. There was no hesitation to what he did next.

The muzzle of his pistol moved, lining up, and he fired two fast shots into Jerome's head, above his eye level. At close range the pair of 9 mm slugs went into Jerome's skull, ripped through his brain and out the back in a spurt of bloody debris. Jerome's head dropped to the carpeted floor, eyes still wide open. His body moved for a few seconds, final spasms before his life ebbed away.

"Bring the computer," the man said, holstering his weapon.

The three men, moving smoothly, exited the room, closed the door and left the hotel.

In the SUV parked outside the shooter took out a cell. He hit a speed-dial number and connected.

"It is done. We have the drive and the agent's laptop. He sent an email with an attachment, to a man named Baker. Chuck Baker."

He ended the call and the SUV drove away from the hotel, heading across the city.

CHAPTER THREE

Langley

In his CIA office at Langley, Edgar Bergstrom sat waiting for Callow's report. He knew it wasn't going to be the news he had expected. His assistant, Jay Callow, had a way of expressing disappointment before he said a word. He had a tendency toward the dramatic.

Today he was less than dramatic. Decidedly nervous. Even his clothing had a crumpled look. His slightly chubby face, with light blue eyes, was pale and he fidgeted on the edge of his seat.

"You going to make me wait all day?" Bergstrom said.

"Alexis is dead," Callow said. "So, no more snooping from him. But there's a downside."

"Just tell me, Jay."

Callow rubbed his fingers across his broad forehead. "It seems Alexis did have a contact. That's where he was going when Inigo's team cornered him. He took a knife to the stomach but he broke away and ran. When the team caught up to him this contact shot it out with them. He killed two of them and wounded the third before he ran."

"Jesus," Bergstrom said. "Does it get any worse?"

"I'm afraid so. Alexis passed something to his contact just before the shooting started."

"The file. He handed over the data?"

"It was assumed so. But here's the kicker," Callow said. "Alexis's contact was Harry Jerome."

Bergstrom was silent for a few moments.

"Do we know where he is now?"

"The follow-up team trailed Jerome to his hotel in Sofia. They went in to put him out of his misery. But it looks like Jerome had already sent an email with an attachment. There was a flash drive in Jerome's hand. I'm guessing Jerome sent the contents of the drive to a private email address. He would be smart enough not to send it to any official site."

"Damn. Let me take a stab at this. Jerome sent the contents of the flash drive to Chuck Baker."

"How'd you guess that?"

"Because Baker is the only man Jerome would ever trust with what's on that fucking stick. He probably figured he might not get out of Sofia alive, so he took out insurance. Baker. Mr. Honest-to-God Baker."

Callow stayed silent for the moment.

"What a grand fuckup," Bergstrom said. He jabbed a finger at Callow. "We need some damage control here, Jay. The whole house of cards could come down on us if we don't. Get some feelers out. Test the water and see if anything links to the operation. If there are possible leaks, fix them."

"I'm on it," Callow said. He stood, making an attempt to straighten his untidy clothing.

"And we need to neutralize Baker."

"As in…"

"Yes, Jay, as in a personal neutralization. I don't want Baker coming out of this alive."

When Callow left, Bergstrom swung his chair around and stared out the window. There was a lot going on inside his head, not least how he was going to explain what had happened to the main man.

He realized he was tapping his fingers against the arm of his executive chair—a nervous habit that revealed itself more and more just lately. No matter how many times he told himself he was in control, his self-doubts maintained a hold on him and he was unable to totally ignore what might go wrong.

Too many damn things.

Like someone breaching security to the point where he had been able to walk away with his gathered intel. Well, almost. Alexis might have got clear if his final act of treachery hadn't been spotted by one of the team. Truth was, Alexis might still achieve what he had set out to do if Baker acted on the file he had inherited. And knowing Baker as he did, Bergstrom understood it was what the man would try to do.

Baker had a mile-wide streak of honesty that wouldn't allow him to suppress what he would learn from the file. He *would* act on it.

If he managed to get the information to the right people it would blow the whole damn thing sky-high. Once that happened there wouldn't be any room left to maneuver. The hounds would be let off their leashes and the fallout would spread unchecked. A nervous smile edged Bergstrom's lips when he realized the implication behind his last conscious thought.

Fallout.

There was a slip.

He pushed to his feet, paced behind his desk and caught his reflection in one of the tinted office windows. He paused to adjust his suit jacket. Stroked his thick, just-starting-to-gray hair. Bergstrom made a daily effort to always look smart. He bought expensive clothes, paid attention to his looks. At six feet, with a smoothly handsome face, Bergstrom exuded confidence.

That confidence cloaked a devious and ruthless inner self ideally suited to his CIA black ops division. His true character. Edgar Bergstrom had little time for the weak. He believed in the power of knowing what he wanted and going for it regardless. The people he commanded knew that and understood what would happen if they crossed him. Unfortunates who failed to realize that paid for their mistakes.

Now, with the news Callow had delivered, Edgar Bergstrom felt a little of the apprehension others experienced when they upset him.

Now more than ever he realized he was getting out of the business at just the right time. This thing he was involved in was going to be his swan song. His payday. The big one that would set him up for life, and to hell with them all. He really had swallowed enough shit for the Company, and the country. Dealing with the overspill of crap created by the government had burned him out in more ways than one. This deal was for him.

He opened a drawer in his desk and took out one of the burn phones he kept there. It would be used once then destroyed. Another safeguard against detection. He tapped in the number he knew by heart and listened as it rang out.

"Yes?" That familiar soulless voice.

"You free for lunch?" Their simple code for "I need to talk urgently."

"An hour."

"See you then."

Bergstrom ended the call.

BERGSTROM SAT ACROSS from Senator Hayden Trent in the dining room of the exclusive Washington Club. They were well into the main course now, surrounded by the quiet ambience of the room, with only the low murmur of voices and the clink of cutlery on the china plates.

"Steak is exceptionally good today," Trent said.

Bergstrom only nodded.

"About as rare as your conversation, Edgar," Trent said.

"This isn't easy," Bergstrom said. "We've had a setback."

Trent paused in his slicing of his steak. His tanned, handsome face lost any semblance of goodwill.

"Just tell me," he said.

"Someone gathered intel on the operation. He was spotted too late. Made a break with his evidence. The contractor I've employed put a team into Sofia and went after him. It didn't go well. The guy, Jean-Paul Alexis, made contact with an accomplice before he died. We know he passed the stolen data to this contact. There was a shoot-out. The insertion team was taken down by this contact before he ran. One of the team survived. He identified Alexis's contact. Harry Jerome. Jerome was with the Agency. The team tracked him to his hotel and silenced him. But not before Jerome had sent the data Alexis collected to another agent here in Washington. CIA's Chuck Baker."

Trent continued eating. He didn't speak for some time. When he did, his words were measured.

"Edgar, you are in charge of maintaining security for me. Finish your lunch, then get back out there and do your job. I don't care what you have to do—just make this go away. You know what's at stake. Right now we don't need someone like this Baker screwing things up. Clean up this mess. It's on your watch, so deal with it. Christ, man, you're CIA. You maintain your own covert section. That must come with some advantages."

"It does, Senator. But even I have to tread carefully.

Baker doesn't come under my purview. And the man is the CIA equivalent of an Eagle Scout. If he suspects something he'll bend over backward to drag it into the light."

Trent refilled his wineglass. "Then get to him and bend him until his back breaks."

"Leave it with me," Bergstrom said. "I'll handle it."

He left the club half an hour later, his car brought around and ready for him. He slipped behind the wheel. From the glove box he took out another prepaid cell phone and tapped in a long number. He eased the car away from the parking spot and joined the traffic. When his call was answered he spoke quickly.

"I need your help to track and remove a target. His name is Chuck Baker. A CIA agent. Is that a problem?"

"No problem, sir."

"Baker needs to be neutralized very quickly."

"Understood."

"And one that you will be paid extra for."

"Fine."

"Give me a half hour and I will send you the information you need on Baker."

"I'll make my arrangements."

Bergstrom made a further call when he returned to his office, again using his burn phone. His call was picked up after a delay.

"Simple question, Laker. Are we on target?"

"The documentation is complete. I just need to finalize the identity papers."

"The media material?"

"Not a problem. The recordings are finished. Vocal tracks are excellent. If I didn't know where they really came from I'd be fooled myself."

"Nothing better than a man who takes pride in his work."

"Look, I'm never going to win any awards for my work, so I'm allowed to tell myself I am brilliant."

"Good. As soon as the package is complete, call me and I'll collect."

"No problem. Send your man anytime now. It will be ready. As soon as it's in your hands I'll destroy all the recordings and the proofs. There won't be anything left. Just the one-off originals."

"Your commission will be transferred to your numbered account when the package is collected."

"Nice doing business with you."

"Yeah. Here's to the next time I need you, Laker."

Bergstrom put the phone down, smiling to himself. He leaned back in his executive chair, pleased with the outcome.

Here's to the next time I need you.

That would never happen. His asset was going to take early retirement, courtesy of Bergstrom's cleaner, the man who swept away matters that were surplus to requirements. One of the pluses of running a deep-cover black ops division was the access it gave Bergstrom to out-of-house operatives, individuals who carried out a multitude of functions. They were very handy when a special need arose.

Bergstrom used his burn phone to call his own specialist, giving him time and place. He added the details for the money transfer that would need to be processed. Laker would not turn over the material until he had proof positive the funds were in his account. There was no doubt Bergstrom's assassin could force the information out of Laker. That would take time and effort, and using that kind of extreme persuasion could add complications. Bergstrom had no time for that. It was simpler to hand over the fee and lose it. Two million dollars was small change when it was weighed against the cost of the rest of the operation.

It wasn't coming out of Bergstrom's pocket so he didn't really care.

"Make sure you have the package before you put Laker down. He's no idiot. Give him his money and let it gather interest in his account. We might be able to get it back someday, but I don't care about chump change at this moment in time. Understood? Good. Let's clean up loose ends as we go along. The less we leave behind, the better."

LAKER LIVED IN A split-level house overlooking lakes and square miles of forest. It was surrounded by snow-crested peaks and timbered hills. There was a late-model 4x4 Jeep parked next to the house, a powerboat tied up at the small wooden jetty. Smoke from the stone chimney was scattered into shreds by the rotor wash from the helicopter as it landed in the clearing a few hundred yards from the house.

Bergstrom's man was alone, having flown the chopper himself. He was conservatively dressed in a light gray suit, white shirt and maroon tie. His dark hair was thick and brushed straight back. He carried an aluminum attaché case in his left hand. He made his way from the helicopter and climbed the steps onto the railed porch. As he reached the front door Laker opened it. He was a slender man, his sandy hair starting to thin. He peered at his visitor over steel-framed eyeglasses. He was casually dressed in expensive jeans and a dark shirt.

"Mr. Laker, my name is Warren Kildare. I am here to conclude your business arrangement with Mr. Bergstrom."

Kildare exuded friendliness, holding out a hand to take Laker's.

"I need to verify who you are," Laker said. "You do understand?"

"Of course. It pays to be careful."

Laker led the way inside.

The main room ran the length of the house, a living room and kitchen in one. Laker's work space was in a section at the rear of the room. The walls were decorated with genuine prints and racks holding replica frontier rifles and revolvers. The whole place was well furnished. The floors were smooth timber. A log fire burned in the large open fireplace.

"Gets chilly up here, I guess," Kildare said, smiling benignly, as he stood by the fire.

Laker used his sat phone to call Bergstrom.

"Your man is here." He listened. "Yes, that describes him exactly. Warren Kildare is the name he gave. Once he has transferred the fee, I'll hand over the package. Would you like to speak to him?…No? That's fine."

Kildare had placed the attaché case on the wooden coffee table and opened the top. He leaned it back to expose an electronic transfer unit. He powered it up, then stood back.

"If you will enter your account password and account number, Mr. Laker, I will then initiate the transfer."

Kildare stood aside, away from the machine as Laker bent over and keyed in his details. The display showed his password and account number as a series of dots. When that was done, Kildare moved and tapped in a key sequence.

"Press the enter key," he said, still with a benevolent expression on his face.

Laker tapped the key and the readout screen began to scroll a series of responses.

"It may take a little while for the transfer to complete. When it does, the screen will display your account details."

Kildare showed no impatience, no expectation of wanting to see the package. He simply stood back a little, watching the screen, then scanning the interior of the house.

"Very nice," he said. "You have a very pleasant home."

"I prefer the isolation," Laker said. "My business needs quiet so I can concentrate. Here I have just what I want."

"Yes," Kildare said. "It's good to have what you need."

The readout screen resolved itself and Laker experienced a mild surprise when he read the account total even though he had been expecting it. On top of the four hundred thousand he already had in his account, there was now an additional two million dollars.

"Would you like to log out of your account, Mr. Laker?" Kildare asked. His face showed his pleasure at being the man who had just delivered a healthy bonus to his employer's client.

When Laker had logged out, Kildare gently closed the attaché case's lid.

"Are you happy with the arrangements?" Kildare asked quietly.

"Yes," Laker said, trying to hide the slight tremor in his voice. This was the largest fee he had ever been paid, and it offered him a future full of promise.

He turned and crossed the room to where a wide desk stood in one corner. He slid open a drawer and took out a leather document case. He handed it to Kildare, who accepted it and placed it on top of the attaché case.

"Mr. Bergstrom will find everything he asked for. All the documentation and the flash drives."

"The originals have been destroyed?"

"Yes. I do this after each package I create. The FBI could walk in here tomorrow and wouldn't find a thing except my files and computer data for my work as an illustrator. Book covers. Artwork. Even comic-strip layouts. Tell Mr. Bergstrom he has nothing to worry about. He's safe."

"Nice to know," Kildare said.

He was standing at the main window, looking out across the placid surface of the lake.

"Like the view?" Laker asked, moving to stand to one side.

"Yes. As you said, a very isolated spot. Do you get many visitors?"

"Not really. In fact you're the first I've had in a couple of weeks."

"So, I guess if you dropped down dead right now no one might find your body for a long time."

Laker gave an unsure laugh. "Never thought of that. Most likely you're right."

"That gives me a great deal of comfort," Kildare said, the pleasant tone of his voice changing to a hard, strident cadence that was alien to Laker's ears.

Kildare turned fast, his left hand snapping forward. His powerful fingers gripped Laker's hair and he jerked the man's head up and back. His right hand flashed into view and Laker had a blurred image of a lock knife blade snapping into position a split second before the extremely sharp steel edge slashed across his throat, back and forth, back and forth, cutting deep from ear to ear. It severed everything in its path. Kildare had anticipated the severe gush of hot blood and stepped away, letting go of Laker as the gurgling man clutched at his throat. The attempt to stem the absolute outpouring was useless. Blood simply spurted between Laker's fingers as he sagged to his knees. It splashed down the front of his soft cotton shirt, drenching the fabric. Laker flailed, even as his life ebbed away along with the massive loss of blood. The primeval need to stay alive. The final urge to stave off death. Laker's wounds ensured that would not happen.

Kildare had already put his knife away. He made his way to the desk and the workstation where Laker's computer sat. He pulled a pair of black latex gloves from his pocket and put them on. Powering up the computer, he initiated a complete purge of the system, clearing files and hard drive. Even after that was complete Kildare disconnected the machine from the power. He took a compact tool kit from his jacket and removed the computer case. He stripped out the hard drive and took it with him.

He retrieved both the attaché case and document folder. He ignored the feeble spasms coming from Laker, now on the floor in a spreading pool of his own blood. He left the latex gloves on so there would be no print transfers to the door handle. He had not touched anything in the house prior to pulling on the gloves. When he took a final glance back Laker had ceased all movement. The deep, open wounds in his throat had stopped pumping blood now the man's heart had shut down.

Kildare walked to his helicopter, climbed in and commenced the powering-up sequence.

When he was airborne, swinging away from the lake, he used his own burn phone to call Bergstrom.

"Mr. Bergstrom, I'll be back in a couple of hours. Meet me at the strip. I have your package. Scratch Laker off your contact list. He won't be available for any future work.... No, sir, no problems. I'll see you then."

He was flying over dense timber and rocky outcroppings. After a few miles he flew over another isolated lake. Kildare slid open the side window and threw out the computer hard drive. It dropped into the depths of the water. Only then did he strip off the latex gloves and push them into his pocket, settling back for the rest of the flight to where he would meet Edgar Bergstrom.

BERGSTROM'S BIG SUV was waiting when Kildare touched down. It was raining, the tarmac glistening in the late-afternoon gloom. Kildare shut down the power and took the attaché case and the leather document folder with him as he exited the aircraft, sprinting across to the black Cadillac Escalade. He climbed into the rear and settled beside Bergstrom on the plush leather seat.

"Take us to town, Jay," Bergstrom said to Callow. "And don't rush."

Callow drove out of the private field and picked up the highway, the Escalade's V-8 engine making barely a sound.

"Here you are, sir," Kildare said, handing over the leather folder.

Bergstrom opened it and slid out the documentation Laker had so beautifully created. He looked it over, then examined each document, shaking his head in admiration at the professionalism of the items.

"Truly remarkable," he said. "Laker's demise is a loss to the world. But there was no alternative. Knowledge can be a double-edged sword. In the right hands a weapon for good, but something that needs to be kept under control."

"I agree, sir," Kildare said.

"Nothing left behind?"

"Laker told me he had deleted everything. To protect himself as much as you."

"Did you believe him?"

"Yes. He wasn't an idiot. Holding back so he might be able to coerce you in the future would have backfired. Laker knew that. He would have been happy with the two million."

"Would have been?" Bergstrom said in mock surprise. "Whatever do you mean, Mr. Kildare?"

"Our friend Laker had a tragic accident just before I left him. Seems he fell on something sharp and bled out."

"Oh well, life comes up with these occurrences."

"I handled the matter of his computer system, too," Kildare said. "Nothing left on it to be found. I double-checked but at a thousand feet the wiped hard drive some-how fell out of my helicopter into a wilderness lake."

"Excellent," Bergstrom said. "Jay, drop Kildare and myself off at the club. You can carry on and make certain that cash transfer is sent to his account."

Callow nodded. "I'll see to that, sir."

"As soon as possible I'll take a flight out and deliver these documents to our friend Inigo. Arrange that, as well."

CHAPTER FOUR

Stony Man Farm

"An agent of the French CDII, Jean-Paul Alexis, dead in Sofia, Bulgaria. And so is a CIA agent, Harry Jerome," Barbara Price said. "From what the cyber team has gleaned, neither man would normally have been in the presence of the other. This is what you were asking about?"

Price, the Farm's mission controller, passed a printed sheet to Hal Brognola and stood aside as the director of the Special Operations Group scanned the data. He read the information a couple of times before raising his eyes.

"This all you have?"

"Wait until you read my next piece of prose," Price said.

Brognola sighed, taking more hard copy from her. He scanned the printed words, quietly grumbling as he digested the text.

"And don't miss this last one."

"Hell, Barb, is this some kind of text jigsaw?"

Price allowed the SOG director time to scan all of the information before she sat in one of the chairs facing his desk. She watched Brognola's face register surprise, then concern as he absorbed what the documents were telling him. Finally he looked across the desk.

"Just remind me what CDII is again," he said.

"Central Directorate of Interior Intelligence," Price answered. "They're responsible for counterintelligence and counterterrorism. Aaron picked this during a scan of internet chatter. It jogged his memory about that face-to-face you had with the Man yesterday. The one where the President called you in."

Brognola nodded. "The one with Chuck Baker. An issue about a possible security concern involving Israel and Iran."

"Your friend Baker had issues about some deep-cover, off-the-books operation?"

"That's right. He's got some suspicions he can't pin down but has fixed in his mind. He picked up background chatter and it just wouldn't go away. Chuck is that kind of guy."

"And the President?"

"We both know Chuck Baker. Solid guy. He doesn't play games. I've known Chuck a damn long time. He has intuition. I trust him."

"That's why you had Aaron run some background?"

"Yeah," Brognola said. "Chuck had intel from one of his contacts about this suspicion with Mideast ties. All in the wind at this stage, but Chuck has picked up rumblings and, like I said, he can't let it go. Then he received the information on his laptop from Jerome just before the guy was killed. That's made him even more determined to drag this into the light."

"Any names?"

"Only suspicions. Edgar Bergstrom. His was the name that came up in the data Jerome emailed through to Baker. Runs a black ops facility at Langley. Chuck's had run-ins with the guy before. Says the man is hard-nosed and protects his operations like a pit bull. And Bergstrom is connected, too. Mainly with Senator Hayden Trent."

"Is that the Hayden Trent who believes we should be putting U.S. Forces into Iran?"

"The same. The guy who advocates taking out the Iranian nuclear capability before it becomes a real threat. The man is promoting that policy as part of his presidential running policy. If he was president, we'd have troops on the ground by now."

"Trent has a lot of support from voters who sympathize," Price said. "Lot of people out there who believe we should strike first and level the Iranian regime. Take down their nuclear infrastructure."

"Look what happened when we did the same in Iraq. A lot of Americans dead and the country still in a mess."

"Hal, you don't believe Trent would drag us into a shooting war with the Iranians? It could shake up the whole region."

"Men like Trent have the unshakable faith they are walking the righteous path," Brognola said.

"You think?" Price shook her head. "First civilians and then our guys in uniform are the ones who pay the price. It sucks, Hal."

The cell in Brognola's pocket rang. He checked the caller ID, then smiled, holding up the phone for Price to see the name on the screen.

The President.

"Mr. President, what can I do for you?"

A THIN, CHILL RAIN was falling as Brognola coasted off the Theodore Roosevelt Bridge and onto Constitution Avenue. The Potomac was behind him as he took the route in the direction of the Vietnam Veterans Memorial park. When he spotted Baker's Agency SUV ahead, already parked, Brognola eased his own vehicle in some yards behind it. As he stepped out he pulled on his tan trench coat, wrapped it around himself and turned up the collar.

He saw Baker climb out of his SUV. The CIA man raised a hand in greeting.

They met near the rear of the SUV. There was a taut expression on Baker's lined face. Brognola thought his old friend looked as if he was carrying a heavy weight around his neck.

"The call from the President sounded urgent, Chuck."

"Not the half of it," Baker said.

"What is it you couldn't tell me over the phone?"

"Remember what I told you at the meeting?" Baker swatted at the chill rain beading his face. "About the Mideast and Bergstrom."

"I remember."

"Since that heads-up with you and the President I've been running down every contact and informant I have in the region. I don't have a complete picture but it seems it might be tied in with that file Harry Jerome sent me before those bastards murdered him. Enough of a story to make me more than curious."

"Who else knows about this, Chuck?" Brognola said.

"No one except the President and you. Soon as I got this worked out I called the President. Hal, this is bad. I knew I could trust you. Asked the Man to get you involved, but to keep it in-house until I can dig up some more information. Everything I have is on my laptop at home. Encrypted files. I couldn't risk putting it on the Company system."

"You think this thing goes deep?"

"If Bergstrom *is* in the mix, it can't go any deeper. That man is bad news. Going over to the dark side is nothing compared to Edgar Bergstrom. Hal, watch your back. If Bergstrom figures you're involved he'll sic his black ops hounds on you. That man doesn't step back from anyone. That's why I wanted this meeting off the record. Then I can fade away while I work this out."

Brognola shrugged. "Story of my life, Chuck. You sure you don't want company right now?"

"Only when I have something I can pin on someone. All I have now is Jerome's input and the starter information Alexis got his hands on. I believe it's the truth but I'll need more before I can point the finger at Bergstrom and Trent. Hal, watch him, he's a slippery son of a bitch and he's got so much protection he's bulletproof."

"Take your own advice, Chuck, and watch *your* back."

Baker smiled. "It's always against the wall. Hal, I'm Mr. Cautious. You know where my apartment is. Go pick up my computer and take a look at what's in there. I'm not going back. I need to stay on the loose. Maybe the Justice Department can offer some backup."

As much as he was a friend, Baker only knew Hal Brognola as a top man in the Justice Department. Nothing about his Stony Man operation.

"So, what about you?" Brognola asked, his phone in his hand, dialing Stony Man.

"Staying mobile. I want to see if anyone is paying me close attention. I'll keep in touch."

They parted company and turned toward their respective vehicles, Brognola already relaying his request to pick up Baker's laptop.

Behind him Baker had opened the SUV door and climbed inside the vehicle.

He didn't even have time to close the door before the SUV exploded.

The powerful blast engulfed the 4x4 in a fireball. The big vehicle disintegrated, metal and plastic debris hurled in every direction.

The resultant concussive wave picked up Hal Brognola and threw him across the hood of his car, slamming his body into the windshield. Flame engulfed the back of his coat as he was pushed partway over the roof of his car. He skidded off the roof and fell to the tarmac, his limp form protected from the main fallout by the bulk of his badly damaged car. The falling rain dampened the flames on his clothing before they became too intrusive.

Brognola lay motionless as the heavy sound of the explosion rolled away, leaving the wreck of Baker's SUV burning, black smoke rising over it.

The driver's door of the SUV hung from one twisted hinge. The interior was demolished. Chuck Baker's remains were burned into the seat, one shriveled and black hand still gripping the melted steering wheel.

As stunned pedestrians started to move in the direction of the explosion, a dark-colored SUV three hundred yards down the street eased away from the curb and drove in the direction of the Potomac River and the Roosevelt Bridge. In the passenger seat a man lifted a cell phone to his ear and made a call.

CHAPTER FIVE

"They wouldn't let me through the bloody door until I received that call on my cell from the President," said David McCarter, leader of Phoenix Force, the elite international covert antiterrorist team. "After that the buggers were almost bowing and scraping. Thought they were going to lay down a red carpet for me."

"What it is to have friends in high places," Price said. "So, how is Hal?"

"One lucky bloke. Bruised from head to foot. Couple of badly bruised ribs. Fracture in his right arm. Slight heat scorches down his back where his clothing caught fire, but his trench coat protected him from the worst. Rain helped to damp the flames down. And he has the bugger of all headaches from a mild concussion."

The Stony Man teams were gathered around the War Room conference table. Along with Phoenix Force were the members of Able Team, the domestic covert strike force. Barbara Price, Aaron Kurtzman and Carmen Delahunt were present. Akira Tokaido and Huntington Wethers had remained on station in the Computer Room to maintain the cyber unit, though they were on an open line in case they had anything to contribute to the meeting.

Hal Brognola's seat at the head of the table remained empty.

Kurtzman wheeled back from topping up his mug of

coffee from his own pot. He stared around the table, looking ever so much like the bear he was nicknamed for.

"Hell, you guys would put Hal right into intensive care if he could see your faces. Let's get this show on the road, people."

Price tapped the folder in front of her. "You all have copies of what we have to date. Everything Aaron and his team have compiled on the names we know."

Kurtzman flicked his hand control and the line of wall-mounted plasma screens lit up.

"Senator Hayden Trent," Price said. "Lunatic-fringe policies. Those are my personal words. But the guy is champing at the bit to start throwing his weight around. If he gets into the White House he'd be our worst nightmare."

"The global-conspiracy groups love him," Calvin James, the black Phoenix Force member, said. "They see a bomb-wielding Islamic radical around every corner. If they had their way Trent would be taking over next week. Be honest, guys, they all scare the hell out of me."

"How powerful is Trent?" McCarter asked.

"He has a large number of dedicated backers," Kurtzman said, putting up another screen that listed manufacturing companies and policy-making groups. "From weapons through to military equipment. The companies who would benefit from another armed conflict. And Trent courts influential people who agree with his policy of getting tough with anyone they believe represent bad news for America."

"You telling me the guy wants to get us involved just so his buddies can make a profit?" Thomas Jackson—T.J.—Hawkins queried. "Even I don't buy that," stated the Texan, and youngest Phoenix recruit.

"Has to be more," Hermann "Gadgets" Schwarz said. Schwarz was Able Team's electronics expert.

"The President feels the same," Price said. "He told me

we need to take this on board ASAP. He has concerns over the implications of the current situation. The shaky state of Mideast politics. Bad feeling between Israel and Iran. The agents killed abroad. And the murder of Chuck Baker and Hal's close call. He feels particularly bad about Hal getting hurt because he had urged him to go meet up with Baker."

"Do we have any details what the meeting was about?" Rosario "the Politician" Blancanales asked. "You said Hal took off pretty fast when he got the call."

"Pol, all he said was that he needed to run an errand for the President. He was meeting Baker near the Vietnam Memorial. That was it.

"Baker's laptop is at his apartment," Price said. "Hal called me about it just before the blast."

"We need to go and collect it," Carl Lyons, Able Team's leader, said.

Price said, "We also need to look into who was behind the bombing. Aaron, can you find out what the D.C. cops learned about the bomb?"

"We're already doing that. But the CIA has their own investigation running now. So has the FBI. And ATF. The Agency will want to shut down any outside investigations and handle it in-house because Baker was one of their own."

Lyons nodded. "More for you guys to dig out, then," he said tautly. "Somewhere in there we could find what we're looking for."

"Any footage from traffic cameras?" Gary Manning asked. The big Canadian was the Phoenix Force demolitions expert. "Maybe a vehicle moving off right after the explosion. A plate we can identify."

"You thinking that bomb was detonated manually?" McCarter asked.

"Baker had already been in and out of the SUV so I

don't think it was a pressure-activated bomb," Kurtzman said. "You set one on a timer, the wrong people could be killed if they're not where you want them, when you want them. I guess someone knew Baker was having a meeting so they wanted to deal with that person, as well. In this case it was Hal. Hence a manually detonated device. Only they hit the button a little too late. Hal was already moving away from the main blast so he got caught on the edge of the burst. Akira is scanning all the cameras in the vicinity right now to see if he can spot the bomber's vehicle."

"So, what does it all mean?" Price asked impatiently.

"Somebody got spooked enough to plant a bomb," Lyons said. "Tells me there has to be a solid threat behind this mess."

"Let's not forget where this all kicked off," Calvin James, the former SEAL, said. "Two agents dead in Sofia. I agree there must be substance behind it."

The phone beside Price rang. She snatched it up.

"Yes?" There was a pause as she listened, then cleared her throat. "Yes, sir, Mr. President."

She leaned forward and touched the controls of the telephone conference unit sitting in the center of the War Room table, then replaced her own handset.

"You are online now, Mr. President."

"Thank you, Ms. Price. Is everyone present?"

"Yes, sir. Both teams and personnel from the cyber unit."

"Good morning, everyone. I apologize for dropping in unannounced but I'm sure you will appreciate the urgency of the situation."

"Whatever we can do, sir," McCarter said.

"I don't need telling that is Jack Coyle," the President said. "Can't mistake that accent.

There was a general round of introductions as the Stony Man teams offered their cover names in turn.

"You have the advantage of me," the President said. "You all know my name and what I look like. I can run but I can't hide. Come to think of it, I can't even have a run without the Secret Service on my tail."

"Mr. President, we were just having a rundown on the facts we have," McCarter said. "Right now that isn't a great deal."

"From past experience I know you've started out with less. Hal is always letting me know about your intuitive skills." He paused, giving a faint chuckle. "Maybe I shouldn't be telling you that. I expect he likes to play the hard taskmaster."

"Too late now, sir," Price said lightly. "You've blown his cover."

"Do you have any update on his condition, Mr. President?" Blancanales asked.

"He's going to be laid up for some days. But knowing Hal, that man will be giving the hospital staff some grief very soon. I'm going to speak with his family later today. They're praying for his speedy recovery. As am I."

"Sooner he's back, the better," Price said. "It's weird him not chairing this meeting."

"This has not been a harmonious episode," the President said. "Three men dead. One of our own hospitalized. Information suggesting some kind of undercover operation that could, if it's based on truth, become extremely threatening. I want to hear your take on it."

"Before we get into that, sir," McCarter said, "I need a quick word with our domestic team. It's relevant to the situation."

"Then carry on."

"We still need Baker's laptop," McCarter said.

Lyons nodded. He beckoned to Blancanales and Schwarz. The Able Team trio quietly left the War Room.

"Sorry about that, Mr. President," McCarter said. "Something that needed moving on right now."

"Don't apologize. We need all the help we can bring to the table. All right, gentlemen and Ms. Price, what do we do?"

"This supposed threat appears to center on Iran and Israel," McCarter said. "My take is something that's going to stir up animosity between them. To be honest, it won't take much to do that. If real hostilities break out, the Mideast region could turn upside down. And like it or not, Senator Trent's wishes could come true."

"If he's involved in engineering an incident, the current administration will receive the backlash if we don't act accordingly. If one or more of the big powers push themselves in the picture, backing Iran," the President said, "Trent will jump on the situation and use it to bolster his policy."

"Are you suggesting something like this could end up a shooting war?" Price asked.

"The whole of the Mideast region is in a jittery state," the President said. "Any provocative moves could generate the spark that sets the place alight. And Israel maneuvered into hitting out at Iran would be fuel to the fire."

"Excuse me for asking," Price said, "but could we be talking nuclear fire?"

The President's hesitation, slight as it was, gave Price the answer she needed. Her face paled and she threw a glance in McCarter's direction as if she was expecting a comforting rejection of the President's statement.

"This can't happen," she whispered, her normal composure shattered. "And if it happens, *we* get dragged in?"

"Israel is our friend. We have an unspoken alliance we

couldn't just ignore, because it's a given Iran would get support from the one country that will jump at the chance to strengthen its hold in the Mideast."

Price cleared her throat. "You mean China?"

"Cutting all connections with Israel and stepping back would allow China to gain the advantage in the region. Like it or not, we can't allow that to happen."

"Oil."

"One of the factors I can't deny, or ignore," the President said. "A future scenario of China becoming a fixture in the region would be cutting off oil supplies for us and a good portion of the free world. One thing the U.S. military needs is oil. Without it we become an endangered species."

"If hostilities break out," Rafael Encizo said, "we move closer to having China jumping to aid Iran. China has blocked every attempt to broker a climb down by Iran over their nuclear policy. Even Russia doesn't favor Iran being held back. If two major powers back Iran it's a given that America will be dragged into the arena."

"We won't let Israel stand alone. She's our biggest ally in the region," the President said. "China flexing its muscles and giving Iran its support can't be ignored."

"You only need to look at a map of the region," McCarter said. "Israel is in a vulnerable position if neighbor states also decided to side with Iran. Wouldn't take much for the region to go on a war footing. If nukes start falling, any previous alliances would be forgotten. Fallout from radiation doesn't pay attention to borders drawn on maps."

"America standing by Israel puts the country right in the enemy camp as far as China would see it," James said.

"It would give them the excuse they need to up the stakes," McCarter added.

"But surely no one is going to let themselves be drawn into an actual nuclear exchange?" Price said. "Even the most blinkered extremist knows there wouldn't be a winner."

"It's not as simple as that," Manning observed. "National pride. Religious fervor. Long-standing hatreds. Sanity goes out the window at a time like this. And once nuclear weapons start being used, it could become more than a localized issue."

"By that you mean *we* could come under threat?" Price said.

The heavy silence that followed gave her the answer she did not want to hear.

Price shook her head in disbelief. "So, the world blows itself apart through bigotry and utter stupidity. Haven't we learned a damn thing over the past hundred years?"

"There are men who believe they can get away with such things," the President said. "They talk themselves into a corner. Can't get out and figure let's roll the biggest dice of all and see if we hit the spot."

"Sitting around this table isn't going to get it done," Price snapped. "Your files hold all current information on the situation. When Able Team gets back with Baker's laptop, we analyze the information and come up with a solution. I suggest you all get your butts off those chairs and work this out. Pardon my French, Mr. President. If you'll excuse me, I have work to do."

The Stony Man mission controller scooped up her own files and left the War Room.

An uneasy silence drifted around the table.

"Never seen her like that before," Kurtzman said.

"She's good and mad," Manning agreed.

Hawkins shook his head. "Not mad," he said calmly. "She's had a glimpse of a possible future and she is plain-and-simple scared."

"That she is," McCarter said. "And so should we all be."

"I take it Ms. Price has left the room," the President said. "Hal being hurt and now our nuclear exchange discussion has been a step too far. I'm sorry she's been affected."

"She'll be okay," McCarter said. "She's one tough lady, sir. She'll be back."

"Right now, gentlemen, you have to make your assessment. I'll leave you to it. We need preventative involvement. Look at what we have. If it broadens out, do what you can to stop it by any means. There's a lot riding on the worst possible scenario here. I'll leave you with just one comment. I am at the end of this phone whenever you need me. For all our sakes I don't want this affair to reach any kind of successful outcome. America doesn't need another set of confrontations. So, whatever you decide, whatever you want, you have my full support. I don't care how many toes you tread on, or how many rules you need to break, you have my permission to do it."

"Business as usual, then, Mr. President," McCarter said.

"I have to agree, Mr. Coyle. I'll prepare myself for the usual round of diplomatic complaints if they start rolling in." The President paused. "Good luck, gentlemen. Be safe, all of you."

The line went dead.

CHAPTER SIX

Georgetown

"There it is," Blancanales said. "Mr. Baker's place is around the intersection and about a hundred yards along on the left."

Lyons shifted around in his seat to stare at his partner. "How the hell do you know all that?"

"Google Earth," Blancanales said casually. "You can practically zoom in through the apartment window."

"I'll keep my blinds down from now on," Lyons said.

Schwarz eased the SUV to the curb. He cut the engine. The Able Team trio sat scoping out the building. It was still raining so the sidewalk was almost deserted.

Lyons was checking out both sides of the street, examining vehicles that were parked in view. He slid his hand inside his leather jacket and gripped the butt of the heavy Colt Python holstered there.

"Is he starting to develop a fetish over that gun?" Schwarz asked.

"Good question," Blancanales said. "I get worried when he does that stroking thing."

"What stroking?" Lyons snapped. "I was not stroking it."

"Defensive," Schwarz said. "Sure sign of embarrassment."

"Embarrassment is having to listen to you two."

"Transfer of guilt," Blancanales decided.

Lyons sighed as he realized he was losing this discussion.

"Let's do this," he said, and pushed open his door.

His teammates followed him to the entrance, Schwarz locking the SUV as they stood under the entrance canopy.

"Third floor," Blancanales said. "Apartment 45. On the front. Overlooks the street."

"Google Earth?" Schwarz asked.

"Yeah. Pretty cool."

They made their way inside and took the stairs out of habit and an inborn mistrust of elevators. In the event of a violent confrontation, being caught in the confines of an elevator was an invitation to disaster.

A notice on the wall indicated which way they needed to go for apartment 45. It was midway along on the left side of the corridor.

"Nice place," Blancanales observed to no one in particular.

"You could pass that along to Google Earth," Lyons said, his voice heavy with sarcasm.

They stopped at door 45.

"A key would have been useful," Schwarz said.

Lyons was already leaning his shoulder against the door, testing its strength.

"We're okay," Blancanales said. "Carl has brought his universal door opener."

Lyons eased back, one hand gripping the door handle. He took a breath before he slammed his left shoulder against the panel, utilizing the pent-up strength in his powerful upper body. The door creaked. Lyons repeated the move. There was a cracking sound and the door opened, Lyons's hand holding it from flying wide.

"Doors just don't hold out like they used to," he muttered.

"Let's hope Baker didn't have the place alarmed," Schwarz said as they went inside.

Lyons checked the wall beside the door. "No alarm," he announced.

"Hope he's right," Blancanales said. He closed the door as he moved inside.

The apartment was midsize. The open-plan layout combined a living area and a kitchen. Big windows looked out onto the street. Baker had not been married. He had kept the place neat and functional. A large flat-screen TV was fixed to one wall. Shelf units held neatly stacked CDs and DVDs. The floor underfoot was smooth pine with a couple of rugs in front of the leather sofa and loungers. Doors led into two bedrooms and a bathroom.

Able Team made a swift search of the apartment. It was empty.

"Clear," Blancanales called as he emerged from the bedroom and heard similar calls from Lyons and Schwarz.

"Over here," Lyons said.

A plain pine desk stood at an angle to one of the windows. Lyons went through the drawers. Baker's laptop sat in one of them. It was in a zipped cover.

"Let's go," Lyons said, reaching for the laptop. "Nothing else here for us."

The apartment door was booted open, four armed figures forcing their way inside.

"Incoming," Lyons yelled.

He let the laptop slide back into the drawer, his right hand already under his jacket as he completed his turn. The big Colt Python rose in a single movement and Lyons eased back on the trigger as one of the newcomers leveled his own weapon at the Able Team commander. He was way behind Lyons. The powerful revolver made a thunderous sound and sent a 145-grain Winchester Silvertip JHP round into the guy's chest. The big slug went in and stopped the target's heart as it plowed through and lodged next to his spine. The guy dropped like a sack of grain.

The apartment rang to the combined sound of multiple gunshots. With the advantage of being spread across the apartment, Able Team had a stretch of time, small as it was. Blancanales and Schwarz fired their 9 mm Berettas almost in unison.

Blancanales took his target straight-on as the guy loosed multiple shots from the squat SMG he wielded. The burst went over Blancanales's head as he dropped to a crouch. His pistol locked in on his target and he placed a double tap that slammed into the man's forehead. The guy stumbled back, his face registering a look of astonishment, quickly followed by the vacant stare of death. He slumped against the wall, sliding down to the floor and leaving a bloody smear on the surface.

Seeing the hesitation in the surviving pair, Schwarz brought his own pistol on target and hit the closest guy with three fast shots, driving him to the floor. One of Schwarz's shots hit the main artery in the guy's neck and he began to lose blood from the gaping wound. It spread in a glistening pool across the wood floor.

The remaining intruder stepped clear of his fallen partners, triggering his SMG in a wild volley, sending slugs across the room. As his weapon arced across the apartment Lyons leveled his Python and delivered a pair of slugs that struck the guy mid-chest and slammed him against the wall before dumping him in an awkward heap on the floor.

Silence fell.

A brass shell casing rolled across the floor.

One of the dead men made a soft groaning sound as his settling body expelled air from his lungs.

Lyons returned to the desk and picked up Baker's laptop.

Blancanales took out his sat phone and speed-dialed Stony Man.

"Hey, Barb, we ran into some unwelcome visitors at Baker's apartment. Need you to initiate liaison with the local LEOs. Stand in for Hal. Can do?"

"Watch me. You all safe?"

"We're fine. Leaving now before the cops show up."

The dead men were quickly searched. The only item of use was a single cell phone that Blancanales slid into a pocket.

They holstered their weapons. Schwarz had his cell phone out and was taking facial shots of the hit team. As they left Schwarz closed the apartment door and the Able trio walked along the corridor toward the stairs.

It was midmorning, so the majority of the building's occupants were most likely at work. Only two doors opened, curious faces peering out. Both elderly.

"What happened?"

Lyons smiled at the pale-faced woman. "We were wondering ourselves. We came to visit an old friend, then heard the racket. Now we don't feel safe so we're leaving."

Blancanales nodded. "I always thought Georgetown was such a nice neighborhood. Go back inside, dear, and close your door."

The other onlooker was a scowling old man, peering at them through his thick spectacles as he wrapped his bathrobe tightly around his skinny body.

"Hey, you," he snapped at Schwarz. "What's going on? Did I hear shooting? Wait, I don't know you."

Schwarz stared at the man. "I don't know you, either. I think I'm going to call the cops."

The guy stepped back, jaw sagging. He watched Schwarz follow Lyons and Blancanales descending the stairs.

"What the hell," he blustered. "I damn well live here."

DISTANT SIRENS SOUNDED as Able Team left the building. They were still a distance away from their vehicle. The rain had kept the sidewalk clear. They walked calmly to their SUV and climbed inside. Schwarz fired up the engine and eased from the curb. He drove away from the approaching police cruisers, taking a left turn onto a busier thoroughfare, where he merged with the traffic.

A block farther on a pair of police cars sped by, maneuvering through the traffic with lights flashing and sirens screaming.

"I think we handled that pretty well," Blancanales said from the rear seat. "After all, those shooters did jump us."

Schwarz said, "Let's hope we can get some facial recognition from the photos I took. Might give us some idea who the opposition is."

Lyons held up the laptop. "And maybe Baker's files might do the same."

"Hey, boss," Blancanales said, "we earn some Brownie points back there?"

"Seeing as how I had to take down two of them myself..." Lyons was stone-faced.

"He's doing Mr. Grumpy again," Schwarz said.

"He hasn't forgiven you for making fun of his affectionate attachment to his gun."

"You think so?"

Blancanales nodded. "Gadgets, you know how sensitive he can get." His cell rang and he picked up the call. "Barb? Go ahead, I'm putting you on speaker."

"…in touch with the local police. Gave them a cover story that didn't exactly pacify their grievances. So, I called Leo Turrin and he stepped in using his Justice Department clout to smooth ruffled feathers. He'll call back when he has anything to tell us."

"Good call," Lyons said. "We're on our way back with Baker's laptop. And a cell we took off one of the perps. That's why I didn't want to hang around. The cops would have detained us for the rest of the day and might have wanted the computer for evidence."

"Aaron and the team are waiting to look at it."

"I'll have some pictures for them," Schwarz said. "Tell the guys to warm up their facial-recognition program."

"Busy morning, guys." Price cleared her throat. "I already said this to everybody else. Sorry for my behavior earlier. It wasn't very professional. I'm not proud of it."

"You don't have anything to apologize for," Blancanales said gently. "It's been a rough day, what with Hal getting hurt and then all that talk about nuclear strikes. And you had a lot to handle in Hal's absence. Then the President gate-crashing the party. Enough to throw anyone off their game."

"We're all allowed an off-the-straight-line moment," Schwarz said. "By the time we get home you'll be back in the saddle."

"We need you, Barb," Lyons said. "Truth is even Hal couldn't run things the way you do."

"Thanks, guys. Too much talk like this and I'm liable to go all weepy again. See you soon."

The line went dead.

"Makes you feel all warm inside," Blancanales said.

"Yeah," Schwarz said. "Hey, Pol, I think Carl here was starting to tear up, as well."

That broke the tension. Blancanales and Schwarz burst out laughing, and even Lyons managed a thin smile.

IN THE CYBER UNIT at Stony Man, Aaron Kurtzman brought up rap sheets on three of the dead shooters. There were files from Homeland Security, the FBI and also Interpol. Kurtzman was waiting for any information from U.K. sources.

Akira Tokaido had taken charge of the acquired cell phone.

"These are some bad boys," Kurtzman said. "Marko Trevosia. Borat Laska. Dino Malko. Serbian. Former military. Nasty pieces of work. They drifted in and out of criminal activities until they moved into the mercenary life. Did some bodyguard work for a couple of human trafficking groups in Eastern Europe before they linked up with a private security setup." Kurtzman raised his big hands in frustration. "*Private security.* Another saying for thugs with attitude and guns for hire."

"Nothing on the fourth guy?" Lyons asked.

"Still running his image," Akira Tokaido said. "Either he's a new kid on the block, or an old one who hasn't been caught misbehaving."

"Okay," McCarter said. "Any idea who runs the outfit these bums worked for?"

"Dino Malko's list of associates does mention one name we've come across recently," Kurtzman said. "It's here on the Interpol file. Background comes from the French CDII."

"Could have been the outfit Jean-Paul Alexis was looking into," Price said.

"Connections coming together," James said.

"So, who's this name linked to Malko?"

"Inigo," Kurtzman said. "Raul Inigo."

He brought up a grainy image that filled the screen of one of the wall monitors: a good-looking man in his mid-thirties, thick black hair and brown Latino features.

McCarter studied it.

"Just who the bloody hell is Raul Inigo?"

CHAPTER SEVEN

The camp was one of the most remote in Yemen. On foot it was five days from the closest village. The way in was dry and dusty, with no provision for wheeled vehicles. This meant everything had to be brought in by helicopter. Being remote also meant it was relatively easy to maintain security. The camp was situated on high ground, which allowed for a clear watch over the surrounding terrain. Anyone approaching on foot could be seen well before they got close. Even aircraft could be spotted. The sky was clear, making it difficult for incoming helicopters to remain out of sight. These factors, though they helped to protect the approaches, were not ignored. There were regular watches stood by the camp's complement. Strictly enforced and maintained by the group's commander.

The current occupants comprised a mix of nationalities and cultures. They trained for close combat, with weapons and hands. There was a large selection of ordnance for them to use, giving them experience with all kinds of weapons. A distance from the main camp a firing range was devoted to intense practice.

The man who controlled the group was a Colombian national who had changed the course of his life some years back and was now the head of his own sought-after organization.

His name was Raul Inigo.

His rule over his men was strong. Any infringement of his rules was dealt with instantly and rigidly.

Inigo was hard but fair. His men understood the need for strength in leadership and they honored him for that.

His enforcement might have made men think twice before they stepped into the ring with him. It did not. Inigo had no problem recruiting to his group. He wanted the best. He got the best. Men who craved the challenges and the risks joining Inigo's group.

They were, to a man, violent outcasts from society. From a number of countries around the globe. Inigo didn't care where they came from. The only thing he demanded was loyalty, plus their allegiance to him alone. He asked them to contribute everything. In return they were paid well, were willing to put their lives on the line if he asked them, and asked to disown all religious and political affiliations.

It left them clear to take on any mission Inigo signed up for. To fight whatever need was current. Inigo offered his services to those who paid well— and he would accept nothing that did not come with an extremely generous paycheck and bonuses.

Inigo had been in business for almost seven years. During those years he had worked for rogue governments, negotiated weapon deals and had undertaken black covert ops for a wide range of governments. That even included the American CIA and British Intelligence. He made people vanish. Set up hostage swaps and had even taken hostages for regimes who wanted people removed. He offered bodyguard protection. If it brought him money, Inigo was interested. He preferred hard cash but was wise to the ways of the financial world. His ever-increasing money balances, maintained in offshore accounts, grew with every deal successfully carried through.

His business skills surprised many people. To many who handed him work he was a cold, diffident man with few social skills. That didn't worry Inigo in the slightest. He had never allowed himself to be seen as anything but what he was. Yet behind that facade was someone who understood the human condition only too well. He played the game by his own set of rules. Never justifying himself because he felt he had nothing to prove.

He was self-taught in everything he felt he needed to understand. He spoke four languages: Spanish, English, French, Russian. He could get by in Arabic and was, with a view to the greater emergence of the country, learning Cantonese and Mandarin. He had already managed two operations for the Chinese government. His desire to improve his knowledge was of overriding importance to Inigo. Second only to his need for increasing his wealth.

That need came from a poverty-stricken childhood in the favelas of Medellín, Colombia. Despite her continuing struggle from the moment of her only son's birth, Inigo's young mother had stood little chance of improving her lot. She'd died after a savage beating at the hands of the man she was living with at the time. Inigo was seven years old, already an experienced street survivor, when it happened. He'd run from the one-room apartment in the heart of the favela and the man who had killed his mother, clutching a hand to his bleeding left cheek where the enraged man had slashed him with a broken bottle. In time the injury healed, leaving him with a thin scar down his cheek, but the horror of seeing his beloved mother brutally murdered stayed with him as he roamed the slums, fighting to survive among the hordes of other street children.

Inigo spent the next ten years as a hustler, growing in confidence and honing his skills. Pickpocket, petty thief. By the time he was fifteen he was a runner for one of the city's drug cartels. His trust earned, he was advanced through the ranks and became a foot soldier of exceptional talent.

A week after his seventeenth birthday Inigo came face-to-face with the man who had murdered his mother.

Two things Inigo had never forgotten were his mother and the man who had brutally ended her life.

He had made a promise to himself that he would one day avenge her death. His expectations had never wavered and the day he recognized the man Inigo reaffirmed that promise.

The man himself did not recognize the boy.

In those ten years Inigo had grown to a height of six feet. He had put on toned muscle and gained in strength. He knew how to survive.

And to kill.

He had tailed the man, following him to the second-floor apartment in a building on the fringe of the favela. Over the next couple of days Inigo had shadowed his quarry until he was satisfied he had enough information to act on.

The first thing he did was to go see his boss, the man who ruled the local cartel. Out of respect Inigo sought a meeting with the man he respected above all others and told him the story of his mother's brutal death at the hands of the man he had just located. Cabrillo, his boss, a deeply religious man who considered family honor a sacred thing, listened to his young lieutenant's plea to be allowed vengeance.

"And you are certain this is the man, Inigo?"

Inigo nodded, touching his fingers to the thin scar that marked his face. It ran from the corner of his eye and halfway down his left cheek.

"Would I ever forget the one who gave me this?"

Cabrillo nodded briefly and gave his blessing. "Then go and make your vengeance so your mother may rest in peace. Inigo, do you need help?"

"Thank you, no. This I must do myself."

Cabrillo had watched the young man leave, knowing the deed would be done. He had total faith in his soldier's capabilities. Inigo had proved himself worthy on a number of occasions and there were the dead to show that.

INIGO WAITED UNTIL DARK before he made his move. His quarry worked behind the bar of a cheap club. He left the club around midnight, making his way to his apartment through back alleys and streets. Inigo had chosen a spot that allowed him to park his car in a side street the man had to pass. He'd left the trunk unlocked and partly raised, then waited until his man appeared.

Inigo had a length of lead pipe in his right hand and as the man stepped by he slipped out of the side street and came up behind him. Inigo raised the pipe, swung it hard and fast, catching the man across the rear of his skull. The victim uttered a shocked grunt, dropping to his knees. Inigo hit him a second time and this time the man fell facedown. Inigo fully raised the trunk lid, returned to take a grip on the unconsciousness man's jacket and dragged him to the rear of the car. He had a thick roll of duct tape in the trunk. Inigo bound the man's wrists and ankles, and stuck a length over his mouth before he lifted him and dropped him into the trunk. He slammed the lid shut and climbed behind the wheel. He drove the length of the side street, eventually emerging on a main road, taking a left that took him out of the city in the direction of a deserted warehouse complex.

Inigo drove into one of the empty buildings. He opened the trunk and dragged the bound figure out, dropping him on the filthy concrete. He sat the man up against the side of the car, then tore off the tape covering his mouth. The man stared up at Inigo, eyes squinting in the semidark. Tears ran down his face from the pain of the blows to his skull. Blood had streamed from the deep gashes and soaked the back of his shirt.

"What do you want from me?" the man asked.

"Your life," Inigo said. "In payment for the one you took."

"I took no one's life."

"You really do not remember me," Inigo said. He leaned closer, stroking his scar. "I remember when you gave this to me. I was seven years old. And you were drunk as you always were."

The man shrank back, eyes fixed on Inigo's scar.

"No… I do not…"

"After you slashed my face you beat my mother to death. So badly even I could not recognize her face. Then you ran and left me with her."

"You cannot do this. No one will believe such a story. I have powerful friends."

"No," Inigo said. "You have no powerful friends. You work behind the bar in a cheap saloon. A piece of scum who is nothing. Less now than you were when you murdered my mother."

Inigo hauled the man to his feet and dragged him across to an open steel barrel he had prepared earlier. He manhandled the man inside the barrel, ignoring the screams and insults hurled at him. When he had finished the man was jammed into the barrel, his face upturned, barely able to move. Constricted as he was, the man found even breathing difficult.

"What are you doing?" His voice was high-pitched, driven by sheer panic.

Inigo leaned over the barrel, a keen-bladed knife in one hand. He deliberately sliced open the side of the man's exposed cheek, cutting deeply so that the blood flowed freely. It spilled over into his mouth. The man shrieked in fear and agony.

"Do you remember now?" Inigo said. "I will never forget."

He crossed to where he had left a metal can, lifted it and returned to the barrel where the man was moaning, blood still pouring from the cut cheek. Inigo removed the cap. The pungent odor of gasoline filled the air. Inigo tilted the can and let the gasoline pour out, soaking the man's clothing. It splashed onto his face, into his mouth and the deep, open gash in his cheek. He kept pouring until the can was empty.

The man was screaming now because he knew what was going to happen. He struggled but he was too tightly jammed into the steel barrel to be able to move. In his sheer terror he lost control of his bodily functions.

"Please, no, do not do this."

"You killed my mother. I heard her plead for her life. Did you stop when she asked?"

Inigo stepped away from the barrel, closing his ears to the shrieks of terror. He took a disposable lighter from his pocket and flicked the lever. When it lit he turned up the adjuster to lengthen the flame. Inigo could see the shimmer of gasoline fumes in the mouth of the barrel. He gently threw the lighter into the fumes, stepping back quickly. The fumes ignited with a soft hiss, the flame expanding. As Inigo moved farther away from the blazing barrel he heard the man's rising screams. It was a piteous sound, wrenched from the very bottom of the man's soul as the gasoline burned away his clothes and ate into his flesh.

As he begged and pleaded, asking Inigo for pity, to God, to his long dead mother.

Inigo stayed until the screams died. Then he calmly climbed into his car and drove out the way he had entered, back to the city where he informed his boss that satisfaction had been achieved.

From that day on Inigo became a changed man. Already a hard, violent soldier, he became even more brutal. His boss saw this change and used it to his advantage. When a particularly extreme solution to a problem was needed, Cabrillo sent for Inigo. And the problem was quickly resolved.

INIGO'S RISE THROUGH the ranks was spectacular. His reputation grew. He became the boss's right-hand man. Over the next eight years he consolidated his position within the organization.

And then an event occurred that altered the course of his life forever.

Intercartel rivalry had already erupted into a savage war. There were daily killings between the drug dealers. Assassinations. Bombings. Brutal slayings. The madness was out of control.

While Inigo was handling a matter ordered by Cabrillo there was an all-out hit on the cartel. Rocket attacks were launched on a number of crucial targets, including the private homes of Inigo's boss, killing him and his immediate family. By the time Inigo became aware of the strikes, it was all over. The cartel crews had also been hit, killing the majority and scattering the rest.

Only Inigo and his personal team survived because they had been in another part of the city. News came to him on the way back, allowing Inigo to divert his journey. They hid out until Inigo received the full story from his street sources. The hit had been orchestrated by the cartel's main rival. It gave them full control of the business across the entire area. Inigo took his people up-country, allowing themselves time to consider their futures.

Inigo saw the drug business becoming a kill-or-be-killed existence. It was bad enough fighting against the police and the quasi-military forces. With greed and treachery becoming the order of the day among the fanatical cartels, simple existence was turning sour.

It was time for a change.

Inigo had around him less than a dozen men. But they were good men. Skilled at what they did. Smart and able to turn their hands to many things.

And they were loyal to Inigo.

He added up what they could salvage from the ashes.

In his position as second in command of the cartel, Inigo had knowledge of where Cabrillo kept the bulk of the money brought in from the ongoing transactions. Money from the U.S.A. From international dealings. Europe. Africa. Parts of the Middle East. The sources were—or had been—extremely profitable. Although those outlets would now dry up, the amounts of revenue already paid ran into hundreds of millions. Inigo's deceased boss had given him access to the deposits, account numbers and locations. Before the hit on the cartel Inigo and Cabrillo had been working on plans to use the cash to move into legitimate business ventures that would launder the money and pave the way to even greater profits.

Inigo realized the way was open for him to change direction and move into an entirely different line of work.

As an enforcer for the defunct cartel Inigo had an ability to meticulously plan and manage even the most delicate of operations. It was something he derived great satisfaction from. He had a way with words and negotiations, and realized he could use those skills for his new venture. He discussed his plans with his team, wanting them to understand his decision. There was no objection. To a man they were all tired of the desperate struggle to stay alive under the cartel mentality and simply wanted out, as Inigo did.

Staying below the radar, they planned their course of action. They would leave the country and establish fresh bases of operations. That was easier to achieve than they might have imagined.

Inigo had been aware of his boss's purchase of a large seagoing motor vessel. It had been purchased with cash from a yard in the Bahamas, where it had undergone a total refit, bringing it up to a vastly superior level of accommodation. The original purchaser had pulled out of the deal when the costs spiraled, leaving the boat company with a broken deal on their hands. Cabrillo had learned of the opportunity and had stepped in with a cash offer, taking advantage of the company's struggles. He and Inigo had flown to the Bahamas, carrying the money with them, and the deal had been struck there and then. The title to the boat had been transferred and the documents kept in the local bank until the completion of the refit. That had happened a couple of months before the hit on the cartel. Inigo had called the boatyard and arranged to take possession.

Before leaving for the Bahamas, Inigo told his team he had one last thing to do. He sent them to the airfield to wait in the chartered plane while he drove off. Although he had not informed them, there was suspicion among them about his plans.

Inigo was gone for just over three hours. When he returned and rejoined his crew he said nothing. Once aboard the plane the pilot fired up the engines and taxied onto the runway. Inigo settled in his seat, a satisfied expression on his face.

Remo, his closest associate and longtime friend, slipped into the seat next to him.

"So, how many did you kill?" he asked.

"Only two," Inigo said. "Menendez and Carazo."

Remo nodded. "The top man and his enforcer. Now you have your vengeance."

Inigo stared out the window. "Our business in Colombia is finished. Today we begin again."

Inigo left Colombia with only one regret—that he had been forced to abandon the SIG-Sauer SSG 3000 sniper rifle he had used to kill the two top men of the rival cartel. He had buried it in the wooded area where he had taken his shots from, seeing the skulls of his two victims explode from the impact of the 7.62 mm slugs through the Barska AC11672 IR Sniper Scope. The long-range targeting had been no problem for him. His skill with a rifle had improved year by year. The fact that the two men had a daily ritual of sitting beside the huge swimming pool inside the high walls of the cartel's villa had made the executions a simple hit as far as Inigo was concerned. The bloodied bodies had dropped on impact, skulls shattered and bone and brain fragments spread across the pristine pool surrounding. By the time the roving bodyguards reacted Inigo had already moved, slipping deeper into the trees and undergrowth, pausing only long enough to secrete the rifle in the trench he had dug earlier before he walked back to where he had parked his car and made the drive back to the waiting aircraft.

The seagoing vessel, the *Boa Vista,* became one of Inigo's bases of operations. Using many of the contacts he had developed during his cartel years, he offered his services as a negotiator, an enforcer and a facilitator. He bought and traded illicit goods. The change in tactics surprised many, interested some and provoked others into doubting Inigo's ability. It took time, but his past achievements could not be denied. In the coming months those who took a chance were more than satisfied with the results. Inigo's reputation grew. The directness of his actions and the delivery of whatever he promised boosted his standing. Within the first two years of launching his organization, which he operated under the guise as a private security company, Inigo was dealing with requests from past and new clients.

His natural abilities at negotiations extended his qualifications. Word of mouth brought him a wide mix of contacts. His reputation as an uncompromising operator, capable of savage violence coupled with adroit diplomacy, went before him. Inigo had no boundaries. He showed no bias where religious or political lines existed. His business was done on a strictly neutral playing field. Muslim or Christian, radical or democratic. None of those things concerned Inigo or his organization. His cardinal rule was that he never cheated a client. Never betrayed them. Never reneged on a deal.

He accepted any mission simply on financial grounds.

He had never discussed his feelings with anyone. His fear of poverty stemmed from his childhood. Before her death his mother had struggled from day to day to maintain some kind of security for herself and her son. The man who had fathered Inigo had walked out the day he'd learned of the pregnancy, so Inigo had never known him. His mother had been barely seventeen, alone in the harsh surroundings of the favela. She had done what she could to protect her child, taking any job she could, having to leave the young child in the care of neighbors. Those early years had burned the fear of poverty into Inigo. He had seen and experienced the degrading squalor, the struggle to bring in enough food to keep the pair of them alive. It had seemed to stretch before them. An unending journey of uncertainty with little prospect of ever being able to drag themselves free. His mother fighting to provide. Inigo himself existing on the streets, begging, stealing simply to get through another day. And then the shock of seeing some stranger his mother had gone with kill her in a drunken rage. The attack on Inigo himself. The man vanishing, leaving a seven-year-old bending over the bloody body, wondering why his mother was not moving, would never move again or hold him in her arms.

Survival took over. Inigo knew, even at his young age, that he could depend on no one. If he was to live he had to do it by himself. And that was what he did. Learning to survive in a world that held little regard for his misfortunes.

He survived. He hoarded what money he made, with the specter of poverty always lurking in the shadows. Every back step, often painful, taught him something new. He never repeated a mistake. Never allowed sentiment to cloud his actions. If he needed to kill to rescue himself from a dangerous situation, he did.

Even when he had become part of the cartel, his life improving, Inigo never forgot. The driving force behind him was the need to ensure he survived by building his financial stock.

Even now, with his new venture bringing in substantially huge cash rewards, Inigo could not rid himself of his inner demons. They were always part of him, driving him. Never letting him forget. He was able to partially satisfy those fears by going for the highest paying operations, no matter how risky they might seem. Careful planning and execution were top of the list. With his team of people around him Inigo pulled off contract after contract and stayed clear of damaging recognition by maintaining a wall of secrecy around him and his men.

Five more years in and Inigo felt more certain of his destiny than ever before.

The boat was his main, floating HQ. Fully equipped with state-of-the-art electronics it was the heart of his operations. He also now had a number of land-based centers in the U.S., Latin America, Africa, the Mideast and even Europe. These were secondary bases that provided him with up-to-date situation reports and swift deployment of teams on local ground. They were manned by his people and were capable of bringing in, if required, handpicked operatives for local work.

Inigo had morphed from the younger cartel enforcer into a well-organized handler of situations. His back catalog of missions included both civilian and military. He had been called upon by clandestine arms of national security agencies to carry out black ops that reached beyond boundaries. Off-the-wall operations deemed necessary by shadow men who stayed out of reach of even their own governments. Inigo's discretion and his impartiality appealed to these people. It gave them deniability while at the same time having their needs met.

I.O. Security, as it was known, had found its place in the sun.

Instability in the Mideast had brought Inigo a varied number of offers. From equipping groups with hardware and weapons to kidnapping and to retrieval of people and information. Inigo's group had accepted offers from al Qaeda, been instrumental in negotiating a deal for the CIA. Inigo did not question the why and wherefore of any transaction. He took them on board, assigned his people and usually ran the ops from his seagoing HQ. It was a satisfactory way of doing business.

And always, with no exceptions, payment was made in hard cash. Inigo preferred U.S. dollars but he was flexible. A case full of rials was as welcome to Inigo as wads of shekel banknotes. Chinese yuan. Russian rubles. They were all the same to Raul Inigo.

Inigo had an accounting manager who handled income. The man was a financial wizard who had the world of cash distribution at his fingertips. The man understood banking practices on a global scale and even in the current climate of restrictions on offshore banking, knew how to get around new regulations. His small team of agents carried cash amounts around the fringes of the financial hinterlands, the deposits being made with little fuss and large incentives.

Inigo's current involvement was with a man he had done business with before. An important man who operated at the extreme edge of the CIA. Edgar Bergstrom, a powerful and shadowy figure with incredible power in his grasp. As director of a black-on-black division Bergstrom operated on the edge. His missions were never scrutinized, very seldom questioned because his influence was such that no one understood the rules by which he played. His personal team of agents was not even on the cards at Langley. Because the things they did for the government were too delicate to own up to, there was a strict deniability protocol. Bergstrom's people did not exist. Anything they did was pushed aside and never spoken of. When a special op was passed down to Bergstrom, he was on his own. Left to solve the problem his own way. It suited the government departments who asked for a result, and it certainly suited Edgar Bergstrom.

This time around, the mission Bergstrom wanted activated made even Inigo take a breath when it was first proposed. When Bergstrom expanded on the matter, Inigo became intrigued. It was an audacious plan. An extremely dangerous and possibly far-reaching plan. But the more

Inigo read into it, the more enthusiastic he became. He wasn't sure why it took him so. It was far above anything he had been involved in before. Certainly the financial rewards would be astronomical.

It was the money side that really pulled Inigo in. He could see that the amount he would make from Bergstrom's scheme would not only benefit him greatly, it would also mean vast amounts for his men. It meant, if Inigo chose, that he could withdraw from his business and retire a wealthy man. Able to choose anywhere he wanted to live. To have whatever he wanted. The incentive was too great to turn down.

There was also the technical side. The purchase of the required hardware. The organization and the delivery. A grand scheme that would test Inigo and his organization.

Even as he sat thinking about it he *knew* he had to take it on.

The challenge was too great to ignore.

When Bergstrom had left the *Boa Vista* that day, Inigo was already working out in his mind how he would obtain the main ingredient for the deal.

It wasn't every day he went out to purchase a nuclear device.

CHAPTER EIGHT

France

"This is a bad time for us all," Senior Agent Sebastian said.

His English was excellent, tinged with a French accent. He looked every inch the archetypal Frenchman—impeccably dressed, even down to his ultraneat tie. McCarter, in his sport jacket and slacks, felt like a street urchin.

"Alexis was a good friend as well as a respected colleague," Sebastian, the CDII agent, went on.

"You knew him well?"

"*Oui*. We came up through the ranks together. Jean-Paul did not want to come out of field duty. He preferred to be in the middle of the action. So, I became his commanding officer. It worked well."

Sebastian stood at the window, staring out across the city. The tall Frenchman absently rubbed the back of his neck. He appeared to be debating with himself, and McCarter left him to it, glancing across at James as they waited for the man to continue.

"I knew he was on some kind of investigation that was bothering him," Sebastian said. "I feel somewhat guilty because I allowed him to go his own way. But it was how he liked to operate. We had developed this way of working over the years. Alexis did better on his own. It suited his temperament. Especially when he was infiltrating. He would call me when there was something to report. But there were times when I might not hear from him for some time. Perhaps this might not have happened if I had monitored him more closely."

"Don't blame yourself," McCarter said. "He was an experienced agent. I'm sure he would have confided in you when he found the time was right."

Sebastian turned to face the Briton. "Perhaps you are right. And your CIA agent? Jerome."

"They were in close touch, it seems," James said. "Realizing the information that had come to light might adversely affect the U.S.A., they must have decided to handle it between themselves until they were sure there was nothing to compromise them both. Alexis read something in the data he had uncovered that had the potential to draw the U.S.A. in. So he contacted Jerome to pass it along."

"And you say there is a suggestion of some plot to involve Israel and Iran?"

"We have to admit we're reading between the lines," McCarter said. "But there seems to be substance to it. Since we became involved, the situation has escalated."

"How so?"

"The information Jerome inherited was sent to a trusted CIA agent. That agent was killed shortly after by a device planted in his car. Our superior was also injured in the blast. Fortunately not badly. But it proves there is enough in these actions to warrant looking into the matter."

"*Mon Dieu,*" Sebastian said. "Tell me your thoughts."

"We're piecing this together as we get more information," McCarter said.

"Along the lines of a manufactured strike on Israel that might incite them to hit back against Iran," James added.

"To what purpose?" Sebastian asked. "Wait. This goes back to something I heard about maybe two, three weeks ago. Some vague report about escalating tension in the Mideast region. Not that it was anything new. Unrest there is an accepted condition. But now I recall one of our monitors mentioning a reference about some kind of action that would cause a great deal of disturbance in the Mideast region. No concrete evidence, and I have to admit we pick up a great deal of this kind of—what is it you say?— yes...*chatter*."

"Our listening agencies are monitoring all the time," James said. "Looking for key words. Phrases. Names."

"The bulk of it comes to nothing," McCarter said, "but sometimes they latch onto something important. And Alexis picked up enough to make him contact Jerome."

There was a tap on the door and an attractive young woman came into Sebastian's office carrying a tray holding cups and an insulated jug. The smell of freshly brewed coffee issued from the jug. The tray was placed on Sebastian's desk and the girl walked out of the office, leaving behind a trace of perfume. Sebastian poured coffee.

"Please, help yourselves."

"Alexis happened upon information supplied to him by one of his own contacts," McCarter said. "This is what our people found in the flash drive he passed to Jerome. A man named Rashid. This guy works as a dealer of information. According to Jerome this wasn't the first time Rashid had dealt with Alexis. When he realized the extent of the information, Alexis must have figured it needed passing to Jerome because there were definite connections to America."

"I understand that," Sebastian said. "Alexis made decisions in the field and acted on them." He smiled. "He hated having to go through official channels. He thought they slowed things down. He was right. I am the first to admit we French are strong on procedure. I just wish he had put me in the picture, also."

"He was doing what he thought was right, Commander," James said.

"Yes. Thank you for that. So, how can I be of help to you?"

"This contact, Rashid. Can you point us in his direction?" McCarter asked. "He could be our lead to the people behind this operation."

"Alexis once told me that Rashid was a solid source of information. As always he looked to the future and told me if he ever had to relinquish his CDII status, then Rashid would still be an asset." Sebastian gave a slight shrug. "I am sure Alexis had no idea his thought might turn into reality. He gave me details about Rashid. Said he had briefed the man about me. I pulled the file when I confirmed you were coming to see me." He slid a thin file from a drawer and laid it on the desktop, then opened it and passed it to McCarter. "If it will be of help."

The file held a single sheet of paper and a photograph. James picked up the image. A head-and-shoulders shot of a dark-skinned Arabic man. Mid-forties. He wore a neat beard and mustache. His dark hair was side-parted. A handsome man with sharp eyes.

"Would you mind if a took a shot?" James asked, lifting up his cell. "Help us to identify him."

"Of course not."

James held his phone over the image and clicked off a shot. He checked the result. It would be useful.

McCarter finished reading the printed information. He handed the document back to Sebastian.

"Commander Sebastian, thanks for everything," he said. "We need to move on this."

Sebastian rose and reached out his hand. "You have come a long way for such a short visit. I hope it has not been wasted."

"Nothing's wasted if it pushes us in the right direction. Rashid looks to be our best hope right now. We don't have any choice."

"May I contact you if I learn anything more myself?"

McCarter gave the French agent the number for his sat phone.

As McCarter and James reached the office door Sebastian said, "I hope you find what you are looking for, my friends, and that you can reach a satisfactory conclusion to this affair. If only for nothing else than Alexis and Jerome. *Bonne chance*."

BACK ON THE SIDEWALK McCarter took out his sat phone and made contact with Stony Man.

"We're done here," he told Price. "Get us on a flight to Tangier. We picked up information on the bloke who fed Alexis the data. Turns out he's a longtime contact Alexis used. We have a location, so we need to talk with him. If anything comes of it, the rest of the team can meet up with us. Cal is going to send you a picture of this contact. Have Bear run a make on him. See if he has a sheet on any database."

"Don't you trust him?"

McCarter laughed. "Listen, luv, there are only a few people I do really trust. One of them is standing next to me. And I'm talking to one of the others. Outside of my small list, I'd have to say no to your question."

"My mother warned me about you smooth-talking Englishmen. But I'll take what you said on advisement."

"Any word on the headmaster?"

McCarter referring to Brognola as the "headmaster" made Price chuckle. "Last report had him awake and starting to grumble."

"He's on the mend, then. We'll make for the air terminal. Give us a call when you fix our flight."

"Will do."

James hailed a cab. As it swung in toward the sidewalk, he glanced at McCarter.

"So, you do trust me, then?" he said.

"No," McCarter said. "I only brought you along because I might have needed a translator. You speak better French than me."

"Times are I speak better English than you."

McCarter was still laughing when they settled in the cab and he instructed the driver to take them to Orly Airport.

AT THE AIRPORT McCarter received a call from Barbara Price.

She had them booked on a flight to Tangier logged to depart in two hours. They would be able to pick up their flight documents at the Royal Air Maroc desk. She had also reserved two rooms for them in Tangier.

"Your new friend Rashid has a small record sheet. In his youth he was arrested for minor smuggling offenses. Spent six months in detention. He mixed with lower-level criminals but managed to stay out of prison. Then he started peddling information. Seems to have the knack for finding out things he shouldn't and selling it on. He's built up quite a reputation as a trusted informant. The older he got, the smarter he got. He seems to stay one step ahead of the law, even though he's been on various lists for years. He's been pulled in on more than one occasion but nothing ever sticks. A senior cop on the Tangier police force made some observations that Rashid seems to have a charmed life, or he is being protected by sources unknown."

"If he's been snitching, especially for people like Alexis,

that's likely to be true. A valuable asset is worth looking after."

"You trust him any more now?"

"No," McCarter said. "Haven't met the bloke, so I'll wait until I do. Catch up when we get to Tangier. Thanks, luv."

"I don't like it," James said.

"What?"

"We're hopping over to Morocco without a weapon between us. Look what happened to Alexis and Jerome. And Hal. I don't want to be a wuss, David, but I'd feel safer with a 9 mm under my jacket, or preferably in my hand."

"Point taken, mate. Right now we are in France and you know what the French are like about illegal weapons. We can't carry on the plane, so let's not get all cranky. I've got an old contact in Tangier who can fix us up, so calm down and let's go get some grub. I hope you realize I haven't eaten since my last meal."

McCarter headed for the food court, James following. It took him a few steps before he realized the incongruity of the Briton's last remark.

IT WAS EARLY EVENING when McCarter and James arrived in Morocco. Their plane touched down at Ibn Battouta Airport just after six o'clock and they stepped out into the warm, dry Moroccan air. They passed through customs along with the rest of the passengers without any problems. The majority of the crowd were vacation groups who piled onto waiting coaches. McCarter and James picked up a waiting taxi. It was a six-year-old Citroën. It had been red once, though it was now more a bleached salmon color. The robed driver placed their travel bags in the trunk, chattering all the time. James quickly found out he spoke fluent French as well as fairly good English. He instructed the driver to take them to their hotel, which was located on the Rue de la Liberté.

"You know Tangier?" the man said in French.

"Enough to know it only takes about twenty minutes to get there," McCarter replied. "So, no long way around. Understand?"

The driver grinned and bobbed his head. He understood these passengers were not to be fooled with.

The ride into Tangier took less than twenty minutes, with the driver weaving in and out of the traffic with consummate ease. He pulled up outside the El Minzah Hotel and skipped out of his seat, heading for the trunk. He was already placing the bags on the ground when McCarter and James climbed out of the rear.

"That was satisfactory for you?"

James nodded. He paid the fare and gave the guy a good tip. The driver handed him a creased business card.

"Here is my number if you need taxi again. I have great knowledge of the city. Anywhere you need to go, yes? I am Aziz."

McCarter and James went inside and approached the reception desk. A dark-skinned, smiling young woman in a cool white tunic attended to them. They were signed in and were shown to their rooms quickly. They had rooms next to each other and James joined McCarter after he had deposited his bag.

"Barb can book all my hotel rooms from now on," James said.

McCarter called room service and ordered sandwiches, and fresh coffee and a couple of bottles of Coca-Cola. While they waited, he called Stony Man and spoke to Price.

"Developments since we spoke last," she told him.

"When Able went to collect Baker's laptop they had a run-in with some unfriendly visitors."

McCarter and James had moved out before Able Team had returned, so this was news to them.

"They okay?"

"They are fine. Scratch four hostiles. At least they brought the evidence home. It's being looked at as we speak. I have someone here wants to talk."

Gary Manning picked up.

"How was Paris?"

"Informative," McCarter said. "I've never been in and out of a city so bloody fast. But at least we managed to gain some information."

"That why you're in Tangier?"

"Alexis received his information from a longtime contact. Bloke who has fed him stuff before. If this guy is on the level, maybe he can point us down the road a little more."

"If Bear gets anything from Baker's laptop we'll pass it along. Don't forget there are three of us waiting for the word. Watching daytime TV is scrambling my brain, so don't make it too long."

"Don't knock it," McCarter said. "Remember where we are. Television here makes the U.S. output look classic."

WHEN THE FOOD and coffee arrived McCarter and James broke off to eat. McCarter was happy when he saw his chilled Coke.

"What's the game plan for tomorrow?" James asked.

"A visit to my contact," McCarter said. "Get ourselves some hardware, then go and look for Rashid. If he's around, we need to have a talk with him."

"Maybe I should call our buddy Aziz," James said, holding up the card the taxi driver had given him. "Let him ferry us around the city. Be a damn sight safer than trying to drive ourselves."

"Calvin, you are not wrong."

They turned in early. In the morning they showered and dressed, then went downstairs and had breakfast. James called the number on the card and arranged for Aziz to pick them up from the hotel as soon as he could. By 9:00 a.m. they were in the taxi, in the middle of the city rush hour. There was a great deal of blaring horns and arm waving. Aziz drove with one hand on the wheel, his free one gesturing wildly. Exhaust fumes and dust misted the air at times. McCarter sat back and enjoyed the spectacle. Calvin James wasn't so sure he was having as much fun as his partner.

McCarter had given Aziz an address. It was in the medina, the old walled part of the city. It had been a long time since McCarter had made a visit here, but he knew his way through.

The Medina was vehicle-free. Cars were not allowed. They would have been unable to navigate the narrow streets and alleys. The buildings crowded in on each other. The layout of the place had most likely never changed in hundreds of years.

"Wait for us," McCarter told Aziz. "We have another visit to make later."

"As long as you pay, I will wait," Aziz said, settling down with a crumpled magazine.

With James close behind, McCarter led the way into the busy area. It teemed with people, the open shops and stalls selling everything from trinkets to clothes to food. The hot air was tinged with the smell of spices and cooking food. It was a noisy, vibrant place. James was lost within a couple of minutes, but McCarter strode along with the confidence of someone well used to his surroundings.

It had been some time since David McCarter had visited the antique store. From the appearance of the exterior, nothing had changed over the years. The faded paintwork was a little more faded and the door creaked and rattled as it had the last time he had pushed it open. The cluttered interior was gloomy. It was crammed with objects that suggested they had been there since the day the shop opened. And so had the layer of dust over it all.

"Hey, Randal, they not put you in a box yet?"

There was movement at the far end of the room. A hunched figure emerged from the shadows, moving into what passed for light in the place.

"I know that voice," the man said. He peered up at McCarter. His eyes, sunk into the hollows of the sockets, shone with a fierce glare. "My God. Mac? That you?"

His accent was strongly British, hailing from the Teesside area of the north. A proper Geordie as McCarter would have said.

The figure straightened, threw his arms wide and hugged McCarter. From where he stood James made out a skinny figure, easily as tall as McCarter, but by no means as broad. His face was burned brown by exposure to the Moroccan sun and his shaved head was burnished almost to a mahogany color. His lean features, lined and leathery, made it hard to work out his age.

"Yorky Randal, you old bugger." McCarter grinned. "I was expecting to find black crepe around the door and you dressed in your best suit."

Randal gave a deep, throaty laugh. "Don't be daft, I haven't got a bloody suit. Day I croak they'll just sweep my bones out the door and be done with me."

He looked beyond McCarter and spotted James.

"You with Mac?"

James nodded and Randal pushed by McCarter and held out a big hand. "Any friend of Mac's is welcome."

"Call me Roy."

"Roy it is. Mac looking after you? Mac, why can't you look as smartly dressed as your pal here? You never did dress tidy. Even when you were in uniform. By the look, nothing's changed."

"Ever the charmer," McCarter said.

"Knowing you, Mac, you haven't come to chat about the past, or to buy a priceless Moroccan heirloom. So, I guess you need tooling up."

McCarter nodded. Randal gestured for them to follow him. He led them through to the rear of the shop, pausing briefly to work a concealed button. A section of the wall, complete with shelves, swung open, and they stepped inside a small room that held racks of weapons. James was impressed by the range of the ordnance. Handguns. SMGs. Combat knives. Magazines for every weapon in the place were stacked on a shelf. They were all loaded.

"Nice collection," James said.

"If you're going to do it, make sure you do it well," Randal said.

"And no one knows about this?"

"Only those who need to," Randal said. The remark told James everything and nothing.

"How's business?" McCarter asked.

"Pretty steady," Randal said. "Always a need for tools of the trade."

"We just need a couple of handguns," McCarter said.

"If I know you, Mac, you haven't changed. Nine mil Browning Hi-Power is behind you," Randal said. He turned to James. "What's your preference, son?"

McCarter had picked up a nicely maintained 9 mm pistol. The Browning was still his weapon of choice, a pistol he had used for years and one he refused to abandon. McCarter checked the mechanism. The pistol was smooth and weighed comfortably in his hand.

"I normally carry a Beretta," James said.

Randal handed him a 9 mm 92F. "Nice piece. Dependable. Smooth action."

McCarter picked a belt holster for himself and James. They loaded their chosen weapons and took a couple of extra magazines for each.

"That all you need?" Randal asked.

"We're not looking to start a war," McCarter answered.

"I believe you," Randal said, grinning expansively.

"A pair of lock knives," James said. "Never know when one might come in handy."

"Smart thinking," Randal said. He selected a pair, in soft covers, and handed them over.

With the pistols holstered and the spare magazines in their pockets, along with the knives, the Phoenix pair followed Randal back into the shop. He secured the back room.

"If you can't get those pistols back to me," he said, "don't fret. They can't be traced."

"Thanks for your help, Mr. Randal," James said.

Randal grinned. "He is polite, isn't he?"

"And very clean," McCarter said. "Sorry to cut and run, but we're working against the clock."

"Anything I can help with?"

McCarter shook his head. "Less you know, the better."

"Okay." Randal trailed them to the door. "Hey, Mac, stay safe. It was nice to see you again. You, too, Roy."

The door closed behind them as they stepped out onto the street and retraced their steps back to where they had exited the taxi. It was still waiting and they climbed in. Aziz put down his magazine and turned his head.

"Where to now, boss?"

McCarter gave him the location for Rashid. "Can you get us there?"

"Sure, boss. It is out of town but I know the address. I am very good with addresses. You tell me, I can find you any place."

"Just this one," McCarter said.

As they moved off James said, "Old friend, then?"

"Yorky?" McCarter smiled. "We served together years ago. Randal was a hell of a soldier."

"What's his deal?"

"Maybe later," McCarter said quietly, not wanting to say too much in the presence of Aziz.

The taxi left the old quarter and eventually merged with the heavy traffic moving through the city. The built-up area started to fall behind. The sun was well up by this time, the heat bearing down. Aziz finally switched on the air-conditioning unit. It groaned and made more noise than the engine. The air it pumped out had a metallic tang to it, but it was at least cool.

McCarter settled back in his seat, unusually quiet. James noticed a faint smile on his lips. The Briton was remembering something from his past. James guessed it had something to do with Randal.

"So?" he asked.

"Remind me to tell you about it sometime."

"Don't worry, man, I will."

They were taking a route that meandered across semi-desert. There were scattered trees and patches of parched grasses. The city lay five miles behind them, the sparkling water of the port still visible. There were a few houses, well spaced out.

"There is the place," Aziz said, pointing. "See, I told you I can find it."

He slowed the Citroën as they moved in line with the residence, which was a white villa with six-foot walls. Clay-colored tiles covered the roof. Double wooden gates gave entrance to the property.

The gates were partway open and McCarter caught a glimpse of a couple of big SUVs parked inside. There was big guy lounging beside one of the vehicles. He had a matte-black SMG in his hands.

Bloody great, McCarter thought. Looks like the vacation is over.

"Keep going," McCarter said. "Up to that stand of palm trees. Pull up beside them. Don't get out of the car. Just wait."

Aziz stared at McCarter. "Is there danger? I do not want danger."

"You want to be paid? Then stay there."

Aziz waved his hands in the air. "I stay."

He pulled the taxi to a stop in the scant cover of the trees. McCarter exited the car, loosening his jacket.

"What is it?" James asked as he followed.

"A feeling."

James groaned. "Oh, great. Every time you get those 'feelings' it means trouble."

"No, just a feeling the guy standing inside those gates hasn't come to cut the grass. Not with the SMG he's carrying. Spotted him as we drove by."

"Maybe this Rashid has his own security. Kind of business he deals, he probably needs protection."

"So, let's find out," McCarter said, and led the way toward the villa's side wall.

CHAPTER NINE

McCarter and James skirted the perimeter wall and reached the rear of the villa. There was no access gate in this section. They acted on pure instinct, neither of them needing to speak. James reached up and grasped the top edge of the wall, slowly raising himself so he could peer into the grounds. McCarter, his Hi-Power in his hand, kept watch in case there was a roving guard they hadn't spotted.

"Nobody out back," James reported as he lowered himself to the ground again. "But I saw movement inside. Sliding French window covers half of the back wall. Open patio across the major part of the rear."

"Longer we wait, the worse the possible outcome," McCarter said. "Let's invite ourselves to the party."

James hauled himself up the wall again, checked that the way was clear, then rolled over and dropped out of sight. Holstering his Browning, McCarter did the same. He dropped to a crouch beside James. They both pulled their weapons.

McCarter scoped the big French window. The interior was nowhere near as bright as the sun-drenched grounds, but McCarter could make out dark shapes in the room beyond the glass.

"Take the left," McCarter said. "I'll go right."

They angled away from the window, moving until they were able to hug the side walls. There were no access points on either side of the villa. That meant entry was by the front door or the sliding-glass panels at the back.

McCarter and James edged in the direction of the French window. Peering around the edge McCarter looked in on an open-plan lounge area. He ignored everything except the bloodied figure tied to a wooden chair and the three bulky men bunched around him. They were repeatedly punching the bound man. His face was already torn and swollen. One of the men had a tube, metal or wood, which he was using to beat the captive's body. The glass muted the sounds from inside, reducing them to a monotone, but one of the men was speaking a repeated question at the bound man.

McCarter saw a stainless-steel handle close to where he stood. He checked it and felt the glass panel slide to the side. He gestured to James.

"Do it."

McCarter gripped the handle and pushed hard. The French window slid smoothly on its runners. The moment the gap was wide enough McCarter stepped into the room, with James right behind him.

"Stop right now," McCarter shouted.

He got the attention of the three men.

They turned as one. The guy wielding the makeshift club launched it in the direction of the Phoenix pair and simultaneously reached for the handgun tucked in his pants.

McCarter's Browning lifted slightly and he put a fast 9 mm slug into the man's forehead. The force snapped his head back. The slug went in and through his brain. It exploded out the back, taking a wedge of bloody bone with it. The guy toppled over and hit the floor with a solid thump, one leg going into spasm.

James saw one of the other guys making his move, his handgun appearing with impressive speed. He was not fast enough to win over a weapon already aimed at him. James, gripping the 92F two-handed, put two slugs into the guy's throat. The guy forgot about his pistol as he clutched at his shredded flesh, blood pumping out in bright spurts. It sprayed through his fingers and ran down the front of his shirt, turning it scarlet.

"The guard," James said as a door crashed open at the front of the house.

He ran forward, hugging the wall as the beefy figure burst into sight, the SMG already raised. The shooter opened up hastily, the stream of slugs plowing holes in the wall above James's head. James crouched, angling the Beretta upward, and stitched the guy in the high chest. The slugs turned the guy off track, his SMG firing wild, but he stayed on his feet until James fired again, expending half a magazine into the guy's head and neck. Killing shots that drove the guard to the floor, body jerking and squirting blood across the tiles.

The surviving attacker, deciding this was his chance, launched himself at McCarter. He was a big man with plenty of weight behind him and he slammed into McCarter. Pushed backward, McCarter reached and caught hold of the guy's thick, oiled hair. He could hear the guy's heavy breathing as he clawed at McCarter's face. They struck the wall, McCarter lifting a knee into his opponent's stomach. It drew a ragged breath from the man. A meaty fist struck at McCarter's cheek. The guy wasn't about to quit. McCarter brought up his Hi-Power and jammed the muzzle against the side of the guy's skull and fired a 9 mm slug that put in a ragged hole on entry and blew a bigger one on its way out.

"Didn't know when to quit," McCarter said, taking a breath.

James took out his lock knife and flipped open the

blade. He bent over the bound man and severed the cord that held him to the chair. The man slumped forward.

"Help me get him on the couch," James said.

They half carried the man to the long leather couch and stretched him out. They recognized Rashid from the photo Sebastian had showed them. He lay back, catching his breath through bloody lips. He clutched his ribs with each painful breath.

"Rashid," James said, and the man nodded. "Can you understand English? Do you have a medical kit?"

The man stared up at James. Blood smeared his face. His left eye was swollen shut.

"Yes. Kitchen. Cupboard over sink." His hand reached up to grasp at James's wrist. "My staff. They took them somewhere in the house."

"Don't move," James said. "I'll be back."

He went in search of the kitchen. McCarter began a search of the house. It didn't take him long to find Rashid's domestic help. They were in the second bedroom. On the tiled floor. One man, one young woman. Their throats had been cut wide open and they lay in wide pools of their own blood.

"Bastards," McCarter said.

He realized he still had his Browning in his hand and right then he was wishing he could go and shoot the intruders a second time. The sight of the dead wiped away any regret he might have been harboring for the men who had done this.

Back in the lounge he watched James tending to Rashid's injuries. When his partner glanced at him McCarter shook his head. Even with only one good eye Rashid noticed the gesture.

"Both of them?" he asked.

"Sorry."

The medical kit turned out to be well equipped and James used his skill to clean up Rashid and make him as comfortable as possible. He removed the man's blood-soaked cotton shirt and examined his torso. Red bruising was starting to spread. James probed the flesh over the ribs. He couldn't detect any breakages but suspected the ribs were badly bruised.

"You, my friend, are going to be hurting for a while."

Rashid said, "But I am alive." He winced as he took a breath. "Am I not?"

"Bruised and battered," McCarter said. He looked around the room at the dead. "In better condition than they are."

"I have friends who will take care of them," Rashid said. "But first I have to thank you for saving my life. I don't doubt those people would have killed me whether I spoke to them or not."

"We would be interested in finding out what they wanted," James said.

"We have a common interest," McCarter said. "Jean-Paul Alexis and an American, Harry Jerome."

"Yes, I had heard. I regret what happened," Rashid said. "I feel responsible. When I passed the information to Jean-Paul I had no idea it would result in such a terrible thing. Many times before I had given him leads to follow. Nothing like this ever happened."

"Since their deaths another American has died in Washington," McCarter said. "He was Jerome's superior in the CIA. We're here to find out what is going on."

Rashid considered what McCarter had told him.

"I owe you my life. For that I am more than indebted. Please tell me what I can do. My profession is sometimes considered in a bad light, but I like to believe I am an honorable person. I trade in information. I buy and sell it. I travel back and forth across the region and I talk to my contacts, picking up little pieces here and there. And as we now live in the electronic age I use that, too. Unfortunately, I sometimes pick up things that turn out not to be pleasant. Like some upcoming disturbance that will involve Israel and Iran."

"The information you passed on to Alexis?" James said.

"Yes. I had returned from Yemen. A bad place to be in currently. Dangerous. I spoke to an old friend who told me about a training camp in the desert. It was being run by a man named Inigo."

"Raul Inigo?" McCarter said.

"Yes. You know this man, too?"

"Know of him," McCarter said.

"He's a mercenary. Inigo will hire his people out to anyone providing the money suits him. He came from Colombia. Medellín. Worked for one of the cartels until a war destroyed his organization. He moved on. Took the cartel money and started his own business. Built it up over a few years. Hires the best and pays them well. Inigo has a simple philosophy. He doesn't care about his clients' motives. Ignores religion, so he can work for Muslims one week and a Catholic the next. The same with politics. He takes no sides."

"So, who's flavor of the month right now?"

"From what I picked up after it happened, the hit team in Sofia belonged to Inigo. He has people all over. A very organized man." Rashid held up a hand. "Very dangerous if you cross him."

"What about these men who came into your home?" James asked.

"I recognized two of them. They are from the city. No more than hired muscle. I suspect they were given a contract by Inigo to find out what else I might know. Inigo must have traced back and learned that I was the one who furnished Alexis with the information he would pass to your American friend Jerome."

"From the data we have," McCarter said, "there looks to be some sort of plan to cause agitation between Iran and Israel. That part we can figure out. What we don't yet know is how this disruption is supposed to work."

With James and McCarter helping, Rashid sat up, favoring his side where James had tightly bandaged his body. He sat for a moment while he gathered his strength. James went to the bedroom and found a fresh shirt he brought back and helped to put Rashid's arms through the sleeves.

"Those idiots who beat me had no idea the answers to their questions were no more than feet away," Rashid said. "In my safe."

"But you weren't going to tell them that," McCarter said.

"Of course not. I keep contact information in there that I have collected over many years."

He pulled his lean body upright and walked slowly across the room. A hung painting, which turned out to be solidly fixed in place, swung aside when he touched a concealed switch. He reached up and tapped a code into the keypad next to the safe. The door clicked open and Rashid reached inside. He withdrew a black iPad tablet and came back to where McCarter and James waited. He powered it up and when the screen brightened he activated a file.

"This is the location of the training camp in Yemen. Coordinates. And a second location that the local tribesmen maintain on behalf of Inigo's Yemeni contractors. Like a jail. I haven't learned who they have there. Perhaps it might provide more information for you." Rashid sat again, sweat beading his brown face. "You were right," he said to James. "It is going to hurt."

"You should call in a doctor. Even go to the hospital. Get yourself thoroughly checked over."

Rashid picked up a cell phone and held it up.

"Yes, yes. I will call my people and they will deal with what has happened. My friends, you should go now. But listen to me. When I told Alexis what I had heard and found, he was most concerned. Even then he saw that any aggression between Israel and Iran could grow to something bigger. He told me he saw the involvement of America if Iran attacked Israel. A friend coming to the aid of a friend. And of course, if that happened, it might be possible that China would back Iran. It is known that China favors stronger ties in the region. Hostilities from Israel would give China a way in. Alexis was a clever man. He understood the complexities of the political consequences. How it all might come to a clash between stronger nations. He even mentioned nuclear weaponry. If that happened then we would all suffer. That is why he said he must seek out his CIA contact and hand the information to him. You must not allow that to happen. May the blessings of Allah be upon you, my friends."

As he followed McCarter out of the villa, James said, "Amen to that."

CHAPTER TEN

Stony Man Farm, War Room

"So we have a suggestion of a plot to stir things up between Israel and Iran," Kurtzman said. "Interference that strengthens the facts. Two agents dead in Sofia. A CIA operative blown up in Washington and Hal hospitalized. Add to that Able Team attacked at Baker's apartment and David and Cal clashing with some guys trying to beat information out of this Rashid character."

"Pretty good summation," Blancanales said.

"The data from Baker's laptop has only confirmed what we've been discussing," Kurtzman said. "The stuff Alexis passed along to Jerome just adds to the mix."

"Don't forget names," Manning added. "Raul Inigo. The guy who seems to be running the deployment side of the operation. And a mention of this Edgar Bergstrom. He's in there somewhere."

Price leaned forward. "Can we ignore Senator Hayden Trent? Tenuous as it seems, he does appear to have a connection with Bergstrom. And an Iranian hostile face-off with Israel would really rack up points on his agenda for putting pressure on sending in U.S. forces. The man was on TV last night again, rallying support. He's using Iranian threats to blockade the Straits of Hormuz as an example of their reckless attitude."

"Trent is a powerful guy," Encizo said. "Check his connections. The list of his friends and supporters. He is one influential hombre."

"Doesn't give him the right to try to affect U.S. policy," Price said. "Especially in somewhere like the Mideast."

"We'll go and look into Bergstrom's involvement," Lyons said. "See if we can trace him back to Trent."

Able Team made their way out of the War Room.

"David and Cal are on their way to Incirlik Air Base in Turkey," Price said. "You will rendezvous with them there. Arrangements have been made to transport you over to Turkey courtesy of the Air Force. The 39th Mission Support Group at Incirlik will fly you to the U.S. base on Masirah Island, Oman. From there you will be ferried into Yemen in a helicopter piloted by a civilian contractor. All your equipment will be generic. No connection to U.S. Military. This has to be a total covert operation. The copter will drop you as close as possible to the training camp Rashid described. It will then return to Oman. All contact to be maintained with Stony Man via your sat phones. When you complete, we'll arrange pickup from one of the task force carriers in the Arabian Sea. Right now there isn't anything close, but by the time you complete your mission there should be one in chopper range." She took a breath and gazed around the table at Phoenix Force team. "Any questions?"

"Couldn't you have found us something risky to do?" Hawkins said lightly.

Price said, "With the restrictive window we have, there hasn't been time to cover risk assessment, guys. I wish we could have made it safer but—"

"In his quaint, old-fashioned way," Encizo said, "T.J. is saying don't worry. We understand. Situations like this don't allow a week for preplanning."

"This seems to have been arranged pretty fast, Barb," Manning said. "No slight intended, but did you have help?"

Price smiled. "My new best buddy, one President of the United States, interceded and used his rank as Commander in Chief to push things along. Like borrowing an Air Force plane to ferry you to where you need to go. He has made it clear to all concerned that the mission is critical. You are tagged as a covert team with the highest security rating. Cooperation has been demanded at all levels with no questions asked. National security. Need-to-know."

Price pushed a loaded pack across the table. "New sat phones. GPS compatible. Fully charged. Also power chargers to keep them topped up before you hit the desert. You'll find your individual handguns there, as well. Extra magazines. Courtesy of 'Cowboy' Kissinger. He said to tell you he's serviced and set up each weapon so if you can't hit targets it's down to poor shooting and not the guns. You'll find com sets in there, too. When you get to Incirlik the rest of your ordnance will be waiting."

"When do we leave?" Encizo asked.

Price smiled. "Oh, why are you still sitting around here? Your helicopter is waiting to ferry you to your flight out."

"I'll be glad when Hal gets back," Hawkins said, his face wreathed in a grin. "This woman is getting really feisty."

"You'd better believe it," Kurtzman said. "Now haul your asses out that door."

The War Room door closed behind the departing team. The silence hung over Price and Kurtzman. Her eyes betrayed her feelings.

"Aaron," she said, "every time. Every time."

He cleared his throat. "I know. Hey, they'll be back. Just like always."

McCARTER AND JAMES disembarked from their flight from Morocco at Turkey's Atatürk International Airport and waited in the lounge for the connecting flight to Adana, where they would be met by a vehicle from the Incirlik base. They had a couple of hours to wait. James wandered off to find coffee and McCarter took the opportunity to call Stony Man. He found out that the rest of Phoenix Force was on its way to Incirlik. Barbara Price brought him up to speed on the details of the arrangements that had been made. McCarter was impressed. Despite the sophisticated encryption provided by the Stony Man sat phones, he didn't stay on the line for too long.

James returned with hot, spicy black coffee.

"Bloody hell, Calvin, if I drink all this I'll be awake for a week."

"In the circumstances," James said, "that might be a good thing."

"Hey, I'm a growing lad. I need my beauty sleep."

"*Beauty* being the operative word."

When McCarter tasted the coffee his face screwed up.

"Same wherever you go. Coffee in plastic cups just doesn't work. Let me go see if I can get a can of Coke."

When they had moved on from Rashid's home they'd found Aziz and his taxi still waiting for them. They'd had him drive them back to the city, where they'd made a detour to return the handguns and the knives to Randal. Aziz had waited outside the hotel as they'd collected their hand luggage, then taken them to the airport. McCarter had settled the substantial fare, adding a generous bonus. Aziz had accepted the money with a wide smile, telling them to look him up if they ever returned to Tangier.

Stony Man had booked them on a flight to Turkey, where they would touch down at Atatürk Airport and pick up the additional flight to Adana, where they were now sitting out the two-hour waiting period. As always the waiting part was the worst part of the deal.

CHAPTER ELEVEN

"This is not acceptable," Inigo said. "Two teams cut down like they were amateurs. Plus the ones in Sofia. More damn men lost over the last week than since we started operations. I want to know who is doing this to me." He lurched to his feet. *"I want to know."*

The anger was bubbling below the surface, made even more frightening by the fact that he spoke in a low whisper, not a violent scream of rage. The members of his team looked at each other, each daring the other to speak. None of them dared to break the silence. They knew Inigo's rage. The rage that could erupt with blinding speed, striking out at anyone close by.

Inigo didn't like any form of defeat. It crawled under his skin like a poisonous tic and spread through his body. Inigo had brought this malady with him from the favelas and he never forgot it. He refused to favor anything that encroached on his power. Allowing something to weaken him was not allowed. In his mind he was all-powerful. A man of stature. Not the shivering orphan who had survived without support. He had sloughed off the cloak of deprivation and poverty. He would never let it embrace him again. In his mind the dark shadow of his past was always present. He was determined to conquer his inner fear. It drove him. Forced him to strive for better things than his bleak origins.

Remo entered the cabin. He became aware, instantly,

of the tense atmosphere. If anyone understood the demons driving Inigo, it was Remo. He had risen from the streets himself and knew how Inigo hated that part of his life. He admired Inigo. Admired the way the favela boy had pushed himself into his current position of power. The success he had achieved when he had taken the remnants of the cartel and transformed it. Because of Inigo, Remo enjoyed the luxurious lifestyle, the power and the worldwide influence the organization wielded.

The recent disappointments they had suffered would have affected Inigo more than anyone else. He had reached a pinnacle and hated to have even the slightest setback.

Remo moved into the cabin. He turned to the assembled men and made a quick gesture, dismissing them. The group retreated, thankful Remo had allowed them to escape. When the cabin door slid closed behind the last man, Remo turned to face his friend.

"Remo, perhaps you should take a job with the UN," Inigo said. "Become a peacemaker."

Remo smiled. "I prefer to stand at your side. We have come through a lot, Inigo, and we will survive these setbacks. Sit down and I will pour you a drink. Then we will discuss what we need to do."

Inigo sank into one of the soft leather seats and stared out through the cabin window. The *Boa Vista* moved serenely through the blue-green waters of the Indian Ocean, below a clear blue sky. The scene of tranquil beauty calmed Inigo. The open windows of the main cabin allowed a warm breeze to drift into the cabin.

"Here," Remo said. He pressed a heavy tumbler of amber whiskey into Inigo's hand, took his own glass and sat facing Inigo.

"This is not the first time we have lost out," he said.

"Not on such a scale," Inigo reminded him. "I don't like

it, Remo. This contract is important. The money apart, it will bring us into contact with powerful people. For the future. So, we can't let ourselves be made to look weak."

"I understand. We need to concentrate on moving forward. Keep everyone on their toes. Send out people to run checks on these men. See if we can get a lead on who they are. There has to be a trail we can follow. Get Bergstrom to follow up on the Washington incident. He has the facilities to look into it."

Inigo nodded. "Yes. But he has to move carefully. If he makes any errors he could compromise himself. We should also get our own people to look into it, too. This time choose someone discreet. Someone who will use brains over brawn. The ones who hit Baker's apartment didn't plan it out and because of that they are dead."

"Leave it to me. Now, what about the man in Tangier—Rashid? Do we send in someone to kill him? He survived. We know that. If he passed over what he knows to the ones who saved him…"

"Then the damage has already been done, Remo. Killing him now would serve no real purpose. And after what happened he has probably surrounded himself with his own protection team. Sending in a removal squad would only entail more expense and expose our people to more risk." Inigo waved a hand in the air. "We have more immediate concerns. The first being the next stage of the operation and making sure we do not leave anything that can be traced back to us."

"The training camp in Yemen?"

"It has served its purpose. Speed up the removal of everyone there. If Rashid gave any indication of its existence, this mysterious force could descend on it. Clear the camp. Leave nothing behind. Level it to the ground."

"What about the captives?"

"The locals we caught snooping around are nothing of consequence. Have them dealt with. The desert will hide their bodies."

"And the Israeli?"

"He still interests me. We should bring him here so we can talk to him without having to look over our shoulders all the time."

"Who do you think he is? Mossad?"

"He was armed. He carried an encrypted phone we can't break into. Yes, I believe he's Mossad, Remo."

"Mossad are bad people to upset."

Inigo smiled. "Remo, if this contract succeeds, the Israelis will have enough to handle without worrying about one missing agent."

"Are you ready to fly out to see Koretski?" Remo asked.

"I go tomorrow."

"A long way, Raul. All the way to the back end of Russia."

"I think of it as a way of expanding my knowledge, Remo, but yes, it is long. And it will be fucking cold, so don't stand there with a grin on your. facc or I might send you instead."

CHAPTER TWELVE

Oman

Phoenix Force touched down at Thumrait Air Base at 3:00 a.m. The flight from Incirlik, on board a USAF transport supply aircraft, had been noisy and uncomfortable. The Air Force didn't worry about things like cossetting passengers. It was a military plane, not a long-haul luxury ride. The Phoenix Force team was well used to the lack of amenities. They spent their time checking their equipment and taking quick naps. It was business as usual for the Stony Man team. Being thrown straight in at the deep end was nothing they hadn't done before. The unknown was what they might encounter at the end of their journey. Whatever that might be, Phoenix Force would face it without complaint.

As well as their chosen handguns, they had been provided with 5.7 mm FN P-90 autoweapons. The P-90 utilized a top-mounted translucent magazine that held fifty rounds, with semi- or full-auto delivery. Gary Manning had also been handed a Dragunov sniper rifle. They also had a selection of fragmentation and flash bang grenades.

It was still dark when the lumbering transport landed. Phoenix Force was met by an Air Force major named Pierson. After a brief exchange he drove them across to a briefing room where they were able to have a look at current maps and charts of the area.

"Your pilot is an expat called Jeff Lowry. He owns an old Huey." Pierson couldn't hold back a grin. "And I mean old. That chopper has been around the block so many times it's going to meet itself coming back one day. But I have to say Lowry holds it together. Most likely with duct tape and spit. Just don't make any remarks when you see it. Lowry is proud of that bird. He's run a few off-the-book missions for us and always got our guys there and back in one piece."

"Sounds like my kind of bloke," McCarter said.

"He'll pick you up at first light. I'm figuring you fellers haven't managed a decent meal since you left Turkey. Let's go across to the mess hall and get you something."

THE FAMILIAR whump-whump of the Huey's rotors informed the Phoenix Force veterans their ride was on its way. In the first light of day it came in over the base and made a textbook landing.

"Pierson wasn't joking," Manning said when he laid eyes on the Bell helicopter.

The chopper's military paintwork was faded and dull, except for where some panels had been replaced. There were a few dents and scratches in evidence. Both passenger doors were missing and sections of the windows were either cracked or slightly yellowed with age.

"Oh, mama," Hawkins whispered. "Guys, I think I'll walk."

"Be nice to the man," McCarter said as the lean figure of Jeff Lowry extracted himself from the cockpit and crossed to meet them.

He was well over six feet tall, a wiry, sunburned man dressed in a wash-faded khaki shirt and pants. His blue eyes surveyed Phoenix Force from an amiable face. A long peaked ball cap was pulled down over his straw-colored hair and he wore a pair of Nike trainers on his feet.

"Well, don't you boys look the real deal," he said. His accent was Kentucky backwoods.

McCarter introduced Phoenix Force. He gripped Lowry's hand.

"Nice to meet you, Jeff."

"You good to go?"

McCarter nodded.

"Take your seats, gentlemen, and we'll go take a flyby over the Yemeni back country."

As soon as Phoenix Force was on board Lowry powered up and the Huey rose smoothly. The UH-1H was a noisy machine. Despite that, Lowry's aircraft showed remarkable power as it picked up speed under his expert hand. It was clear that he had spent a great many hours working on the Huey's turbine engine, achieving maximum power from it.

McCarter dropped into the seat next to Lowry.

"Still noisy," he said, "but you've done a great job on that engine."

"The old Huey was never going to win any prizes for silent running." The pilot grinned. "What the hell. You can't have everything."

"You were in the service?"

"Yeah. I spent twelve years coaxing these babies to stay in the air. Did tours all over. Then I figured it was time to do it for myself when I ended my last tour. Heard about a machine here in Oman that was going for a song. Came to look at her and decided she was meant just for me. Scraped together the price. Managed to dicker it down some and there you go. Since then I been working on her and flying charters back and forth. Oil companies. Agency ops. Anything goes." Lowry's grin widened. "Hell, I done a few trips under the radar. Military used me a couple times.

Like you guys. No questions asked either way. Fast trips in and out, been shot at time or two but, shit, who wants life to get too quiet."

"You good for these coordinates?" McCarter asked, showing the numbers to Lowry.

The pilot checked them and gave a slow nod. "About thirty miles in from the border. In the Empty Quarter. The local badlands."

"I know."

"You walked the walk?"

"Some time back now."

"With that Limey accent I'm thinking Special Air Service."

McCarter just smiled. The pilot tapped the side of his nose.

"I get it. No talkee-talkee. Fine. But they're a good bunch. The best."

Lowry showed McCarter the map he had taped to a clipboard. He traced the route with his finger.

"There she is," he said.

"Put us down about three klicks short of the target," McCarter said. "You good to hang around for us?"

"No problem. And it's what I'm being paid to do. Look, it won't be a long trip," Lowry said. "You fellers enjoy the ride."

McCarter moved back to squat beside the rest of the team as the featureless landscape flashed by below the Huey. He placed his back against the bulkhead and sat until Lowry motioned to him.

"Coming to your landing coordinates," Lowry yelled above the engine's racket.

The chopper began to descend, the sandy terrain stretching as far as they could see. It was empty.

A desolate place.

"The badlands" described it perfectly.

Encizo tapped McCarter's shoulder.

"There," he said. "Armed men."

McCarter picked up the straggling figures. The chopper was slowing now as Lowry took them toward a landing.

The line of armed figures had seen the Huey. They were stringing out, weapons rising.

Men from the camp?

A patrol?

"Oh, bloody hell," the Briton said.

His keen eyes had recognized the weapon one of the men below was carrying. He saw the guy swing the object to his shoulder.

"That's an RPG," McCarter yelled. Over his shoulder he called to the pilot. "Jeff, get us clear fast. Hostile fire on its way."

The helicopter began to turn at a steep angle, Lowry working the controls with a sure hand. As fast as he was, the RPG shooter was faster. McCarter saw the brief flash of flame and smoke as the missile was launched, then watched its wavering course as it snaked up toward the chopper.

"Incoming," the Briton called out. "Right at us."

The Soviet rocket hit the tail end of the helicopter, the blast ripping it apart. Lowry struggled with the controls, but he had lost everything. The chopper began a dizzying fall, a series of spinning swoops.

"Hang on," James shouted.

The five Stony Man warriors grabbed hold of anything available. Cargo straps and struts.

"Lowry?" McCarter yelled.

"Just hang tight," the pilot replied. "Coming in now…"

They came in on a shallow curve, Lowry managing a final stall as he boosted the power of the rotors to the maximum, helping to lift the nose just before they hit the ground. The stricken helicopter plowed a deep furrow in the earth, trailing a thick spume of dust in its wake.

Inside the aircraft the occupants were bounced around like loose beans in a can. The structure of the chopper creaked and groaned, outer sections shearing off. Under the impact of landing the metal skids simply collapsed so the resultant slide was on the underside of the machine. It came to a sudden and grinding halt, the nose trying to bury itself in the earth. Dust billowed around the wrecked aircraft. The smell of aviation fuel filled the cabin.

"Grab your gear and let's get the hell out of here," McCarter said, picking himself up off the cabin floor. "Anyone hurt?"

"No more than usual," Hawkins said.

McCarter swung through to check on Lowry. The front section of the flight deck had collapsed inward, the aluminum structure enveloping Jeff Lowry. The American pilot had taken the full force of the crash and his body had been cruelly pinned in the crush of metal. McCarter could only see the man's head and shoulders. One arm was severed at the elbow, and his lower throat was torn wide open. Blood glistened in thick streaks in among the twisted metal.

Calvin James appeared at McCarter's side. He leaned in and checked Lowry's pulse. "Nothing," he said. He closed Lowry's staring wide eyes. "Sorry, man. You did us proud."

"Let's go," McCarter said.

White smoke was starting to coil into the cabin, the distinct smell of hot electrical wiring underlying it.

With their backpacks in place and weapons ready Phoenix Force clustered together a distance from the downed helicopter.

McCarter checked his GPS unit.

"If this thing is still online we're about four miles from where we should have landed." He jerked a thumb toward the west. "That way. Let's beat our feet before that RPG bloke and his mates show up."

"They already have," Encizo said.

Armed figures appeared over the crest of a low hill back along the chopper's flight path. As soon as they spotted Phoenix Force they opened fire. Slugs began to impact the ground around the Stony Man team, but the gunfire was sporadic and not accurate.

"No way," Manning muttered as he slid his sniper rifle from his shoulder and pulled it into position. The Dragunov SVU, chambered for 7.62 mm ammunition and with a mounted PSO-1 telescopic sight, had been the only non-U.S.A. weapon available at short notice. The bullpup configuration was familiar to Manning. He had used the rifle before and knew its capabilities. It had a gas-operated rotating bolt. It was fitted with a 10-round curved box magazine. And there was the added bonus that Gary Manning was Phoenix Force's official sharpshooter.

Ignoring the short-falling fire, Manning snugged the rifle to his shoulder, locking in on his first target, and put a single 7.62 mm round through the guy's chest. The impact kicked the man off his feet and dumped him on the ground in front of his buddies. The echo of the shot was still rattling off the rocky slopes when Manning fired his next round. A second man went down, the back of his skull taken out by the through-and-through. In his stride now, Manning executed a third shot as the distant attackers broke apart, seeking cover. He had chosen this target deliberately. The man wielding the RPG that had brought the helicopter down. The 7.62 mm slug hit the guy side-on as he turned to run. It went under his left arm, traversed his body and sectioned his heart before erupting through his right shoulder in a spurt of red.

The rest of the attacking group dived for full cover, aware they were under a gun that could reach farther than theirs, being used by a shooter with superior skills. Whatever else they were, the opposition was smart in that respect.

"Great shooting, Gary," Hawkins said.

"Too damn easy," Manning said. "Like fish in a barrel."

"He being modest?" Encizo said.

"Not really," McCarter said. "Now let's get the hell out of here before they start using their bloody brains."

Fire began to creep out from the helicopter's engine compartment as smoldering cable came into contact with fuel vapor. The fire spread quickly, finding the mass of spilled fuel. As Phoenix Force moved away they heard the solid whoosh as fire engulfed the midsection of the machine.

They started west, Manning bringing up the rear in case any of the enemy showed their heads above the parapet.

The effects of the helicopter crash began to manifest themselves. Every member of the team felt aches and discomfort from the solid impact when the aircraft had reached ground zero. None of them made any comments over their individual hurts. Not out of some macho bravado. They kept their feelings in check because they didn't want to have other team members worrying about each other. The mission was their prime concern. Until it was resolved personal complications took a backseat.

During their approach to the objective the team heard the crack of Manning's Dragunov on three separate occasions. They maintained their steady pace, understanding that the Canadian was cutting down the numbers on the back trail and knowing Manning would close up again.

They located their destination without further interruption, crowding close in the wide shadow provided by a dusty overhang of rock.

The camp lay in front of their position. What was left of it. Tents had been burned to the ground, leaving nothing but blackened remains. A few wisps of smoke still trailed up from the site. The same thing had happened to a couple of prefabricated wood huts. A scattering of abandoned items lay in the churned sand.

"Damn," McCarter said. "Looks like they scarpered."

"Looks like we just missed them. Maybe they figured we might pay them a visit," James said.

"Or they'd completed what they needed to do here," Manning said.

"We need to take a look at the other site," Encizo said.

McCarter nodded. "Let's go take a look." He scanned the GPS unit. "Over to the north. Come on, my beauties. A little more exercise will set you up nicely."

"For what?" Hawkins asked.

"Getting out of Yemen," James said.

"Why the rush?" Encizo said. "We've been shot down. Lost our ride and pilot. Reached our target and found it burned to the ground. Now we go looking for another site before we hike out of the country. What's not to like?"

"Said like that, I have to see your point," McCarter agreed. "Let's go."

"This Inigo," Hawkins said. "He's using his head. We've taken down a number of his operators, so he's cutting his losses and backing off."

"Gets his people out of Yemen because he figures we'll come looking for him," Encizo said. "Leaves his local Yemeni guys to deal with us."

"And they nearly succeeded," McCarter said. He peeled

off his ball cap and ran a hand through his damp hair. "This bloody place is hot in more ways than one."

They trooped up a long, gritty slope. The sun hit them from overhead and the ground under their booted feet radiated heat. At the top of the slope they dropped to their stomachs, staying below the ridge line. McCarter took binoculars from his pack and edged forward to scope out the terrain. He spent long minutes surveying the way ahead until he was satisfied there was no threat. He put the glasses away, taking a minute to moisten his dry throat with warm water from his canteen.

"A chilled Coke and fag," he muttered. "A fag, a fag, my kingdom for a fag."

Beside him James gave a chuckle. "You don't really mean that. It's all in your mind."

"You think?" McCarter said. "Listen, chum, my mind wants a smoke, as well."

At the Briton's command they started out again. Single file, McCarter in the lead and Hawkins bringing up the rear.

Fine, gritty sand swirled across their path as a hot wind blew up and created a mini dust storm. It lasted for no more than twenty minutes. By the time it blew itself out the Phoenix Force team was spitting sand particles out of their mouths, even though they had wrapped their neck scarves over their faces. The sand managed to infiltrate their clothing and seek out the crevices in their flesh. As soon as the wind rose they pulled their weapons in close, protecting the mechanisms from becoming clogged. McCarter called a halt once the wind died and they took shelter in a hollow where they cleaned and checked their weapons before moving on.

"Hey, that was fun," Hawkins said.

No one answered, so he fell silent.

The delay added to their trek. It was just after midday, the hottest time, when McCarter held up a hand and they dropped to the hot ground.

"Rashid came through," Hawkins said, studying the cluster of buildings and a couple of tents.

"I see three guards," McCarter said. He was scanning the layout through binoculars from his backpack. "All carrying. AK-47s. There's an open truck parked alongside the largest building."

The hot and dry wind was gusting down in their direction from the higher ground. It swept pale dust at them, seeping into their clothing again and clinging to their skin.

James dragged a hand across his mouth. "Damn stuff," he said. "Can we get this done, David?"

McCarter managed a grin. "We getting tetchy, mate?"

"Actually, *mate,* yes."

"Take Rafe and assess the situation. See if you can eyeball any other opposition around the far side. I'm going to update Stony Man. Then we'll go."

James and Encizo slid away, staying with the ridge until they were well clear of the main objective, then working their way around to the side and then rear.

"Any movement along our back trail?" McCarter asked Manning.

The Canadian shook his head. "All down," he assured the team leader.

McCarter didn't need to probe any further. If Manning said the crew was down, that was it. Manning wouldn't make a statement without absolute guarantees.

He keyed the sat phone and waited while the sequence resolved itself into the ring tone. He recognized Barbara Price's voice.

"Hello, luv. This is your English uncle calling."

The relief in her tone was easy to pick up.

"You all okay?"

"Yes. We're at the target location. Getting set to go in."

"Right. Any problems?"

"We did lose our ride," McCarter said. "And our pilot."

"What happened?"

"There was a welcoming party. Not friendly. Hit us with an RPG. Lowry brought us down but he didn't make it. We engaged and handled our hosts. Had to walk in to the location."

"Sorry about Lowry. How will you get clear once the target has been taken out?"

"Still working on that," McCarter admitted. "First things first. You have anything new for me?"

"Uh-uh. Aaron and the guys are still working flat-out on more information, but I'm leaving them alone. You know how grouchy Bear gets if he thinks he's being pushed."

"Just keep us in the loop."

"Will do. Hey, good luck."

McCarter put the phone away.

His earpiece clicked and he picked up Calvin James's calm voice.

"In position," he said. "We have one guy watching the rear. We're set."

"Roger that. You'll hear when we move. That's your go."

One of the armed men outside the building took a cell phone out of his robes. He listened to what the caller was saying, his head nodding in agreement. The call ended and the guy spoke to his partners. He threw a thumb in the direction of the building. Two of the men lifted their weapons and made their way inside.

"What's happening?" Manning asked.

"Not sure but I'm getting a bad feeling."

The two guards reappeared. They were dragging a third man with them. He looked in a bad way. His filthy clothing was streaked with dried blood and when he finally raised his head McCarter could see the brutal marks of heavy bruising. He struggled weakly, feet dragging in the dust. His captors pushed him to his knees and stepped back. The guy knelt in the dirt, barely able to raise his limp arms.

The three guards watched him, one of them saying something that brought a round of harsh laughter. The man in the middle moved forward.

Without any preamble he thrust his hand inside his robe, pulled out an autopistol and aimed at the kneeling man.

McCarter realized what the man was about to do.

The pistol cracked heavily, a pair of slugs coring into the back of the kneeling prisoner's skull. The man jerked forward as a spurt of blood erupted from his head before he slammed facedown in the dust.

"Bastard," Manning said.

McCarter saw the Canadian's rifle swing up to settle on the guard with the pistol. His single shot took the man in the chest, the impact slamming him back against the wall. The guy stared down at the bloody hole in his chest and began coughing up blood before he dropped.

"Go, go, go," McCarter yelled into his com set.

Phoenix Force pushed to their feet and made their frontal strike. They pounded across the open ground, dust powdering from beneath their boots. McCarter signaled for Hawkins to break left and cover the side area. Manning stayed on McCarter's heels.

The Briton hammered a burst at one of the remaining guards, his slugs ripping through the layer of clothing and puncturing the flesh beneath. The guy made a half turn, then went to his knees, dropping his AK. He fumbled under his robe for a concealed handgun, half clearing it before McCarter put a shot through the side of his head.

The slug, mushrooming as it struck bone, tumbled through the brain and detached a larger chunk of bone on exit.

Manning had shouldered his rifle, drawing his autopistol, and as he edged around McCarter he triggered three close shots that punched into the third guy's throat and opened up a stream of blood. The target went down without a sound.

Movement at the open door became an armed figure, robed and wearing a kaffiyeh. The guy opened fire without taking a pause to track in on the racing figures. His burst chunked into the dry earth inches from McCarter. The Phoenix Force commando leveled his P-90 and hit the shooter with a burst that ripped through his lean torso and blew out his back, taking flesh and spine with it. The shooter toppled back.

McCarter and Manning flattened against the stone wall. Manning plucked a flash bang from his harness and primed it. He leaned sideways and lobbed the grenade in through the open door. McCarter and Manning clamped their hands over their ears and turned their heads away from the doorway. The hard crack of the stun grenade still managed to make itself known as it detonated. The effect on Phoenix Force was minimal.

"Go," McCarter yelled, and led the way inside.

A haze of thin smoke hung in the air. Armed figures stumbled around the untidy room.

McCarter took out the closest figure, hitting the guy with a 5.7 mm P-90 burst that kicked him off his feet. Manning repeated the move, his pistol thundering in the confines of the thick stone walls, hitting the second man. With the occupants out of commission Phoenix Force crossed the room and reached the opening that exposed the passage leading to the rear.

A robed figure appeared and his AK-47 raked the walls

with heavy fire. Slugs ripped chunks out of the crumbling stone, filling the air with fragments and acrid dust. The firing went on until the shooter's weapon ran out of ammunition.

McCarter gave a wild yell and hurled himself along the passage before Manning could stop him. He hit the floor, arcing his P-90 around, and lining it up on the hooded terrorist who was still ramming a fresh magazine into this SMG. The guy's face turned toward the Briton, mouth opening in a yell of defiance as he realized his fatal mistake. McCarter didn't give him much time to reflect on it. He thrust his FN at the guy's chest and triggered a burst that ravaged flesh and bone, sending the man back against the wall, bloody debris spattering the stone. McCarter pushed to his feet and kicked the dropped AK clear of the jerking body.

The passage ended in a heavy wooden door, bound with iron straps. A solid bolt held the door secure.

Encizo grabbed the bolt and slid it back. He pushed the door open, the hinges protesting. The cell beyond was dark, the stench coming from it overpowering. Shadowed figures could be seen inside the cell.

"Bloody hell," McCarter said. "How long have they had these poor buggers in here?"

A stumbling form detached itself from the other figures and moved with infinite slowness in the direction of the open door, reaching out to lean against the frame.

"Too long," he said.

The voice was low, rasping, coming from a throat that lacked moisture. The eyes fixing on McCarter were dark-ringed, recent bruises marking the flesh. A partly healed gash showed ragged edges across the left cheek. Thick black hair, matted and dull, framed the sunken-cheeked face. The lower part of the face was edged with thick black stubble.

McCarter stared into the eyes, something familiar in the steady gaze.

"Ben? Ben Sharon?" he said.

The Mossad agent returned the Briton's stare, his dulled senses struggling to catch elusive memories. His cracked and bloody lips formed a thin smile.

"What do I call you this time?"

McCarter grinned. "Jack Coyle." He reached out to support Sharon as the man slumped. "Give the man a hand," he said to Manning.

As Manning moved to assist the Mossad agent, Sharon said, "Left arm's fractured."

When he stepped away from the door McCarter saw that Sharon's arm was bound tight against his body to hold it immobile.

"Hard time," McCarter said.

"You could say."

Manning helped the Israeli along the passage.

Hawkins appeared, easing by Manning and Sharon.

"Clear out there," he said. He peered into the cell. "What about these other guys, boss?"

"Let's get them outside."

There were three more inside the filthy, cramped cell. One could barely walk on his own. McCarter and Hawkins half carried the man out into the open, where they sat him against the outside wall. One of the walking prisoners held his right arm close to his body, shielding the crudely bandaged stump where his hand had been. All the prisoners showed signs of harsh physical beatings and their filthy clothes were torn to rags.

James and Encizo showed up, having dealt with the guard at the rear.

"All clear," Encizo said.

"You find any…" James said before his gaze fell on the assembled prisoners. "What the hell have they done here?"

"Well, it isn't a Holiday Inn," McCarter said.

"These poor bastards need a medical team," James said.

"Well, they'll just have to make do with your packet of Band-Aids and antiseptic cream."

James broke out his medic kit and began to check out the prisoners.

Manning, silent for a while, stepped forward, then faced McCarter.

"What the hell is Ben Sharon doing here?"

"It wasn't to give the place a five-star rating. Haven't had much time to ask him yet."

Manning crouched in front of Sharon, attracting his attention.

"How did they catch you in their net, Ben?"

"I got lucky?" Sharon croaked. "I was working a lead and fell in with the wrong crowd."

"What were you after?"

Sharon didn't appear to understand the question, his thoughts drifting away. He was in no fit state to make conversation, so Manning backed off. After James had examined him and assessed his condition he pulled McCarter and Manning to one side.

"Don't expect too much from him now. He needs time to clear his head. Badly dehydrated. He's lost weight, too. Not much I can do for him out here. Same with the others. Hospital's what they all need. ASAP."

"I'll see what Stony Man can conjure up," McCarter said. "Do what you can for them, Cal. Gary, set up a defensive perimeter with the rest of the team. In case we get visitors. I don't want us here for any longer than necessary, but I'd guess bloody miracles are in short supply today."

McCarter pulled out his sat phone and keyed in for Stony Man. It took time before he got a response. Hearing Barbara Price's calm voice just emphasized how far from home they all were.

"I know this isn't like calling in a big yellow taxi, luv, but we need a lift out of here. Four freed prisoners. All in a bad way. They should be hospitalized. Listen, Barb, one of them is Ben Sharon."

"Mossad's Ben Sharon?"

"The same. He isn't ready to talk to anyone right now, so how he ended up in this place is still a mystery."

"Rashid's intel turned out to be useful."

"Looks that way."

"Are you thinking Sharon being there has something to do with this mission?"

"Hoping so. With Iran and Israel in the mix, it makes it likely. That's why we need to airlift out of here. Pull some strings. Use your charm. You do have charm, I presume?"

Price burst into laughter. "Cheeky," she said. "You leave it to me. I'll get back to you as soon as I have it sorted."

"Thank you, Ms. Price."

"No problem."

McCarter was about to end the call when a thought came to him. "Might be useful to have a word with the Man. See if he can get through to Israel and ask if they can bring us into the loop about Ben's mission."

"I'll pass that on."

FOUR HOURS AFTER nightfall the bulk of a U.S. Navy Seahawk helicopter, guided by the GPS transmission from McCarter's sat phone, set down just short of the site. Phoenix Force and their four guests hustled over to the waiting aircraft. Once Sharon and his companions had been lifted inside, the Stony Man team followed. The helicopter took off without hesitation, rising swiftly and swinging toward the coast, the Arabian sea and the U.S. Navy aircraft carrier waiting in international water.

CHAPTER THIRTEEN

"Another grand screwup," Inigo said.

At any other time he might have been angry, but he was exhausted from his flight to Russia and his trip to see Koretski. After making the deal he had trekked back from the isolated spot and caught his flight home.

Inigo nodded. "I wanted the guards to eliminate all the prisoners but now I find out this fucking commando team raided the base and took the captives away after killing the guards."

"So, we have lost the Israeli, too."

"Remo, the man has been in that cell for almost a week. Even under duress he gave nothing away. We know he'd been checking us out. But we also know he hasn't been able to tell Mossad anything because we caught him before he did. His cell's call list was clean. When Rudolpho accessed his backlist on our computer there was nothing on that, either. He's a Mossad agent, I know that, Remo, and Mossad agents do not waste time on calls to order pizzas. He would have informed his superiors if he had something vital to tell them."

"You were going to have him brought here to the *Boa Vista* for further interrogation. Why change that?"

"Because with him dead anything he may have unearthed dies with him. It won't harm us if no one finds out what he may, or may not, have found out. Simple logic. One more problem out of the way."

"You could be right."

"I usually am. Now I have to contact Bergstrom before I fall asleep. He needs updating."

Remo handed over the sat phone.

"Are we safe?" Inigo asked when Edgar Bergstrom came on the line.

"If I can't have a secure line we're in deep shit. Let's keep this brief, though."

"The camp has been cleared. Our mysterious hit team showed up. Killed the guards and took our prisoners away."

"Even the Mossad guy?"

"Him, too. It's a pity but it has happened so there's no point in whining. It might have been interesting to find out what he knew, but we need to move on."

"So, how are the arrangements progressing?"

"You will be pleased to know everything is going fine. I have just returned from my visit to Russia with Koretski."

"And?"

"I will tell you…"

MIKHAIL KORETSKI reached out a gloved hand to take Inigo's. "Welcome," he said. "You came a long way."

The Russian was a big man, very broad, his head sitting on a short neck. He wore a thick mustache on his upper lip and his face was pitted and scarred.

"Sometimes one must travel far for specialist equipment," Inigo replied.

Koretski offered a fatalistic shrug. "This will not come cheap. As we discussed. You understand this?"

"My client is aware he is asking for an expensive piece of hardware. Money is no object."

"Music to my ears."

Koretski glanced at the gray sweep of the sky. He patted Inigo's shoulder and gestured for him to follow.

The bleak landscape of the Russian steppes was an unsociable place. The ground underfoot was iron-hard, streaked with frozen ruts, and the wind blowing in across the inhospitable terrain held a threat of more snow. A scattering of buildings was the only reminder that this had once been a Russian missile base. Long abandoned and left to decay, the place now served as one of Mikhail Koretski's operation facilities.

Koretski and Inigo had done business many times in the past. He had innumerable suppliers in anything and everything illegal. The man's contacts were spread far and wide, and Koretski had yet to fail in procuring a product. Even this time, when Inigo had told him what he wanted, Koretski's only comment was that it might take a little extra time to obtain. He had, in fact, got his hands on it within two weeks, surprising even Inigo.

A deal of this magnitude could not be handled by one of Inigo's hired hands. It required his presence. Inigo subscribed to taking care of important deals on a one-to-one basis. So, he had subjected himself to the arduous trip to meet Koretski himself. Now, with the chill wind cutting through his clothing, he followed the Russian inside the hut that served as Koretski's distribution point.

A rush of warm air hit Inigo as he stepped inside. The hut smelled of the paraffin fueling the hot-air blower set in one corner. It stung Inigo's eyes but was preferable to the freezing exterior temperature.

Apart from the heater the hut was empty save for the four-foot-square wooden crate and three of Koretski's armed security team. The front of the crate was hinged and had been opened, exposing the thick canvas cover of the device sitting inside.

"What you asked for, *tovarich*," Koretski said. "A present from the defunct Soviet arsenal. Special Atomic Demolition Munitions. Known as SADMs. Much easier to say. One and a half kilotons of punch. It will make quite a bang. Purchased from an ex-major who has been trying to move it on for over a year. The man, who is an idiot, sold it for a knock-down price. He wasn't even sure if the thing was still active, but I had my weapons tech take a look and he gave me the nod it was okay." Koretski laughed. "The major was not told. I let him believe it was a risky sale but I was prepared to pay. He had finished off a second bottle of vodka by this time, so we came to an agreement I would take the thing off his hands on the understanding there would be no comeback if it proved to be dead. I think he believed he had screwed me. If I had told him it was fully workable he would have pushed up the price he was asking. Not that it was going to make any difference to the outcome."

Inigo sensed something in the man's voice. He crossed to make a closer inspection of the device. The canvas cover was faded, the stenciled serial numbers barely legible. He glanced over his shoulder.

"Tell me, Mikhail, how is the major?"

Koretski smiled. "It seems he had a nasty accident a few days after I had completed the deal. A car knocked him down near his apartment building. Hit and run. No one saw or heard anything."

"Unfortunate for him," Inigo said. "But a way of making certain he could not point the finger. A wise move cleaning up after yourself."

"It was known he was a heavy drinker. And drinkers have a habit of talking too much. Plus, of course, he had come into all that money suddenly. If the authorities noticed his increase in spending it might have aroused their curiosity. He insisted on being paid in cash. A great deal of money that he kept in two large carryalls in his apartment. Until some visitors removed it."

"Mikhail, your business practices amaze me. You procured the device *and* reclaimed your money."

"I hope that is not a problem, Raul. The money you advanced was for the bomb."

"Which we now have. You regained the money and you also have your fee. Both of us are satisfied. All we need now is to work out how to move that device from here to a pickup point where I can take delivery."

"Tell me where you want it and I will have your package on its way in the morning. I will work out the delivery schedule."

"You make it sound so easy, Mikhail. Why don't you surprise me and say it will go by DHL."

"Come into my office," Koretski said. "I can show you how we'll do it…"

"THAT'S THE BEST NEWS I've heard lately," Bergstrom said. "When can we expect final delivery?"

"Soon," Inigo said. "Koretski is well on with the delivery even as we speak."

"Good."

"I am going to push things forward, Edgar. Move everything into place as soon as possible. I'll be honest. This team, whoever they are, is still persisting. I hate having to admit it, but they are good. Which puts more pressure on us all."

"I have faith in you. You've always come through before. I see no reason why it can't happen again."

"Edgar, I am going to go to sleep now. I have flown to Russia, made the deal and flown back. My jet lag will be kicking in any second. I'll be in touch."

Inigo put down the sat phone.

He stared out the cabin window. Despite the upbeat talk he felt a slight apprehension growing. He didn't like that. He had confidence in his abilities and his people. Yet he couldn't dismiss how he felt. In the far distance, still on the horizon, he made out a line of dark clouds.

A storm?

Inigo smiled. If he had been a religious man he might have taken that as a portent of bad times ahead. He was not a man of any faith. He believed in his inner self, not some imagined deity. He made his own luck, his own destiny. It lay in *his* hands. Even so he found it hard to push aside the flickering shadows that skittered around the dark recesses of his mind.

His old hang-up had to do with his poverty-stricken childhood, when he had nothing and life overwhelmed him with its bleakness. Even though he had risen above it, beaten away the bad years and amassed a great deal of wealth, the specter remained. Taunting him from the fringes of his subconscious thoughts. Inigo knew it would never leave him completely. Yet despite his fear, the shadows helped to keep him strong. As long as they existed he would strive continuously to rise above any problems and beat any challenges that plagued him.

CHAPTER FOURTEEN

The brief inquiry Commander Valentine Seminov, Moscow OCD, had received on his personal sat phone came from his American contacts in the covert agency he had worked with before. He knew the source because no one else would have requested his help on such a matter. He had read the text, with its coded urgent prefix. His cop's brain had engaged immediately because as thinly worded as the message was, it struck chords.

Valentine Seminov had his own string of informants that stretched far and wide. His OCD brief meant he kept a close watch on matters that might affect Russia, even laterally. He knew about Raul Inigo, had a file on the man and his organization, and was aware of the far-reaching implications of any Mideast conflicts. So, when his information grapevine came up with a thread that had the names of Inigo and a Russian weapons dealer named Koretski together, Seminov pulled the two together and chose to pass the information along.

He understood his information was sketchy, flimsy even, but Seminov was a cop at heart and his heart was telling him to go with it. He had founded cases before on thin implications. If it helped, all well and good. If not, all that had been wasted was a little time.

He reached for the sat phone he kept in his desk. The number it held was one he had used before to connect him to the people he understood would be able to make use of

what he had to say. Seminov had had face-to-face contact
with the operatives in the field. Apart from that he knew
nothing of the background of the people. He knew they
were dedicated people who combated the enemies of the
U.S.A., and on a number of occasions had assisted him
during missions that involved Russia, as well. Seminov
knew the organization was totally covert and had nothing
to do with standard American security agencies. He knew
nothing more about it. Not where it was based or who the
people were, apart from the obvious cover names they
used. That didn't concern Seminov. He counted them as
strong allies. He respected them because they had proved
themselves on more than one occasion.

Now he pressed the key that would connect him to his
friends. He heard the hum of the sat phone as it commenced the sequence that would route his call through
various cutouts and security systems. When his call was
answered Seminov recognized the voice of the young
woman he knew only as Sarah. He had never met her and
had no idea what she looked like. But something told him
she was attractive and she was definitely not a Sarah. It
amused him to create an image of her in his mind.

"Commander Seminov," Price said. "Good to hear from
you. It's been some time."

"And how many times do I tell you, you should call me
Valentine. 'Commander Seminov' makes me feel old, and
it is so formal."

"*Dobroye utro,* Valentine," Price said.

"Very good, Sarah," Seminov said. "And a good morning to you."

"I take it this call was not to see how my Russian has
improved, Valentine."

"Unfortunately not. It seems we only ever speak when

a crisis has arisen. And so it is again. I believe I may have information that could be of use to you."

"Tell me."

"Through my channels of information, of which I have many, there has come to my attention rumors of a very bad deal that has already taken place. It concerns the possible negotiation of a device bought illegally."

"Let me guess that this is more than a few AK-47s or some high explosives."

"Correct, Sarah. What I am talking about here is a nuclear device. A relatively small one, but with enough power to create an explosion that will do much damage. I believe the popular name for it is a suitcase bomb. You have heard this before?"

"Yes. Not overly powerful but with a radioactive emission that would rate a great deal of suffering over a long period."

"Exactly. Small but effective. Now this device that has been traded is somewhat larger than a real suitcase. It is housed in a medium-size outer shell. About four foot square in your American measurements. When I read your inquiry text I knew there was a definite connection."

"What pointed to that?"

"Names, initially. The dead agents. Then one name that stood out."

"Let me guess. Raul Inigo."

"Inigo. Not the first time I have come across that name. A man who has created a reputation for himself as a negotiator. A supplier of all things for sale. Weapons of any kind. A man who will enter into any contract as long as it serves his main purpose. To make himself and his organization even more wealthy than it already is. He is well-known in my country. Every black marketer has dealt with him. Inigo buys and sells people as much as he negotiates the purchase of weapons. He appears to be indifferent to the harm he causes. The people who suffer. I believe you have a word that defines him. *Immoral?*"

"Amoral," Price said. "A man who stands aside from accepted limits of behavior. He sees no wrong in anything he does, regardless of the effects it has."

"That is Inigo. He was spotted briefly in Kursk with a known seller of black-market weapons. A man named Mikhail Koretski. One of our informants saw them together. They were in a café and from what the informant saw, their negotiations were extremely intense."

"If Koretski was selling what you suggest, I'm not surprised he was nervous."

"Inigo's presence would suggest a very important deal. For him to attend in person is unusual."

"Did your man give any indication how the delivery might be handled?"

"No. After their Kursk meeting Koretski and Inigo vanished for a few days. All my informant managed to find out was that they flew to the far north. Possibly to view this item. At present I have no additional information."

"So, have we lost the trail?"

"Ah, Sarah, illegal goods are shipped by many routes. Too many for us to keep an eye on them all. My informant is looking into this but it may be too late. Such a delicate item as this one would have to be handled in great secrecy, as you will understand. My informant is attempting to locate Koretski. He has apparently dropped out of sight since his meeting with Inigo. It is most likely he is arranging the shipment of the device. It is a puzzle."

"That's the problem, Valentine. This whole affair is giving us headaches. We've been working on theories and suppositions. Dealing with small pieces of information. And since it came into our view, matters have escalated."

Seminov noticed the hesitant way "Sarah" avoided direct details.

"I do not wish to pry into your operational procedures," he said. "But if there is anything I can do, please let me know."

Price made the decision to provide Seminov with some information. The Russian was in a position to offer his own data and anything Stony Man could gain would help.

"Our teams are in the field as we speak," Price said. "One is abroad, the other handling the domestic side. Since the original data fell into our hands a security agent has been killed from a bomb planted in his vehicle. Our own superior was injured in the explosion. Luckily not seriously, but he is recovering in hospital."

"This is terrible news. And your people?"

"The domestic team were attacked when they went to retrieve the dead agent's computer from his home. They survived and we are analyzing the computer as we speak."

"And your other team?"

"Tracking Inigo and his involvement in this affair."

"If it is not asking too much, Sarah, what alerted you to all this?"

"It came via information received by the agent who died in the explosion. One of his people died sending the information to him. This agent was killed in Sofia, where he had arranged to meet an operative from a French agency—"

"The CDII?"

"You know?"

"Only that Jean-Paul Alexis had been murdered. He was known to us, Sarah. A good man. I had heard about his death but not much more."

"It was Alexis who collected information that convinced him to pass it to his CIA friend, an agent named Jerome. But when they met in Sofia, Alexis was attacked. He managed to pass his information to Jerome. Jerome shot his way out but was tracked to his hotel and shortly after he had sent the data to his CIA superior he was also killed."

"And the data was enough to arouse your suspicions something was being planned?"

"Yes. Inigo's name was in the gathered data. There were other names but I can't reveal those, Valentine."

"I will double our efforts and try to locate Koretski. If we can find him, he might be persuaded to let us know where the device has gone. I will contact you the moment I learn anything."

"Thank you, Valentine."

"Sarah, a nuclear device on the loose can be a threat to us all. Especially when we do not know where it may be detonated."

"I couldn't agree more, Valentine."

CHAPTER FIFTEEN

"Can I see him?" David McCarter asked.

The Navy doctor nodded. "Just remember he's still pretty weak. Body fluid level is low. And he's been subjected to some severe physical beatings. He's on sedatives to help him rest, so he might be sleepy."

"Understood," McCarter said. "I just need to ask him a few questions. If it wasn't urgent I wouldn't bother him. I'll keep it brief." The Briton touched the medic's shoulder. "Thanks for looking after him, Doc."

The Navy carrier's medical bay was quiet. Ben Sharon was the only patient. He lay still in his bed, his splinted arm resting on the covers. He had been cleaned up, and with the grime gone the ugly bruising on his face stood out even more. McCarter thought he might be asleep, but as he neared the bed Sharon's head turned and he stared at his visitor. His cracked, sore lips curved in a crooked smile.

"*Shalom,* my friend," he said. His voice was low and it was obvious even speaking was an effort.

"I won't say you're looking better," McCarter said, "but at least they brushed your hair."

"Always the diplomat. Jack—it is Jack this time? Thanks for getting me out of that hole. Pass that on to the rest of your team."

"So, how did you get into that hole?"

"Wrong place, wrong time," Sharon said slowly. "I was tracking Raul Inigo and his group. Into my third week it took me to Yemen. I heard about a training camp he had in the desert. I had local assets in country and they picked up intel about it. Inigo had been paying the Yemeni radicals for its use. We managed to track the location, but somewhere along the line our presence had been noted. We were jumped two miles from the camp and dragged in. He was there, Inigo, and he became very angry that his cover had been exposed."

Sharon paused and indicated the plastic cup of water on the locker. McCarter held it to his lips so he could refresh himself.

"Looks like they gave you all a hard time."

"Yes. Inigo made it clear he wanted information. How we had found him. Who we had told. The thing is, I hadn't told anyone because by the time I realized we were really close to the camp I didn't get the chance to call it in. I should have done it earlier, so I can't blame anyone except myself."

"You mentioned to Landis it had been close on a week since they grabbed you," McCarter stated, referring to Calvin's cover name.

"I'm certain it was something like that. They came for us every day at noon. Took us to one of the tents and started the questioning and the beatings all over again. Sometimes, after the sessions, they dragged us outside and left us in the open, exposed to the sun. Inigo was there most of the time when we were being questioned. Cold bastard. He would watch with never a flicker on his face. Even when they cut off Razul's hand. A helicopter came a few times and I think he must have left because for a day or so he wouldn't be there during the questioning."

McCarter noticed the Israeli's speech was slowing down. He was tiring again. He knew he needed to let Sharon rest. First, though, he needed a little more information.

"Ben, do you have any idea what's in the wind?"

"Only that it's something to do with Israel and Iran at each other's throats. An engineered strike to escalate tension. Coming soon."

The information tied in with what they already suspected.

"A French agent from the CDII picked up similar chatter."

"Alexis?" Sharon nodded. "I know him."

"Inigo's people got to him in Sofia. Sorry, Ben, but he's dead. He managed to pass his information to a CIA agent. Inigo's local boys found him, too, but not before he sent the data through to Washington. Which is how we became involved."

"I think this plan means to pull in the big guns," Sharon whispered. "Get the U.S. behind Israel and China rooting for Iran."

"Our take on it, too."

Sharon's hand reached out, his fingers gripping Mc-Carter's wrist. "Don't let it happen." He paused again, summoning enough strength to make one final statement. "I have a man in Kenya. A good man. In a town near the border with Somalia. He knows where Inigo has a supply base near the Somalian coast. Before I went into Yemen he told me there had been movement at this base. He saw Inigo there with an American. Caught a name. Bergstrom. There was a lot of stuff being brought in. Maybe to do with this destabilization plan. I don't know. My contact can get you into Somalia if you think it's necessary."

Bergstrom, McCarter acknowledged.

With Inigo.

That connection again.

"Give me his name, Ben, and how we can get in touch."

THE U.S. CARRIER had a communications center that was beyond state-of-the-art. McCarter was in the MTAC—Multiple Threat Alert Center—operations room, faced by a bank of plasma screens.

He was online with Barbara Price, who had just showed up, looking tense.

Isaac Tauber, the Mossad section chief Ben Sharon reported to, was on another screen.

And the President of the United States was on a third screen.

"I have already expressed my thanks to the President," Tauber said. He was a stern-faced man in his mid-fifties, graying hair cut short. "Now I say thank you, Mr. Coyle, for what you have done for Agent Sharon. There was great concern for his well-being since his vanishing act. Sharon is an exceptional agent, despite his sometimes individual traits, and losing him would not be acceptable. So, once again, thanks to yourself and your team. Your President tells me he is in the capable hands of the U.S. Navy and is improving."

"Yes, sir," McCarter said. "I have just been speaking to him. He gave me some useful information we would like to act on ASAP."

"I'd like to hear that myself," the President said.

"Ben told me he suspected this man Raul Inigo has a base of operations in Somalia. This came from Ben's contact in Kenya. There have been consignments to this base, and the contact believes they may be related to the operation Inigo is running. If we keep up with our suspicions then it follows we need to check out these items and find out just what they are."

Barbara Price spoke up. The tone of her voice suggested what she had to say was vital to the discussion.

"I may have a lead on that, gentlemen. Just before I

came in on this meeting I was on the phone to one of our contacts in Moscow. Commander Valentine Seminov of the OCD. He had acknowledged a query text we sent out. We had asked for any information certain parties might be able to help us with. Commander Seminov passed along a sighting of Raul Inigo in Russia. He was in the company of a Mikhail Koretski—a known black-market dealer in illegal weapons. From what Commander Seminov has learned the possibility exists that a Russian nuclear suitcase bomb has been negotiated. Easily portable from what I've heard, the SADM carries a one-and-a-half-kiloton payload."

"You trust this Russian policeman?" Tauber asked.

"Yes, sir," McCarter said. "He has liaised with us before. He plays it straight down the line."

"If this device information is true," the Israeli said, "it adds weight to this possible threatened scenario."

"No question," the President said. "This needs to be dealt with head-on, Jack."

"No argument from me, Mr. President," McCarter said.

"If Inigo has a base in Somalia where he stores items, it seems a likely place to start looking," Price said.

"Agreed," McCarter said.

"A bad place at this time," the President said.

"I concur," Tauber agreed.

"With all respect, Mr. Tauber, we don't have much of a choice," McCarter said. "If our speculations are correct and we don't terminate this operation there's no telling what might happen. Whatever we do needs to be done now. We take the chance this nuke might be in Somalia because, to be truthful, we don't have any other place to go."

"We can mount an operation," Tauber said. "But it would take time to get everything in place."

"Jack," the President said, "is your team ready to move?"

"Yes, sir. The Navy can arrange for us to get into Kenya fast. Once there, we can link up with Sharon's man and make an incursion into Somalia."

"You make it sound almost like a walk in the park," Tauber said.

"Far from it," the President said. "But these men are the best. If there is any chance of putting a stop to this situation, I'll bet on them every time."

"Then we have to go with what we have. We will mount alerts here in Israel. Please contact me if there is anything we can do to help. Thank you for your input, Mr. President. It is appreciated." Tauber looked directly at McCarter. "Mr. Coyle, good luck. *Shalom*."

His image vanished from the screen, leaving McCarter with the President and Barbara Price.

"As far as Section Chief Tauber understands, your team is a covert arm of the military," the President said. "Your existence in reality is safe."

"I couldn't help but notice there was no mention of Bergstrom or Trent," McCarter said.

"He's very keen, Ms. Price," the President said.

Price smiled. "Sir, you have no idea."

"I think we'll keep it that way. Jack, I kept those names back because I saw no profit in advertising the fact that it's possible a member of the CIA may be in league with the enemy. Admitting Bergstrom might be working against us wouldn't go down well with a foreign security agency. Especially when that agency happens to be Mossad. Trent is another matter I don't want in the open at this moment in time. I'm hoping both teams can bring this matter to a successful conclusion. For all our sakes. Ms. Price, please keep me apprised. I'll repeat what I said before. You need any backup, just call."

"Thank you, Mr. President."

"Jack, make this happen. Godspeed to you all."

A second screen blanked out.

"Down to you and me, Barb," McCarter said.

"Just to let you know," Price said, "the hospital is close to kicking Hal out. He's being a bad patient. Just wants to leave so he can get back to work."

"Signs of a good recovery. Tell him from me he's got to behave. Make the most of his time off."

"From Bear. They've got all the detail from the data that originated with Alexis. Bottom line is mainly confirmation of what we've been running with. A threat to destabilize relations between Israel and Iran. But no mention how the thing is going to be set in motion."

"If it's true about this nuke, we can all make some keen guesses how it's going to go down."

"This won't be your first visit to Somalia," Price said. "Come out safe."

"Do our best, luv."

McCarter stared at the blank screens.

"Here we go again," he said, so softly no one in the MTAC operations room could hear.

CHAPTER SIXTEEN

Kenya

Henry Chaka was six feet five inches of solid black muscle, his shaved head gleamed. He had a cheerful temperament, an easy manner and a deep voice. Chaka operated a three-vehicle taxi service that catered mainly to tourists. He operated his business from his residence, which was an old house that harked back to the time when the U.K. had ruled most of Africa.

Before they left the carrier, Sharon had insisted on borrowing McCarter's sat phone. He had called Chaka and told him he was fine and that he was sending along some friends who needed to pick up where the mission had stalled. By the time he had completed his call the African was fully briefed on Phoenix Force and their imminent arrival in Kenya.

"He'll be ready for you," Sharon said. "He's a good man. I trust him. He won't let you down."

The insertion of Phoenix Force into Kenya was achieved with stealth and the professional help provided by the U.S. Navy. A nuclear-powered deep-water submarine had made its rendezvous after being rerouted from its patrol in the Arabian Sea. It had taken Phoenix Force on board, diving immediately to alter course for the Kenyan coast. It surfaced in the prearranged position adjacent to an isolated strip of coastline and Phoenix Force climbed into the launched F470 Combat Rubber Raiding Craft. Two members of the sub's crew were in charge of the CRRC, which sped through the water and deposited Phoenix Force on the beach. As soon as they left the amphibian rubber boat it turned and headed back to the waiting sub, which took the CRRC and crew back on board, then submerged.

Phoenix Force were dressed in plain civilian clothing and had stored their equipment in two large carryalls.

McCarter slipped a compact signaling device from his pocket and activated it. The device transmitted a silent signal over a preset frequency across a short range. It received a recognition signal within thirty seconds.

An SUV rolled out from a stand of palms fringing the beach. It came to a halt only yards from where Phoenix Force stood waiting. The driver's door opened and they had their first look at Henry Chaka.

The tall Kenyan held out a large hand. "You are Coyle. Allen. Constantine. Landis and Rankin. *Shalom,* as my friend Ben would say. I am Henry Chaka." He spread his long arms. "Welcome to Kenya."

McCarter took the offered hand, his own big fist almost swallowed by Chaka's. "*Jambo,* Chaka," he greeted.

"Already you speak Swahili."

"That about covers my knowledge," the Briton admitted.

Chaka laughed. "It is more than Sharon knows. Tell me how he is."

"In the U.S. Navy's hands, being well looked after."

"Good. He is a brave man and I feared he might be dead."

"He'll mend," James said.

"Let us go. Safer to be on the road than standing around here."

They placed their bags in the back of the SUV, then

climbed in, McCarter sitting next to Chaka. He started the engine and drove away from the beach. The trail they were on was rough. After a quarter hour they moved onto a narrow road.

"From here it is a long drive to the border. But do not worry. I'll get you into Somalia."

"Getting in doesn't bother me," McCarter said. "It's staying alive and getting back out that does."

The remark struck Chaka as funny. He roared with laughter, shaking his head. "Sharon said I would like you. He was right."

"Any likelihood of being stopped?" McCarter asked.

Chaka shrugged. "It can happen, but things have quieted down since the recent troubles. The government is trying to maintain a low profile when it comes to a military presence, so there are not so many soldiers around at present. More local police patrols than military."

"I'm not sure which is worse," James said.

"At this time any police will be snoring in their beds," Chaka said. "They'll show their faces in the daylight, but we will be over the border by then. Oh, there is a cool bag behind you with bottled water."

At first light they reached a small village. Chaka informed them it was just over a mile from the border with Somalia. He parked the SUV behind a wooden building that had a rusting corrugated iron roof. Smoke issued from a tin chimney. A few chickens strutted around the dusty back lot. A skinny dog barely bothered to lift its head as Phoenix Force climbed out of the SUV.

"Now we walk," Chaka said. "It will take us until midday to reach where we are going. Getting caught in Somalia would not be pleasant, so if you have weapons now is the time to bring them out and be ready to use them."

It was the signal for the Stony Man commandos to gear

up. The large bags they had brought contained clothing and ordnance. Desert camo pants and shirts. Combat boots and ball caps. They each donned a lightweight vest that had a selection of pockets and clips for extra magazines and sat phones. They shared a selection of fragmentation grenades and smoke canisters. Handguns were stowed in high-ride holsters and they each carried a sheathed Cold Steel Tanto knife. They were still carrying their FN P-90 autoweapons.

Chaka watched the transformation with a smile on his lips. He had simply changed into khaki pants and a black T-shirt, pulling a floppy bush hat over his head. He took an AK-47 from the rear compartment of the SUV along with a cloth satchel holding extra magazines. He also had a panga, a machete-type broad-bladed weapon. He slipped the item into a leather loop on his belt.

"You look like you mean business," he commented. He passed out more of the bottled water and the Phoenix Force commandos stowed them in the small backpacks they carried. "Go easy on this. Not many places you will be able to buy more once we get into Somalia territory."

"Sounds like an ideal place for a trekking vacation," Hawkins said.

Chaka thought about that for a moment. "No. Not really," he said.

"Your vehicle going to be safe here?" Encizo asked.

"Yes. Didn't I mention that this house belongs to one of my family? Uncle on my mother's side. I always leave it here when I'm on business."

"It had to be something like that," Manning said.

Chaka took the lead. "Have your visas and passports ready for inspection," he said.

Their way took them along a faint path that snaked through sparse vegetation, the ground underfoot hard and stony. Chaka moved quickly, sure of his way. Phoenix Force followed close, trusting the tall Kenyan.

Two hours in and the sun was high, a sullen heat bearing down on them. In those two hours they had seen no signs of life, nor heard anything. This was barren and inhospitable terrain. From rocky underfoot to parched and loose sand that barely sustained clumps of scorched grasses.

"Is it like this all over?" McCarter asked.

"No," Chaka said. "Some places are really bad."

Even McCarter had to grin at the flippant reply.

Midmorning they took a break, resting in a shallow trough and trying to stay out of the full glare of the sun.

"To the east is a village. Good people who only want to live their lives in peace. We can rest there. It would be advisable. Walking this distance can take your strength. And the people may be able to give us information."

"I'm with Henry on this one," Hawkins said. "They have a McDonald's franchise there?"

"No, my friend. But there is a Coca-Cola refrigerator in the store."

"Bloody hell," McCarter said. "Sounds like my kind of town."

"A word," Chaka said. "Be wary of the man who runs the store. His name is Saran. I don't trust him. Don't know why, but there it is."

They reached the outskirts of the village an hour before noon—a straggling collection of huts and some larger buildings, mostly timber, though some of them had part mud-brick construction. The place had a shambolic feel to it. Chaka kept them all under cover as they looked the place over.

"The people here have no alliance to anyone but themselves," Chaka said. "Not that they should be blamed for that. For too long they have been badly treated by everyone. The changing governments. Self-appointed administrators who want to strip them of everything valuable to line their own pockets. The country goes to ruin around them. The pirate community attacks boats that stray into the waters along the coast. I am sure you know the stories. They have given Somalia a bad name, but these people are just simple beings who ask little, yet are generous to those who offer them friendship. Wait here while I go talk to them, make them see you are not enemies."

Chaka slipped from cover and walked across the dusty square in the direction of the huts. He held his arms clear of his body and began to call out in the local dialect. He stood facing the huts, waiting. After a couple of minutes figures began to appear, watching, then becoming more animated when they realized who it was calling to them. First one, then another crossed to meet Chaka. His infectious, booming laugh rang out. Children appeared, smiling broadly as they recognized him. Now they gathered around him, chattering freely.

Phoenix Force picked up on something they all shared. Everyone, adults and children alike, was thin to the point of emaciation. Under their simple cotton clothes their bodies were pared almost to the bone. The children showed it more than the grown-ups. Faces that had yet to be fully developed showed sunken cheeks and eyes that appeared too large.

"Man, I'll never complain about being hungry again," Hawkins said.

"*¡Por Dios!*" Encizo whispered. "Who lets these people starve like this?"

"The ones who take what they can from them," Manning said.

"How do you steal from people who have nothing left?" Encizo asked.

The excited chattering dropped to a murmur as Chaka spoke earnestly to the crowd. He turned and beckoned for Phoenix Force to join him.

McCarter slung his P-90 across his back, the others following his example. With McCarter in the lead the Stony Man team walked slowly into the open and across the square to join their Kenyan guide.

At first sight of the five obviously armed strangers there was a nervous reaction. Some of the older villagers shrank away from Chaka. He began to speak to them again, coaxing and calming their anxiety. Whatever he was saying had a soothing effect on the Somalians. It was the younger children who showed less fear. With the inborn curiosity of the young, they moved out to meet the strangers. McCarter was confronted by a large-eyed girl of five. She stared up at the tall Briton, eyes moving back and forth. McCarter smiled at her and held out a big hand. The girl took it without hesitation, her young face taking on a grave expression as she led him into the loose group of villagers.

"You realize you've just become engaged to be married," Chaka said. "They do that kind of thing very young around here." Then he grinned, unable to maintain a serious face.

"Hey, congratulations, boss," Hawkins said.

"Funny guy," McCarter said. "You're off the guest list as of right now."

Tension started to ease, and the Phoenix Force veterans found themselves surrounded by smiling faces and hands reaching out to touch them. Chaka translated as much as he could.

"I told them you are here to stand against Inigo and his men. They know Inigo. That he has made a bargain with the pirates, paying them much money to sail safely in their waters. He uses the fishing village along the coast for a base to store goods and conduct business. The people in the village are under threat if they say or do anything. These people have friends and families in the port and they understand how powerful Inigo is."

"Hell," Manning said. "I am getting royally pissed off hearing about this Inigo. He keeps popping up wherever we go. Time we caught up with him and yanked his chain."

"Language," James said. "Not in front of the children."

"Chaka, we should move on ASAP. Have our rest and leave. If Inigo gets wind we're around this place, it might go bad for these people."

Chaka said something to the crowd. As his words reached them there was a chorus of raised voices. Heads shaking and hands reaching out to the men of Phoenix Force.

"Roughly translated they are saying to hell with Inigo. He may have men with guns but they refuse to bow their heads to him. Jack, they believe you have come to chase Inigo away and they will not be afraid."

"I bloody well hope you put them right on that."

"I think I must have made a mistake and told them they were right."

James slapped McCarter across his shoulders. "Well done, boss. The great savior."

"Should we call you *Saint* Jack now?" Hawkins said.

McCarter sighed. "I am in the company of madmen."

Chaka pointed at the sagging timber frontage of what he called the village store. He led the way, with Phoenix Force and the villagers following. The interior was only marginally cooler than outside. The shelves held a diminished display of goods, cans of indeterminate age, and on the floor were sacks of maize and rice. A shelf behind the rickety counter held a few bottles and cartons of cigarettes.

To McCarter's disappointment there were no Player's, but he did spot a few packs of Marlboro.

Somewhere out back they could hear the wheezing chug of a generator. That meant electricity. McCarter scanned the interior and spotted the familiar red of a Coca-Cola chiller. He made his way over and placed his hand against the door. It was cool under his palm. He opened the door and smiled at the sight of Coke cans. He took one out, closing his hand around the chilled aluminum.

"Tell me this is real," he said, "and not an illusion."

"Where the hell do they get this from?" James asked.

"The owner, Saran, has a supplier," Chaka said. "It comes in by boat a couple of times a month. Along with a few other contraband items. Believe it or not, customers come from all over to buy."

"But not the villagers?" Encizo asked.

"They can't even afford a bottle between them."

"Son of a bitch," Hawkins said. He stared at the guy behind the counter, not missing that he was in slightly better shape than the rest of the watching crowd, a solid man with a surly expression on his fleshy dark face. "I got nothing against making a profit. But not like this."

"It is the world we live in," Chaka said. "Saran occasionally gives out-of-date food to the village. Not much. But he also lets them run up credit."

"Nice guy," McCarter said. "Does he take U.S. dollars?"

"Who doesn't?"

"Ask him what he wants for the contents of his chiller." Chaka turned to the storekeeper and spoke to him. There was a brief interchange. The storekeeper seemed reluctant to make real eye contact with Chaka or Phoenix Force. Chaka turned and quoted a figure to McCarter. The Briton took out the roll of money always carried in his pack; readily accepted American currency was a useful adjunct to the weapons they held. In certain situations handing over money could ease a difficult moment; it was something that went hand in hand with missions abroad. At this particular time it was about to relieve tension as well as thirst.

McCarter peeled off the amount and handed it to the guy behind the counter. He added a couple more notes and pointed to the Marlboro pack. Saran took a pack down and laid it on the counter with bad grace.

"Find an empty box and load up those cans," McCarter said. "Take them out and hand them around."

McCarter gestured to Chaka and they moved out of the store.

"Is something wrong?" Chaka asked.

"That Saran bloke. You said you don't trust him?"

"Not with my sister," Chaka said. "Not even with my dog."

"That's what I thought. I'm picking up a bad vibe about that bloke. Chaka, go and talk to people. Find out what you can about Inigo—if he's in the fishing village. Soon as the team has rested a couple of hours we'll head out."

Chaka nodded and walked off, leaving McCarter to check out the village and the outlying area. He left his team with the villagers, who were making the most of the unexpected cans of Coke. McCarter wished he could do more for them. Cans of fizzy drink weren't going to change their lifestyle. He knew he was allowing his feelings to cloud his thinking. His priority was the mission, finding out what was behind Inigo and his association with Edgar Bergstrom. The people here in this village were not his ultimate concern. But David McCarter couldn't ignore what his heart was experiencing.

He popped the tab on the can and took a long swallow of the Coke. It was a pleasant, familiar feeling.

AN HOUR LATER the village had settled into its normal routine.

Chaka crossed the square to find McCarter and report.

"I have talked with everyone I know," the Kenyan said.

"Anything useful?"

"There have been reports Inigo is at the fishing village. With a number of his men."

"Still there?"

"A visiting relative said yes. His boat is anchored offshore."

McCarter straightened. "Then it's time we headed out." He called the others to join him.

"We moving?" Manning asked.

"Yes."

Across the square someone yelled a warning.

There was a sudden flurry of movement, dust boiling up as three vehicles swept into view.

McCarter saw armed figures in the rear of an openbacked Mazda truck. He didn't need telling who they were.

Phoenix Force had come to find Inigo.

It seemed Inigo had found *them*.

CHAPTER SEVENTEEN

"Cover," McCarter yelled to Chaka. "Get everyone into cover."

The Kenyan began to scream at the villagers, waving his free arm. The people scattered, adults grabbing up children and running for cover before the vehicles reached the village square.

Along with the Mazda truck was a pair of identical, late-model SUVs. Windows were down on the SUVs, the barrels of SMGs showing. The rear of the Mazda held a crew of three armed men.

There was no time for speculation on how the attacking force had been summoned. Autoweapons began firing even as the three vehicles spun across the square, dust billowing in their wake and adding to the utter confusion. Sense and reason ceased to exist as wildly fired slugs found targets. Bodies twisted and fell under the heavy fire from the shooters' weapons.

"Take them out," McCarter yelled into his com set.

He dropped to a crouch, his P-90 tracking the Mazda. He laid a burst into the cab, the 5.7 mm slugs shattering the windshield in a shower of glittering shards. The driver let go of the wheel as he was caught by a number of the slugs, his face erupting in bloody spurts. The out-of-control truck completed a half circle before it shuddered to a halt, the shooters clinging on to the roll bar as it bounced to a stop.

Encizo and James had pulled their own weapons on target and hit the three men before they were able to recover.

The SUVs turned, one coming to a stop outside the store, the other farther on, armed figures exiting hastily opened doors. It was obvious they had no worked-out plan. They were in the village to cause as much damage as they could while dealing with the unexpected visitors.

Phoenix Force spread out across the square, facing off the attack team and bringing a professional slant to the chaotic action of the raiders.

The village became a battleground as the two sides fought for supremacy. Inigo's attack force may have had the numbers but they were far from being an organized group. Three of them went down within seconds of exiting their vehicle. Others died as they sought cover behind the SUVs. Manning and Encizo had maneuvered around the perimeter of the square, bringing them in line with the opposite side of the vehicles. As the attackers reached the hoped-for cover of the large vehicles, they exposed themselves to the accurate fire of the Phoenix pair. They opened fire and stitched the shooters, dropping them in bloody heaps on the dusty ground.

Hawkins spotted one of the men creeping along behind the stalled Mazda. The guy exposed himself as he reached the front of the truck, in the act of pulling the pin on what was obviously a grenade, prior to throwing it in the direction of McCarter and James. As the raider stepped into full view Hawkins hit him with a burst, his slugs ripping into the target's lower torso. The guy fell back against the front of the truck, the grenade slipping from his nerveless fingers. It struck the ground, rolled an inch or so, then stopped. The wounded raider, too far gone from taking Hawkins's slugs, wasn't even aware of the grenade. When it blew, it took him apart and buckled the front of the truck. The man's shredded corpse slithered to the ground, his legs practically gone and his upper body a bloody mess. The thump of the explosion drowned out every other sound before it faded. Flames from a fractured fuel line shot out in rising fingers that spread. The crumpled hood kept the bulk of the blaze contained but the heat started to blister the paintwork.

Dust had formed a cloud that rolled across the village square, Inigo's men using it to make their advance.

Phoenix Force and Chaka hit back, their weapons crackling as they engaged the attacking team. Slugs pounded the earth, kicking up gritty soil. The target sites were obscured for a time, making it difficult to gain an advantage. As the dust settled, and indistinct shapes became sharp again, both sides were able to track in and determine their objectives.

Phoenix Force had moved apart, creating individual targets, rather than bunching together. It meant Inigo's hardmen were presented with shooters ranged across the square. It forced them to reorganize themselves, choosing their shots, and that lost them time.

And men.

The crackle of autofire increased as Phoenix Force took the fight to the opposition, sending bursts that were tightly focused.

Two, then three of Inigo's men dropped to the ground.

The casualty rate rose.

Inigo's team fired off bursts that were more in panic than pinpoint shots. The closest they came to a hit was when a single slug took a fragment of cloth from Encizo's shirtsleeve. It didn't even graze his flesh; he felt a slight tug at his sleeve and that was it.

"Move in," McCarter's voice growled over the com sets. "Hit these jokers where it hurts."

THE SHOOTING was sporadic. Inigo's force had been reduced but they were still putting up resistance. Phoenix Force and Chaka had spread out, seeking cover as they traded shots with the attackers.

Manning was closer to the store. He saw Chaka turn and head in that direction, his face set and angry.

"It is Saran," the Kenyan said. "He called in Inigo's men. It couldn't be anyone else. That's why he wouldn't look us in the eyes. He knew these gunmen were coming. He has sold his soul to that man."

"Chaka is going after Saran," Manning relayed over his com set.

"Cover his back," McCarter said.

The Canadian went after Chaka when he saw the tall African vanish through the door. He followed some yards behind. As he entered the store he caught a brief glimpse of Chaka already moving through the door that led into the rear of the building. Manning didn't hesitate. He skirted the counter and breached the open doorway.

Ahead of him he heard a noise. Angry yelling. There was a solid thump of sound and a startled gasp, then the crash of someone falling.

"Chaka," Manning called.

He received no reply. He entered the narrow passage that led to an end room.

Chaka was down on the floor. Blood gleamed on his skull, but he was moving slowly, muttering to himself.

The door to the far room was just swinging shut.

"Chaka's down. He's alive. I'm going after Saran," Manning relayed to McCarter.

Manning ignored the response coming over his com set as he lunged at the door and kicked it open, ducking and going in at a crouch.

Manning paused, head turning slightly as he picked

up a brief sound coming from a door to his left. An almost inaudible creak. Someone shifting his weight prior to making a move. The Canadian was level with the door and took time now to notice it was not fully closed. His gaze spotted a shadow of movement and it was followed by another protest from a loose floorboard.

The Phoenix Force pro turned to face the door. He raised his right foot and drove it at the door, kicking it wide. Saran was caught briefly off guard but made a fast recovery and lunged at Manning, right hand clutching the handle of a slim-bladed knife. The guy was agile despite his bulky stature and he swept the knife in at Manning's body. The steel glinted as it thrust at Manning. He turned at the waist, presenting a slimmer target. The blade caught the material of Manning's sleeve. Saran's right hand passed across Manning's body. Manning dropped his P-90 and clamped his left hand around his attacker's wrist, fingers gripping hard. Manning turned the knife hand away and swept his right elbow around, slamming it against Saran's jaw. The blow was delivered with maximum force and snapped the man's head to the side. Manning followed up with a crippling knee to Saran's groin, drawing a hoarse grunt from him.

Gary Manning was no fan of hand-to-hand combat, especially when it included a knife, so his intention was to end it fast. Being in close to his adversary, Manning had no chance to use his own weapons. So he used both hands on Saran's knife wrist, twisting brutally until the man uttered a low moan. He lashed out with his free arm, slamming it against Manning's face, drawing blood when he split a lip. Manning increased the pressure on the storekeeper's wrist. It came to the point where Saran either had to let go of the blade or allow his wrist to be snapped. He chose the first option, releasing the knife.

The knife bounced as it hit the floor and Manning took the opportunity to kick it across the room before leaning his weight on Saran and pushing him backward until their movement was stopped by the wall. Manning let go of Saran's wrist and drove his fists up in a clubbing action that impacted under Saran's chin. His head snapped back, slamming against the wall with enough force to crack the plaster. Blood was pouring from Saran's mouth. He still had enough strength to swing a meaty fist at Manning, catching him in the mouth. The blow hurt, stunning Manning briefly, and Saran took the moment to hit the Canadian a second time.

Spitting blood, Manning swung both hands up, one on each side of Saran's head, and slammed them in hard over the man's ears. The blows were solid, and the impact pressure magnified the effect. Saran sucked in a hard breath, squeezing his eyes shut as he tried to recover from the effect of Manning's strike. Seeing his advantage, Manning clutched a handful of Saran's shirt, twisted and hauled the groaning man over his right hip. The man choked off a cry as he was thrown off his feet. He slammed to the floor, facedown, and Manning dropped quickly, driving his knees into the guy's lower back.

Saran arched up off the floor, hands flailing as he tried to reach behind him to get a grip on the man pinning him to the floor. He had no chance as Manning grasped his head in both powerful hands and hauled back and up. A scream rose in Saran's throat as he realized what was about to happen. He made one desperate attempt to free himself. His attempt lasted just as long as it took Manning to snap his spine. Saran jerked, a ragged breath gusting from his lips before he went limp.

Manning pushed slowly to his feet. He leaned against the wall, his chest heaving from the exertion. He was about to sleeve blood from his lips when he heard the unmistakable metallic snap of a cocking handle. The sound came from beyond the door of the room.

The burst of autofire sent hot slugs through the flimsy wood panels. They struck the far wall, scattering plaster chips and dust. As the rattle of shots died away Manning picked up harsh voices. A second burst splintered more of the door.

Time was running out.

Fast.

Too damn fast, the Canadian decided.

Manning turned and eyed the window on the opposite wall. The room was on the ground floor, so he wasn't faced with a long drop.

Someone fired again. Wood splinters filled the air. The visitors seemed anxious to get into the room.

Gary Manning made his choice.

He had no idea how many were on the other side of the wood. And by the way they were sending burst after burst through the wood, they were not going to back away.

The moment the current burst of autofire stopped, he pushed away from the wall, powering across the floor in the direction of the room's side window. A moment before he hit, Manning hunched his shoulders forward and threw up his muscular arms to shield his face. He hit the window full-on. The flimsy frame splintered and the streaked glass shattered. He threw himself forward, clearing the window, and moved his arms aside as he dropped. His feet hit the weed-choked alley. Manning felt his forward motion threatening to take him off balance and he fought to stay upright. He hadn't realized how narrow the alley was until he slammed bodily into the wall of the building opposite. The impact stunned him for a few seconds. He turned away from the wall, ignoring the ache in his body from the impact.

With no time to check himself out, Manning started to reach for his holstered pistol, then saw the head and shoulders of one of the shooters lean through the window. The barrel of his AK-47 probing ahead of him, the shooter's gaze settled on Manning's moving form a split second before the Phoenix Force commando reached out and grabbed the Kalashnikov. Manning wrenched the weapon from the guy's hands, turned it around and triggered a burst that took the shooter's face and half his skull off. The guy hung motionless for seconds, blood and shredded flesh showing where his face had been, then he slumped forward across the sill.

Manning wasn't waiting to count how many backups there were. He broke for the rear end of the alley, away from the front of the store, the AK-47 clutched ready for use. When he cleared the alley, ready to circle the rear of the store, he saw the additional SUV parked there, a single raider protecting the vehicle, his weapon held loosely across his chest. His head snapped around when Manning appeared. He screamed a frantic warning and pulled his autorifle toward Manning. He was nowhere near fast enough. Manning hit him with a short burst that ripped through his torso, the high-velocity slugs ravaging the guy's body.

"I'm at the back of the store. Another SUV here. On my way around to you," he said into his com set.

"Working our way to the store," McCarter yelled. "These buggers are holding us back."

"More hostiles in the store," Manning warned.

He was level with the SUV when figures burst from the rear door of the store. He had time to count three before the attackers barreled into him, using the butts of their weapons to strike at him. Manning had no time to track his weapon in. He felt brutal blows to his face and body. He stumbled back against the SUV. The burly Canadian was able to take the punishment but the combined efforts of the three men overwhelmed him. He took a hard blow to the side of his head that dropped him to his knees. The day closed down briefly, his senses jarring as he was manhandled by his attackers. His weapons were stripped away from him. Even his com set was ripped away. Hands gripped his clothing and he was bundled into the rear of the SUV. He heard the engine roar into life. Doors slammed. He was driven to the floor of the SUV, still fighting the weakness the physical attack had brought on.

He felt the SUV swerve around the rear of the store, the sound of gunfire still echoing in the background. One of the men in the rear with him kicked at Manning's unprotected body. The blow bruised his ribs. He tried to resist. All that got him was another blow to the back of his skull, and this time Manning blacked out.

THE VILLAGE SQUARE echoed with the continuing firefight. Bodies were spread across the dusty ground. The numbers had shrunk and Inigo's hit team was losing out.

Three of the shooters concealed behind the farthest parked SUV ceased firing. The reason became apparent when the SUV's engine burst into life, roaring wildly as the man behind the wheel hammered the gas pedal to the floor. The heavy vehicle lurched forward, the rear end swinging before the big tires gripped. A heavy cloud of dust obscured the vehicle as it picked up speed and exited the village.

Left alone, the survivors displayed at least some measure of credibility as they stayed to fight on.

CHAPTER EIGHTEEN

Manning felt the effect of the SUV being driven fast over uneven ground. His consciousness returned slowly. His head ached and he could feel where blood had soaked through his hair and down the back of his neck. He made no attempt to move, letting his body reset itself. He knew he was still on the floor of the vehicle. His captors were on the wide seat above him. He could hear them talking. They sounded pleased with themselves, relaxed even. Something in his favor. He cracked one eye. Inches away from his face was the stock end of an AK-47. The butt was on the floor of the SUV. Straining his eyes, Manning followed the outline of the assault rifle. It rested between the legs of its owner, leaning against the front of the seat. The guy's hands were draped loosely against the upraised barrel. A second thing in Manning's favor.

He had no way of knowing how long a journey they might be involved in or if at the end he might find he was surrounded by a greater number of Inigo's men. Manning didn't intend finding out if he could avoid it. So, any action had to be undertaken now.

Waiting was not an option. Manning always tried to take the short route to solving any problem.

His check of the AK-47 had showed him the weapon's selector lever was set for automatic fire.

He took a deep breath, turned his body and closed his hands around the Kalashnikov.

As the weapon was jerked from his loose hands the guy shouted to his companion.

A split second later the interior of the SUV was filled with the hard crackle of autofire. Manning's finger held back the trigger as he swept the muzzle back and forth between the men on the rear seat. Hot shell casings rained down on him, followed by warm blood spray as his close-quarter fire found targets, punching in through flesh and bone. Booted feet jerked and kicked out, catching Manning. He ignored the frantic movement as he exhausted the AK-47's magazine.

Pushing up off the floor, Manning ignored the bloody bodies and made a grab for the other assault rifle that lay on the seat between the dead men.

The SUV was swerving wildly as the driver tried to maintain control and pull his handgun from its holster on his side. He spotted movement in the rearview mirror and saw the blood-spotted face of the man who had just slaughtered his partners. The guy made a successful attempt at freeing his pistol and began to lift it.

Manning jabbed the muzzle of his AK-47 against the side of the man's head and put a single round into it. Bloody gore spattered the interior of the SUV. The guy keeled over. His hand slipped from the wheel and the SUV swerved off the rutted, dusty road. Manning snatched at the wheel with one hand, his other reaching for the ignition key. He switched the engine off and felt the SUV starting to slow. He held the wheel steady as the vehicle wandered and kept it on a near-straight line until it rolled to a stop.

Pushing open one of the rear doors, Manning climbed out. He leaned against the SUV until he felt steady enough to move again. He reached inside and pulled out the two bodies and dragged them clear. He did the same with the head-shot driver.

"That, Gary, was your crazy stunt of the week," he said out loud.

He selected one of the AK-47s and the SIG Sauer pistol the driver had been carrying and placed them on the front passenger seat, along with the spare magazines he'd located. Behind the wheel, he fired up the engine. He was about to reverse so he could return to the village when he spotted a trail of dust behind him and recognized one of the SUVs from the village.

Good guys or bad guys? he wondered.

He received his answer as the SUV moved into range and someone started shooting at him—Inigo's men, and they had seen the bodies on the ground.

Manning slammed the SUV into gear and stamped on the gas pedal. He heard the thump of slugs against the vehicle's body, which really confirmed he was being chased by the opposition.

Manning checked his mirror.

Damn.

The SUV was right behind him, moving at a speed that would bring it close very quickly.

Manning clicked the seat belt into position as he felt the SUV power up.

He remained calm, because panicking wouldn't help, and Manning was not prone to panicking. He took situations as they came, assessed them and acted accordingly.

His judgment on his current situation was simple enough.

He had no backup.

No cover ahead.

The road he was on was open on either side.

It ran straight ahead.

Manning had no knowledge whether the men pursuing him had contact with anyone. For all he knew they might be gathering reinforcements to join the chase or to set up some kind of roadblock ahead.

They knew the terrain.

He didn't.

The only things in his favor were the SUV, which had a full tank of gas when he checked the gauge, and his meager arsenal. Although the SUV was powerful, a current model, so was the identical one behind him. He had all the modern technology such vehicles could offer, but so did the vehicle chasing him.

But he didn't have bullet-resistant bodywork. Manning realized that moments later when he felt the thud of a slug hitting the side of the SUV, penetrating and burying itself in the back of the passenger seat.

He checked his mirrors and saw the pursuing SUV was dangerously close. An armed figure was leaning out of the side window and locking in on Manning's vehicle for a second shot.

Manning jammed his foot on the brake, the speed of the SUV dropping and causing the other driver to brake and pull to one side to avoid a rear-end collision.

"Not on your best day," Manning said.

He increased speed, pulling away from the chase car, leaving behind a tail of dust that momentarily blinded the other driver.

Okay, Gary, you won't get away with that a second time.

"But where do you go to lose these buggers?" he asked himself out loud.

Manning's words bounced back to him from the windshield. He couldn't have deliberately chosen a worse place to engage in a chase. No cover. No relief. Just a dusty trail through a barren landscape.

A quick glance at the speedometer showed Manning he still had the ability to raise his speed. The downside of that was the pursuing vehicle. Same model, so it would have the same range.

Scratch that off his list.

He constantly checked his mirrors, wanting to be alert to any moves his pursuers might make.

He saw a head and shoulders appear above the roofline of the other SUV. He had forgotten about the retractable sunroof. The guy showing himself wielded an AK-47. Leaning forward, he braced his elbows on the roof and tracked in with the autorifle.

Not good.

The shooter's fresh position would allow him a wider range and the ability to keep his weapon steadier than when he had been leaning out a window.

Manning jerked the wheel. His SUV swayed to one side. The pursuing vehicle followed.

The AK-47 crackled, flame winking from the muzzle. The shooter had it on auto and kept firing, his line of slugs closing on Manning's vehicle. He felt the thump as 7.62 mm slugs hit the tailgate, others punching in through the rear window.

As long as he stayed away from the tires.

The shooter dropped his muzzle. His first burst hit the rear fender. Then his shots found their target. The left-hand rear tire blew and Manning's SUV lost some of its stability. The shooter snapped in a fresh magazine and took out the other rear tire after a heavy burst.

Manning felt the rear stray off course as rubber shredded and fell away, leaving the speeding vehicle running on its steel rims. Manning felt the bumps and jolts. His hands gripped the steering wheel tightly, attempting to keep the SUV on its forward path.

He understood his dilemma.

Drop his speed and allow the pursuit vehicle to get even closer.

Maintain his speed and risk losing control of the shuddering SUV completely.

No great choice, he decided.

Any swift decision was taken away as he hit a rough section of the hard-packed road. The SUV began to bounce, the rear wheels scraping the iron-hard earth and throwing the vehicle's rear out of sync. Manning felt the steering wheel snap back and forth and even his powerful grip was having a hard time holding the SUV on track.

Even as he took his foot off the gas pedal to lower the speed, Manning felt the vehicle slew sideways. He touched the brake, realized that wasn't going to help, and lifted his booted foot.

Too late.

The SUV lurched sideways, engine racing, and Manning felt the seat beneath him start to lift. He saw the landscape tilt, roll, as the SUV spun wildly. Without seeing, Manning knew all four wheels had cleared the ground. He slammed both feet into the foot well, tensing his muscles. Beyond the windshield he saw the world turn. Then he heard the solid crash as the SUV came back down to earth, on its left side. The windshield dissolved. Glass from his driver's door window shattered, fragments showering him. It was only the seat belt that prevented him from being thrown around the interior as the vehicle turned again, paneling buckling, more glass shattering. Loose items flew around Manning. The Kalashnikov slammed the side of his head. The windshield, loosened from its frame, slid out of view and a rain of dirt and dust blew into the vehicle, peppering Manning's face. He let go of the wheel and grabbed hold of the straps of the seat belt as the SUV stood on end for long seconds before finally crashing back to earth on its wheels and sitting at an angle. Manning was dimly aware of metallic creaks and groans and the hiss of steam boiling from the fractured radiator. He could smell hot metal, the stench of leaking oil and, somewhere, the pungent odor of spilled gasoline.

His body ached. Warm blood ran down his face. He was dazed, his senses a violent jumble. Manning managed to free the seat belt. He thought about the AK-47. Leaning forward, he scanned the foot well. Saw the autorifle and reached for it.

The door was yanked open, a dark figure showing in the opening. The muzzle of a rifle was pushed hard into Manning's side.

"No," someone said.

Manning turned in the direction of the voice. His vision was blurred but he could see enough to recognize an armed man.

"Get him out."

Rough hands caught hold of Manning's shirt and he was dragged out of the SUV. Once clear he was allowed to fall to the hard earth, half-conscious of a trio of figures clustered around him.

"On his feet. Hold him up."

Hands gripped Manning's upper arms and lifted him upright. His vision cleared enough to allow him to make out the features of the man staring at him, the dark face taut with barely controlled anger.

"You've caused enough trouble," the man said. "Killed our men. Wrecked one of our vehicles. We still do not know who you are but we are going to find out. One way or another."

The guy moved back a little, just enough to give him room to swing his arm. Manning sensed the coming blow. His reactions were too sluggish to let him avoid it. The fist slammed across his left cheek. The force snapped Manning's head to one side. The hitter grunted with the effort, sucking in a deep breath as he pulled his arm back and fired off a second punch that landed with a solid crack. Manning's head rocked from the unrestrained force of the blows, blood spraying from his lips.

"You are putting our plans under threat…"

A third strike.

"And we will not let that happen…"

A slamming blow to the ribs.

"We have invested too much time and effort…"

The rapid round of body and face hits left Manning close to unconscious, head down and dripping blood. It was only the hands gripping his arms that kept the Phoenix Force commando upright.

One final blow that barely registered.

"Put him in the vehicle," the man said, his voice reaching Manning from a great distance. "I want to be away from this place now. We will take him to Inigo."

The Canadian felt himself being dragged. Then he was thrown inside the SUV and found himself on the floor again. Heavy boots thumped down on him as Inigo's men settled in the rear. Manning heard doors slam. The SUV moved away, picking up speed. He had no idea in which direction they were traveling. All he did register was the high speed the vehicle was moving.

His whole body was on fire with pain. The left side of his face was numb; Manning knew the pain would come later. The inside of his cheek had been driven against his teeth, gouging the flesh, and it was bleeding. He was in no position to offer any resistance so he simply lay where he was.

Right at that moment Gary Manning had no choices available.

He was in enemy hands. Until an opportunity revealed itself, Manning had no other option than to play along.

CHAPTER NINETEEN

Unaware of Manning's capture, the other members of Phoenix Force advanced on Inigo's team. With a number of their colleagues having deserted them, the resistance of those remaining began to crumble. Aware they were facing a dedicated, combat-experienced enemy, the Inigo hardmen fell back into the cover offered by their vehicles. Despite that, the accurate fire from Phoenix Force slowly took their numbers down. They were outclassed. They were by no means the cream of Inigo's extensive force. In truth they were local Somalians, paid by Inigo to supervise his incoming goods at the fishing port, little more than armed thugs who enjoyed the prestige and the cash that working for Inigo brought them. This time they found themselves outclassed by others who were a step above the local inhabitants they normally pushed around.

The last man standing went down under the muzzle of Hawkins's P-90. A silence blanketed the village square. The villagers who had fled the fighting slowly emerged from their huts, staring around at the results of the conflict. Wide-eyed children clung to their parents. A body count showed two dead and four with minor injuries. As their courage returned the villagers moved around the fallen attackers. There were pointing fingers and some angry curses at the men who had struck their village.

McCarter finished reloading his weapon. The team gathered together.

"Where are Gary and Chaka? I haven't seen them since they hit the store," Enrico said.

McCarter called him on his com set. There was no reply.

"Cal, with me. T.J., stay close to Encizo. Eyes skinned in case there are more."

He led the way into the deserted store and through to the rear. They found Chaka dragging himself up off the floor, a hand clasped to his bleeding skull. They steadied him as he leaned against the wall.

"Take it easy," James said, breaking out his emergency medic kit.

"You see where Allen went?" McCarter asked, referring to Manning.

Chaka indicated the bullet-marked door. "I remember him going after Saran, then shots. I passed out. Just before I passed out I heard more gunfire, then a window breaking."

"Just relax," James told him.

McCarter kicked the door open. He saw Saran's body on the floor, his head at an odd angle. Turning, he saw the body of a man hanging over the sill of a broken window.

There was no sign of Manning.

McCarter checked the alley. It was empty.

Behind him, James and an unsteady Chaka came into the room. The Kenyan had an adhesive patch over the gash in his skull.

And behind them was a skinny, wizened villager making noise and tugging at Chaka's clothes. Chaka turned and spoke to the old man, who began a long and excited speech, accompanied by arm waving.

"He know something?" James asked.

Chaka nodded. "He saw what happened to Allen.

"The old man had been hiding from the firefight. He

was about to crawl beneath the store when Manning jumped through the window, then disarmed and shot the man who had tried to follow him. Manning had taken the AK-47 and had run around to the back of the store, speaking into his com set. The old man had seen the parked SUV, then Inigo's men emerge from the back of the store. He had witnessed their attack on Manning, overpowering him and bundling him into the SUV before it drove away."

"Which way?" McCarter asked.

"He says east," Chaka said. "That would be in the direction of the fishing village where Inigo has his base."

They retraced their steps, moved to the rear of the store, and went outside. They found Manning's handgun and com set on the scuffed ground, along with his pack. They noted the tire tracks left by the SUV.

The old man began to speak again. As Chaka listened, his face stiffened with anger. He patted the old man's shoulder, then turned and went back inside. McCarter and James followed and saw him standing over Saran's body.

"I should have picked it up earlier. Saran was acting strange," Chaka said. "Now I know why." He bent over Saran's body and slid an expensive cell phone out of the man's pocket. He held it up. "Saran never owned one of these in his life. And look at the watch on his wrist. Would have cost more than he could ever afford. The man was stupid enough to wear it in plain sight. The old man saw one of Inigo's men give Saran the phone and the watch a couple of days back. Then he thought nothing more of it. He figured it was a payoff for something. He didn't know about us going to show up at the time."

Encizo checked the phone, bringing up the recent call list. "He made a call thirty minutes after we showed up."

"To let Inigo know there were armed strangers in the village."

Chaka jerked a thumb over his shoulder in the direction of the body draped across the shattered window. "The dead guy over there. He is one of Inigo's men. The old man said your man was big. Broad shoulders and chest," Chaka said. "Built like a bull."

"Bullheaded, more like," McCarter muttered.

"Not like the rest of us," Encizo said.

McCarter glared at the Cuban. Then his face relaxed and he managed a thin smile. In truth he and Manning were very alike. They both would seize an opportunity and go for it if they thought it might help the mission.

"Ask the old guy if Allen was badly hurt," McCarter said.

After a brief conversation Chaka said, "He believes they took him alive. They beat him but not enough to kill him."

The old man was watching as McCarter lit a cigarette, his bright eyes fixing on it. McCarter handed him the pack. The old man grinned, showing his crooked brown teeth as he took out one of the cigarettes and stuck it between his lips. McCarter lit it for him and the old man took a long drag.

"That's my trouble," McCarter said. "I'm too softhearted."

"Yeah, right," Hawkins said.

"Soft and hearted," James said. "Not two words I'd ever find tattooed on your ass."

"Let's go and find our MIA," McCarter said.

They climbed into the remaining SUV, Chaka behind the wheel. As they pulled away McCarter noted that the old man had followed them through the store. He had helped himself to a couple cartons of cigarettes from the shelf behind the counter and was watching them, happily blowing smoke.

Villagers were moving around the bodies, gathering up weapons and going through pockets.

"Nothing will be overlooked," Chaka said. "Remember, this is Africa. Nothing is wasted."

When they came across the abandoned SUV, McCarter and Chaka checked it out while the rest of Phoenix Force formed a perimeter watch.

"Lot of blood," Chaka said.

They had passed the three bodies Manning had left on the road. McCarter spotted the tire tracks of the second vehicle heading away from the crash site. Still moving east.

McCarter called Stony Man on his sat phone, waiting impatiently while the connection was made.

"Can you track me via the phone?" he asked.

Price, sensing his unwillingness to give too much away, immediately connected him to Kurtzman after advising the cyber chief what McCarter was asking for.

"I have you on screen," Kurtzman said after pinpointing their location via the Zero satellite platform.

"From our position, going east, there should be a fishing port on the coast. Can you scan for anything larger than a generic fishing boat? Probably anchored offshore."

"You want to know the color of the captain's shorts, too?"

"Not really," McCarter said.

There was a silence as Kurtzman initiated his satellite sweep.

"We do have a hundred-foot motor cruiser moored beyond the bay. Not a local vessel. That boat talks big money."

"Thanks. You picking up anything from the port itself we should know about?"

"More vehicles than a place like that would normally have. Akira is doing a check. According to background the port is suspected of being a local rendezvous point for radicals. CIA book figures it sometimes runs supplies and people in and out of the area." Kurtzman paused. "You thinking of paying a visit?"

"We're one man short. Looks like he's been taken there. Maybe for transport to that bloody boat."

"Anything we can do from this end?"

"Try to keep the place under surveillance. Call if you have an update."

"You got it."

McCarter ended the call.

"My information has Inigo running a boat," Chaka said, picking up the reference during McCarter's call. "He likes expensive toys. Even had his own helicopter."

"Trouble with having fancy toys is someone always wants to take them away from you," McCarter said. He waved at his teammates. "Let's go. Looks like we may have a location for our boy."

As they neared the coast, the terrain changed. They encountered a series of serrated ridges, some sparse and sun-dried grasses, the occasional stand of withered trees. But still dust, gritty and plentiful.

"No chance of promoting this as a scenic park, then," Hawkins said. "I've seen prettier country down around the Big Bend in Texas."

"And I suppose it's bigger, too," James said.

"Uh-huh."

"Is everything in Texas bigger?"

Hawkins glanced across at James. "Well, yeah."

"That include the bragging?"

"Hey, boss, can I sit somewhere else?" Hawkins said. "This hombre is starting to get to me."

"You can always ride on the bloody roof," McCarter said.

Chaka grinned. "I think I have joined a touring vaude-ville troupe."

"Now you've done it," Encizo said. "Exposed our real identities. We'll have to turn around and go home now."

"Too late," Chaka said, slowing the SUV and pulling in behind a high ridge.

They all climbed out and moved to the top of the ridge, staying below as they surveyed the scene.

Beyond the ridge the landscape slid down a long slope that evened out a few hundred yards from the coastline—and the scattered buildings that comprised the fishing port Stony Man had detailed.

McCarter activated his sat phone and spoke to Kurtzman.

"Black SUV rolled in about a half hour ago. Couldn't get any ID on the passengers because it pulled in close to a building. It's still there. We did pinpoint a couple of armed sentries on the roof." Kurtzman paused, speaking to someone. "Hunt just saw a power launch coming away from the motor cruiser. Looks to be heading for the shore. We'll see if we can get some close-ups."

McCarter relayed the conversation to the team.

"You figure they're coming to transfer Allen?" Encizo asked.

"Or to carry out an interrogation," Chaka said.

"Either way, we can't just sit back and do nothing," McCarter said.

"You want to take a closer look?" Chaka asked.

McCarter nodded. Breaking out his binoculars, the Briton bellied down and began a long scan of the port, checking for any signs of armed personnel to add to the pair on the roof. When he was satisfied, he turned away from the ridge line.

"What do you figure?" Encizo asked. "Much opposition?"

"Two on the roof of that building," McCarter said. "There are a couple more armed blokes down at the quayside. No machine-gun emplacements. No weapons mounted on trucks. Can't tell how many might be inside with Allen."

"How about that launch coming in?" Hawkins asked.

"Four. Helmsman and three others. Couldn't see any rifles, but that doesn't mean they won't have any around."

"Chances are they'll be expecting us," James said. "They know Allen wasn't alone."

"Which is why they want to get him on board that bloody cruiser," McCarter said. "Be harder for us to get to him then."

Encizo sighed. "Going down there isn't about to get us a welcome."

"You really going down there?" Chaka asked.

"Were you ever in the military?" James asked.

"Yes," Chaka answered. James simply looked at him until Chaka gave a brief nod, a sheepish smile on his lips. "No man is left behind. It's been some time since I needed to remember that."

Chaka watched as Phoenix Force readied themselves, reloading their weapons and giving them a final check. He did the same with his own AK-47. He caught the team watching him.

"You think I'm going to sit here on this ridge and watch you fellows go charging into Inigo's hideout? No chance— I'm in this all the way."

"Can't argue against that," Hawkins said.

"These things can get hairy," McCarter said.

"Don't they all," Chaka noted.

"Let's get on board the suicide express," McCarter said.

"He likes his little jokes," Chaka said.

James adjusted his cap. "This time I don't think he is joking."

CHAPTER TWENTY

Inigo already had the nuclear device on board the *Boa Vista*. He also had the documentation provided by Bergstrom that would implicate the Iranians as the perpetrators of the bomb blast on Israeli soil. The documents would be carefully leaked, as would the recordings identifying Iran as the force behind the nuclear explosion.

The collection of the device had been the primary objective of his visit to Somalia once Mikhail Koretski had completed his delivery.

The arrival of the mystery force in the village had been a bonus, and when Saran informed Inigo of their presence he had dispatched a group to deal with them. But the newcomers had faced down and defeated his men. The only plus side had been the capture of one of the commandos. The man he had under guard right now. Inigo wanted to find out who the man was, where his team originated and who they worked for. So he intended to take the man on board the *Boa Vista*.

Inigo had been informed the launch was on its way. He wanted to get his prisoner out to the comparative safety of the boat. He owed no allegiance to anyone except his employer, but he understood the way things were in the region. Though he had arrangements with the local military and the police, there were no absolute guarantees. Changes in the administration. New men in charge. These could alter his standing and bring about fresh demands. Inigo might suddenly have to find additional money. Bribes to the new man in charge. Money was no worry. He was well supplied from a number of radical sources, all of which wanted unrest and agitation fermenting. It was the nature of the beast to demand upheaval. The far-spread regions were all open to rebellion, to the ever-changing pressures from various influences. Politics and religion. Hatred. The desires of those who wanted change in their own favor.

Above all these were the demanding needs of Bergstrom's secretive unit organizing the strike on Israel. Even Inigo realized the far-reaching and dangerous expectations of the complicated plot. If it came to fruition, there could easily be a violent eruption that had the potential to draw in not only local governments, but outside powers vying for position and desperate to dominate.

The U.S.A.

China.

Even the involvement of the Russians.

On a strictly personal level, Inigo didn't care who came out on top. He saw the affair as a means to further his own ambitions. A simple enough desire. He wanted to extend his influence. But above that he wanted the monetary gain that would be his part of the end result. He had been involved long enough to understand the driving forces behind such matters.

He had never yet met a dirt-poor fanatic. Or a destitute ayatollah. He had seen the expensive cars. The high-end SUVs and the fine residences these people owned. They all played the humble card for their devoted followers but at day's end they didn't squat in the dirt. More likely retreated to comfortable apartments and villas.

Inigo wanted his share. He worked hard to please whoever was his current employer every time he accepted a fresh contract. His teams were the best money could buy.

And as long as he kept delivering the goods, he couldn't lose. He would be the first to admit he enjoyed the rewards. He paid his people well. Kept them content. And when the time came for action they were ready. Inigo's business thrived on violence and death and bringing about the demise of certain parties working against his current benefactor. Assassination. Blackmail and kidnapping. There was little, if anything, on the list that Inigo wouldn't handle. No one he wouldn't take down. Men or women—it made no difference. If they were marked for death then so be it.

His immediate concern was the man they had captured. From what little information Inigo had, it seemed the commando was part of a team searching for answers to what was developing. The prisoner had become separated from the rest of his team during the village fight. The how didn't matter to Inigo. The event had been costly in terms of men lost but had allowed the capture of the man. Inigo's need now was to get the prisoner on board the cruiser before his team came after him. If he could make that happen, the likelihood of a rescue attempt would recede. With the cruiser on the open sea, any operation by the prisoner's teammates could easily be repulsed, unless they gained control of a superior vessel. Which was unlikely. There were no seagoing vessels capable of outrunning the cruiser, and certainly nothing with superior firepower in the region.

Knowing that did not entirely ease Inigo's concerns. He hadn't stayed at the top of his game by being complacent. It was not advisable to let his guard down. He had seen others perish because they had decided they had reached a state of invincibility, only to be proved wrong in a moment of laxity. That would not happen to Inigo. He kept his eye on the ball, as the Americans said. Anticipating possible trouble allowed him the luxury of protecting himself. And right now, even though he had his prisoner, Inigo was not about to sit back and congratulate himself. The time for that would come when he had the man safely away from this stinking fishing port and secure on board the *Boa Vista.*

"*¡Hola!* Cabo, get him on his feet. Down to the quay. I want him ready when the launch arrives."

Cabo, one of his lieutenants, grabbed his AK-47 from where he had left it and crossed the room. He was the man who had engineered the capture of the prisoner back in the local village. Taking the prisoner alive would offer them a chance to learn about the force that had already caused them much trouble. Inigo had been extremely pleased when Cabo had showed up with his captive.

The prisoner sat with his back to the wall, arms across his raised knees, with his head down. He hadn't moved since they'd brought him inside.

"On your fucking feet, white boy," Cabo yelled, using one of his booted feet to kick the prisoner.

Cabo was a six-foot, heavily built man, with plenty of muscle power. He enjoyed knocking people around. Especially those who were unarmed and not able to fight back.

The kick he delivered rolled the prisoner along the wall....

FOR GARY MANNING that kick was the final blow he was going to take from his captors.

During the ride in and the subsequent time he had spent in the hut, Manning had conserved his energy as much as he could. He had remained still and silent, sucking up the pain and building his strength. He accepted his position was difficult. Being separated from the rest of Phoenix Force meant he had only himself to rely on for the time being. He was sure his team was searching for him, most likely on the trail Inigo had left behind. That was fine in theory, but Manning didn't let himself be fooled he was going to be freed anytime soon. Until something came his way, he was going to have to rely on his own skills and use what he could to drag himself out of his current predicament.

As he rolled from Cabo's kick Manning took a sideways glance down the length of the hut.

As well as Inigo there were two of his men lounging near the door, weapons propped against the wall.

Then there was Cabo. Manning wasn't going to forget him. The big guy was readying himself to launch another kick at Manning.

Take time out, Cabo, Manning said to himself.

He waited a couple more seconds. Right up to Cabo pulling his foot back. Then Manning launched a powerful kick of his own, delivered with every ounce of his brawny physique. His boot heel slammed into Cabo's other leg, now taking his entire weight. Manning felt his heel crush Cabo's knee, turning it to mush as everything shattered. Cabo's leg bent against the joint. The guy let out a high screech of agony as his demolished knee collapsed under his weight. He toppled sideways, pulled by his own motion.

Manning sucked in a deep breath, ignoring the protest from his battered body; any pain he had now would not matter if he didn't survive, so he lunged away from the wall. His hands reached for the Kalashnikov slipping from Cabo's hand. He closed his fingers around the Soviet autorifle. It was a weapon Manning had used on a number of occasions and he had spent time on the Stony Man firing range familiarizing himself with its operation. As he slithered on his knees Manning gripped the AK-47, moving the selector to full auto, so that when he tracked in on his targets he was ready.

Inigo was halfway out the door, and he kept moving, leaving his two men to deal with the prisoner.

They made a grab for their redundant weapons.

Cabo's large body slammed to the floor of the hut, still moaning.

The Canadian commando brought the AK-47 up, finger already on the trigger. He eased it back. The Kalashnikov thundered out its hard sound, jacking out 7.62 mm slugs in a deadly volley. Manning traversed between the two men, the slugs tearing into and through their bodies. Bloody fragments erupted as the powerful drive of the slugs cored into and through. Blood spatter stippled the wall. The pair of would-be shooters was driven to the floor of the hut, twisting and squirming beneath the unrelenting bursts of autofire.

Inigo had gone.

Manning could hear him screaming orders and knew he was not going to be left alone.

On his feet, he felt something grip one of his ankles. Thick fingers dug into his flesh. It was Cabo, his left hand around Manning's ankle, his right wielding a thick-bladed knife.

Manning angled the AK-47 down and put a short burst into the guy's skull, spreading blood and brains across the floor.

He checked out the hut. No rear exit. Just crude, scattered furnishings. On a table near the door, bottles of local beer, partly smoked cigarettes.

And a number of the familiar curved magazines for the AK-47. As Manning passed by the table he picked up four loaded magazines and pushed them into the wide pockets of his combat pants. If he was going to have to fight his way out of town, extra ammunition was a must.

He took a spare magazine and quickly reloaded the rifle.

Manning picked up an unopened bottle and knocked the cap off on the edge of the table. The beer was tepid and had a powerful kick. Manning didn't even try to guess what it was made from. He just needed liquid to ease his parched throat. It hurt simply moving his jaw.

The pounding of boots on the dust-dry ground outside caught Manning's attention. He threw the bottle aside and pulled the Kalashnikov into position.

He met the approaching men as they closed in on the open door, their weapons tracking on the opening. Manning hit them with short bursts. The impact from the high-velocity slugs knocked them off stride, sent them stumbling awkwardly. Any previous intent was driven from them by the numbing slam of 7.62 mm projectiles. The lead guy fell forward across the sill of the open door, his AK-47 bouncing from his slack hands. Manning scooped it up and draped it around his neck as he ducked through the door, edging to the left and triggering more slugs from his weapon as another shooter appeared. They both fired at the same time.

Manning felt a searing burn across the muscle of his left arm, heard more slugs thudding into the wall of the hut behind him. He felt the sting of wood splinters across his back, biting through his shirt.

He set his mouth in a determined line and turned the AK-47 in the direction of the approaching shooter. His finger stroked the trigger and sent 7.62 mm slugs at the guy. The shooter's face exploded in a flash of blood and pulped flesh.

As Manning emerged from the hut he saw Inigo close to the jetty, waving the launch in. He shouted orders to the pair of armed men on the jetty, pointing in Manning's direction.

Manning took momentary cover behind a stack of wooden crates as the men started in his direction.

Gunshots crackled behind him. Slugs thudded into one of the crates only inches away. Manning threw himself to the ground, twisting around, and saw a pair of armed shooters on the roof of the hut.

He hadn't noticed them before but they were making their presence known now. He squirmed around the stack of crates, briefly concealing himself from the erratic shots.

Okay, Gary, now you have them behind you and in front. Figure this one out.

More firing from the roof. The slugs were still off target. Hitting the ground inches from the stack of crates. One thing the pair lacked was precision shooting. Not allowing for the higher angle they were firing from. It gave Manning a thin window. Sooner or later they were going to range in.

He rolled and sat up, brought his Kalashnikov to his shoulder, flicking the selector to semiauto, which would allow him single shots. He ignored the slugs kicking up dust around him, gauging angle and trajectory, and worked the trigger. The AK-47 cracked and Manning's target was kicked back from the edge of the roof, a burst of red spraying from his body. Manning fired a second time and caught the guy in the side as his body arched from the first slug. The guy's partner turned to look at his wounded mate, taking his eyes off Manning. The Canadian used the few seconds to adjust his aim and hit the second shooter, triggering a trio of shots that ripped into the guy. He went to his knees, letting go of his weapon. He swayed forward and toppled from the roof of the hut, hitting the hard ground with a crunching thud.

Two down, two to go.

Manning turned and searched for the two men from the jetty.

The sound of an approaching vehicle caught his attention.

More hostiles?

When Manning glanced over his shoulder he saw the dusty outline of an SUV barreling down the slope in the direction of the dock. It swung in a wide, dust-raising curve, coming to a sliding halt.

Doors flew open and Phoenix Force hit the ground running, weapons up as they engaged the pair of Inigo soldiers moving up from the jetty. The rattle of P-90s sounded. The Inigo soldiers were cut down without pause, bodies riddled by intense autofire.

Manning pushed to his feet, calling out as he waved a hand in the direction of the jetty.

"Inigo. Heading for that launch," he yelled.

They were out of time.

Inigo had already leaped into the launch and it was powering away from the jetty. Out of range. It picked up speed, leaving a churning wake behind.

As Manning leaned against the wooden crates, his expended energy draining away and leaving him weak, he saw the tall figure of Inigo standing at the stern of the launch, facing back toward the shore.

The man raised an arm, in a defiant salute, clenching his fist.

"This time, you son of a bitch," Manning said. "But it's not over yet."

"What's not over?" McCarter asked as he joined the Canadian. He looked out to where the launch was fast disappearing into the distance. "Oh, that. We'll get another chance, mate." He took a longer look at Manning. "Bloody hell, Gary, it must have been some party."

Manning was suddenly feeling very fragile. The effects of his handling by Inigo's men and the physical beating began to take their toll. Manning was tough but no one was invulnerable. He let himself sink to the ground, the overwhelming pain crowding in.

James appeared, crouching beside his teammate. He slid off his pack and opened it.

"Going to take more than a couple of painkillers to cure this," he said.

Manning eyed him, a serious expression on his battered face.

"Great to see you, too, pal."

WHILE JAMES ATTENDED TO Manning and the rest of the team, including Chaka, started a search of Inigo's base, McCarter made a call.

"I was about to call you," Barbara Price said.

McCarter picked up the serious tone in her voice. There was no time for banter or levity.

"Am I going to like this?" he asked.

"I don't think so," Price said.

She gave him the details of her talk with Valentine Seminov. The information about the nuclear device and the fact Raul Inigo was personally involved. As she talked, McCarter turned and fixed his gaze on the distant silhouette of Inigo's boat.

"So, our earlier concerns about nuclear weapons doesn't sound like wishful thinking any longer," Price said. "Valentine will keep us updated on everything if he manages to get further information."

"Makes all this a lot clearer now," McCarter said. "No wonder Inigo and his chums wanted to keep the lid on it.

Listen, luv, I want you to pass me every single word on this. Anything you get, I don't care how trivial. You understand?"

"Yes. Is there anything you need right now?"

"Stand by to have us picked up and taken back to the carrier once we've finished here."

"My God," Price said. "I almost forgot. What about Gary?"

"Back in the fold," McCarter said. "Being patched up by our resident medic."

"Good."

"Shunt me through to the computer magician. I'll talk to you later."

Kurtzman's gruff tones came through a minute later. "Hear you got your MIA back. Good. Now, what are you after this time?"

"Simple request for you cyber-space geniuses. That boat you've been watching for us. Can you keep a long-term track on it? When it leaves here?"

"Shouldn't cause us too much of a problem."

"We need to see where it goes. Aaron, did Barb tell you about her talk with Seminov?"

"She did. Is this to do with that?"

"Raul Inigo is the bloke who negotiated the deal for the nuclear device. So, he should know where it's heading. For all we know he might have the thing on board right now. Maybe this was where he was holding it."

"And you want to keep tabs on him?"

"Too bloody right, we do."

"Consider it done."

With his call completed McCarter made his way over to check out Inigo's base. The hut where Manning had been held revealed nothing of interest. But there was a larger storage shed that contained stacks of contraband goods, including a stash of weapons and ammunition and a few bales of plastic-wrapped drugs. There were also a number of glass vessels filled with a clear liquid. The labels read Ethanol. The liquid could be used for fuel or in the manufacture of alcohol.

"The Somalians make their own liquor," Chaka said. "Cheap and dangerous. The last thing those pirates should have."

"I don't think he approves of pirates," Hawkins said.

"I never liked Long John Silver myself," McCarter said.

"Long John who?"

"*Treasure Island?* Nasty pirate. Wooden leg. Parrot on his shoulder. Classic book. Robert Louis Stevenson."

Hawkins shook his head. "I prefer a good Western."

"The youth of today," McCarter said. "No class."

"We have to do something about all this," Chaka said.

"Burn it," Encizo said. "Pour the ethanol over it and burn it."

"A man after my own heart," Chaka said.

He used his panga to slice open the packaged drugs, then took the tops off of the ethanol vessels and poured it over the drugs. Ammunition boxes were opened and scattered around the autorifles and handguns. More ethanol was splashed over the ordnance. There was a good number of glass vessels. By the time they were empty, the inside of the hut reeked from the fumes.

"Everybody out," McCarter ordered. "We breathe in any more of these fumes, we'll be as lit up as this bloody shed is going to be."

Chaka used a bottle to make a trail leading outside. McCarter lent him a lighter and Chaka touched it to the pooled ethanol. It flared brightly, the flames racing back along the trail and inside the open door. Nothing happened for a time, then there was a loud whoosh of sound and a wall of flame spread across the shed's interior. The flames were soon licking at the walls and roof. The dry, weathered wood caught easily. Smoke began to rise into the sky.

Phoenix Force withdrew to a safe distance as heated ammunition began to cook off.

McCarter stared out to Inigo's boat. He was sure the man would be able to see the blaze.

"Just be watching, you arsehole, because sooner rather than later it'll be your turn to be burned. And that's a promise."

CHAPTER TWENTY-ONE

The anger Inigo felt was hard to contain. He stood at the rail of the *Boa Vista* and watched the smoke rising from his warehouse. Returning to the boat without his prisoner had been humiliating enough, but to have his base seized by the team of commandos hit him hard.

Remo brought him binoculars and Inigo scanned the area. Flames rose from the warehouse, with thick smoke rising into the air. He tried not to think of the valuable merchandise being consumed by the fire. The weapons and ammunition, plus the cache of liquor, being destroyed meant a large monetary loss. Yet against the large consignment of narcotic drugs, they were pocket change. The resale value of the drugs ran into the millions. Inigo could have wept. On top of the financial aspect was to have let the client down. Inigo didn't like to disappoint his customers. As with all his dealings, reliability was the key to his client base. With the drug consignment being willfully destroyed, Inigo was going to have to resupply at his own expense. That was because much of the drug cache had already been bought and paid for. There would be no problem actually replacing the consignment. He would go to his main supplier and obtain a further batch. Paying out of his own pocket was the part of the deal that would hurt.

Inigo lowered the binoculars. He didn't want to look any longer. It was bordering on painful to see his valuable merchandise being turned into ashes. He handed the binoculars to Remo.

Inigo banished the incident from his mind. He had the main prize on board. In the boat's hold.

The nuclear device.

In truth it was the only thing that concerned him at present. Deliver that and then he could start to deal with the men who had plagued him recently.

"Time we left," he said. "Nothing we can do here."

Remo nodded and made for the bridge. As well as being Inigo's right-hand man, Remo commanded the *Boa Vista*. He was an excellent seaman and handled the boat with ease.

"To the Pakistan rendezvous?"

Inigo nodded and walked away. He went into the main cabin and poured himself a large whiskey. He stood at the window facing the shore, unable to resist a final look at his burning warehouse.

"I will not forget, my friends," he said.

THE TRIP through the Arabian Sea was without incident. While the boat cruised the distance to the meeting point, Inigo busied himself with running his organization. He slept well that night, despite his restless anger at what had happened in Somalia. He woke, showered and had coffee before he slumped in one of the comfortable leather armchairs and reached for the sat phone. As he keyed in the number he felt the *Boa Vista's* powerful engines rumble into life.

"Yes?"

"*¡Hola!* Edgar," Inigo said.

"Are you about to tell me good news, or should I sit down?" Bergstrom inquired.

"As far as you are concerned, the news is favorable.

We have just dropped anchor and I will be on my way to complete the transfer shortly. On a personal note, not so good. That hostile group has wiped out my base in Somalia and put the warehouse to the torch. A valuable cargo has been destroyed and I was unable to prevent it. I barely got away myself."

"Sorry to hear that, Raul. I wish I could pinpoint who these people are but we've had no luck identifying them. Our predicament is similar here. A small unit has hit one of my covert teams back home and made them look like idiots. I have a terminate-with-prejudice order out for them. Raul, the sooner we finalize this deal, the better. I have a feeling if we don't, these sons of bitches are going to whittle us down to nothing. Whoever they are, and I hate to say it, the bastards are good. Too good to be allowed to stay alive."

"You seem to be expressing what I am feeling. I am starting to develop a personal aggravation toward these men. Since they came on the scene their tactics have become more tiresome. The moment our business is over I am going to put all my efforts into locating and destroying them. Believe me, Edgar, it is a long time since I've allowed my feelings to become so strong. Emotion should be pushed aside but these men…ah, I should not think about them at this time. First we deliver the device. Is your deployment team in position?"

"We're waiting, ready to transfer the device to the waiting freighter. Then we move it into Israeli waters as part of an expected cargo. Right under the authorities' noses."

"You are sure this will work? Getting into Israel is not an easy task."

"You forget who is managing this. It won't be the first time my people have undertaken such a mission. We are not amateurs, Inigo. This is our job."

"Good luck. Flight time from the *Boa Vista* will be just under an hour. We will make the handover go as smoothly as possible."

"Good."

"One last question…"

"Raul, the minute you hand over the device I will make the call. The money will be deposited within ten minutes. I'll wait until you check your account. Satisfied?"

"No offense intended, Edgar. It's the way I always do business. Old or new client. Money on delivery. You know that."

"Sound strategy. I can't fault it. So, deliver the package and you can go cruise the Arabian Sea."

"Edgar, with what you have planned, I think I'll move a lot further away than that."

Bergstrom was still laughing when Inigo ended the call.

He stood and made his way from the cabin and down to the deck level, where he inspected his Bell helicopter. The pilot, Hernandez, was carrying out a thorough pre-flight check. He barely acknowledged Inigo's presence. The pilot was a dedicated man. He prized the helicopter as if it were his personal possession, making certain there were no problems that might interrupt a flight. Inigo found that reassuring. And especially today when they were going to be carrying an extraspecial cargo.

He slid open the cabin door and stared at the four-foot-square, canvas-covered cube. The kiloton device waited under the cover for the final adjustments and time settings that would ready it for detonation. A blast that would send shock waves throughout the Middle East and set the stage for Israel's undoubtedly hostile response. Staring at the device, Inigo felt no reaction. The nuke was, as far as he was concerned, simply another piece of hardware he was supplying to a client. Transactions were simply that. Inigo never thought further than the delivery. Closing the sale was his prime motive.

He slid the cabin door shut and watched Hernandez ticking off his check sheet.

"Let me know when it's done," he said. "We need to go."

Hernandez simply nodded.

Inigo stood at the stern. A warm breeze pushed in. His thoughts went to recent events. If he had been a fatalist the events might have suggested a downturn in his life. Inigo was not. He accepted that life did not always present him with perfect situations. So, disappointments had to be accepted. The loss of men and merchandise was unfortunate but not in itself enough to destroy either his existence, or his future. Inigo would move on. He would, however, exact his due from the team of commandos. As he had dealt with the rival cartel leaders in Colombia, he would make certain to deliver a blood vengeance on the opposition. It was something he refused to let slip by. A matter of honor. Also a matter of necessity. If word got out that Inigo had been bested, his reputation would be left with a stain on it. And Inigo's reputation was important. Any future clients needed to know he stood by his word. Not by inaction but by striking back at those who desired to take advantage.

Inigo had the means and the money to mount an ongoing search for the commando team. He would find them and he would have each and every one of them eliminated.

But not before he made them suffer.

Just as he had made his mother's killer suffer.

Before they died they would, to a man, be sorry they had ever crossed Raul Inigo's path.

CHAPTER TWENTY-TWO

"That cell the guys brought in only had a couple of numbers on its call list. Number was for a burn phone so there wasn't much to work with. Until I tried remote activation. Switch the cell phone on and then we can track its position."

"You can do that?" Price asked.

"Doesn't work on every phone," Tokaido said, "but we got lucky this time. The number from the cell turns out to be located in Maryland. It's for a landline. An address for Franklin Meyer. And guess what? Meyer heads a security outfit called Black Watch Incorporated. Small company. Employs ex-military personnel. Now, Black Watch isn't on many Recommended lists. But one name came up that rings bells. Jay Callow. And Callow works out of Bergstrom's office at Langley."

"Joining the dots. Great work, Akira," Price said. "I'll hand this to Able Team."

"Now we have this lead," Kurtzman said, "we'll follow through and see if we can dredge anything else up on Meyer and his organization."

Price turned to make her way out of the cyber room. "Just keep looking, guys," she said.

Back in her own office she raised Able Team and spoke to Carl Lyons. He listened as she related the information Tokaido had found.

"I'll text you the address and sat-nav coordinates."

"Gives us a way in," he said. "Feed us anything else you get."

"Will do."

"THIS BERGSTROM IS SHARP," Blancanales said. "He's in bed with Inigo. Working the strings to pull this deal off. He's CIA but his black ops status means he can operate outside the system."

"Leaves him pretty well isolated," Schwarz said. "Must spend a lot of time looking over his shoulder."

"He's sure of himself. Arrogant. Guy believes he's bulletproof."

"He's got that wrong," Lyons said. "You can bet on that."

Lyons drained his coffee cup and without another word headed for the door. Blancanales and Schwarz glanced at each other in silence, then followed the Able Team leader out of the coffee shop and across the parking lot.

"You can drive," Lyons said, tossing the keys to Schwarz.

At the edge of the parking lot Schwarz asked, "Where to?"

Lyons had his sat phone in his hand, checking the text Price had sent him. He offered a breakdown of the Stony Man findings. "Meyer's office," he said.

Schwarz caught sight of Blancanales in the rearview mirror. He had a faint smile on his face.

"Meyer it is," Schwarz said, and eased the SUV into the traffic flow.

Lyons had contacted Stony Man and was engrossed in a conversation with Aaron Kurtzman. He was asking for an update on Bergstrom's associates. Kurtzman was plainly giving him chapter and verse because Lyons didn't speak for some time.

"That's fine, Bear," he finally said, breaking the connection and putting his phone away.

"Reader of minds plainly I am not." Blancanales mimicked Yoda. "Explanation give Jedi should."

"I just got some fresh detail that implicates Meyer up to his armpits. This has just come through since I spoke to Barb. Meyer has been doing backdoor work for Bergstrom, with this Callow as a go-between."

They reached the strip where Meyer's company was located. Schwarz parked a few doors down and cut the motor.

"Hard or soft?" Blancanales asked.

"If he plays nice," Lyons said, "that's fine by me. Let's go and stir the pot for Meyer."

They exited the SUV and moved along the sidewalk.

"So, who gets to take the back door?" Schwarz asked, then immediately regretted his question.

"I just love it when someone volunteers," Lyons said.

Schwarz moved ahead and turned into the alley at the end of the block.

The logo on a plate to one side of the front door read Black Watch Inc. Lyons led the way inside, through the glass door that took them into a reception area where a redheaded young woman watched them closely from behind her curved desk. The wall behind held photographs of dark-clad figures wielding high-end weapons.

"May I help you?" Her voice was coolly professional. "Do you have an appointment?"

Lyons gave her a "no and I don't care" look. He slid his leather badge holder from his sport jacket and flipped it open so she could see the Justice Department shield.

The girl scanned the badge, pursing her full lips. Her left hand reached toward the phone.

"Oh, no," Blancanales said quietly. "We wouldn't want Mr. Meyer getting all worked up."

The girl's smooth cheeks flushed, leaving Blancanales wondering if she was embarrassed or angry. Judging by the hard gleam in her green eyes, he decided it must have been the latter.

"You go ahead," he said to Lyons. "I'll keep the young lady company."

"I don't need a babysitter." The professional tone had vanished now. The girl glared at Blancanales. "And you're not my daddy."

"Tut-tut," Blancanales said, "such hostility from one so young."

He leaned on the desk and grinned at the girl.

LYONS PUSHED THROUGH the door that led to the main office area. There was a corridor running the length of the building, with doors leading off each side. As the door swung shut behind him Lyons felt the sat phone in his pocket vibrate. He made a quick check and saw a brief message on the screen. It was from Schwarz, letting him know he was in position.

Lyons read the names on the doors. The only one he was interested in was the one that told him where Meyer was located. When he found it, Lyons worked the handle and pushed the door open. As he stepped inside, pushing the door shut, moving so his back was to the wall, Lyons saw Meyer behind a large, cluttered desk. The man's tanned, jowly face expressed anger. His right hand dropped beneath the desk, jabbing at something Lyons assumed was a panic button.

At the same time Lyons caught a glimpse of a dark-suited man pushing up out of a leather recliner to his left. The man was solid under his clothing. And fit. It showed in the way he moved, coming up off the recliner in a smooth lunge, his long legs propelling him across the carpeted floor.

Lyons turned to meet the guy, observing the easy way he slid a big hand under his jacket, left side.

Soft was going hard fast, Lyons thought.

Before the big guy had time to take a solid hold on his holstered weapon, Lyons made his own move. To a casual observer Lyons didn't seem to do a great deal. That was not true. Lyons delivered two blows: a swinging left, followed by a right. His closed fists cracked against the guy's jaw, jerking his head to one side, then back. The heavy sound of the blows was followed by a stunned grunt from the recipient. As his head rocked from the punches, blood flew from his lips. The guy simply went down, hard, unconscious before he slammed into the carpet, his head bouncing before he sprawled on his back.

Lyons bent over and flipped open the guy's jacket, relieving him of the holstered 9 mm Glock.

He moved to his former position against the wall as the sound of running feet came from the corridor.

Meyer sat upright behind his desk, hands flat on the top. His expression was telling Lyons to expect trouble. Lyons ignored him.

The door swung wide, hitting the wall. The first guy inside, lean, with a thick mop of blond hair, carried a mini-Uzi. A second guy, also armed, pushing in close behind him, caught a glimpse of Lyons as the Able Team commander moved. He lifted the Uzi and angled it toward Lyons.

"Hey, Lonny..." he said, then grunted as Lyons slammed the Glock across the bridge of his nose. The soft crunch was followed by a moan. Blood began to spurt from the guy's nose. It spilled down his face and dripped heavily across his pastel-colored shirt. The guy dropped his weapon and clutched both hands to his broken nose. Blood leaked through his fingers.

The man called Lonny spun around, eyes staring. He swung his Uzi in Lyons's general direction. Lyons had already made a move, his left hand knocking the barrel of the compact SMG upward. As Lonny's finger squeezed back on the trigger a burst of 9 mm slugs exploded from the muzzle, raking the office ceiling. A line of ragged holes appeared. Dust filtered down from the damaged areas. Lyons closed his hand around the miniUzi and wrenched it from Lonny's grasp, then jammed the Glock's muzzle into the man's throat, just below his chin. He stared at Lonny, his expression suggesting Lonny not make any moves.

Movement outside the door signaled Blancanales's appearance. He had his Beretta in his fist. The redheaded girl was beside him, staring.

"Go call the guy outside the back door," Blancanales said to her. When she glared at him, Blancanales added, "Just do it."

"Sit down," Lyons said to Lonny. "Take your buddy with you."

Lonny did as he was told, albeit with reluctance. He understood it wouldn't be prudent to do anything to further upset the blond man.

"So, what do we have here?" Blancanales asked.

"Men with guns," Lyons said. "Who don't ask questions first."

He passed the Uzi to Blancanales.

"Not good for customer relations," Blancanales said.

"You're not customers," Lonny said.

"We're not?" Schwarz asked as he showed up at the open door.

"They just barged in, Mr. Meyer," the redhead said. "Wouldn't let me call you."

"Liv, just calm down," Meyer said.

Schwarz stayed at the door so he could observe anyone coming through from the front reception area.

"Over by the window, Liv," Blancanales said.

She did what he told her. That had everyone facing Lyons and Blancanales across the office.

"Now we've all been introduced," Lyons said, "we can talk."

"You barge into my office, attack my staff and now you want to talk," Meyer said. "About what?"

"We can start with your association with Edgar Bergstrom," Lyons said conversationally. "And Senator Trent."

Lyons heard Lonny's sharp intake of breath at the mention of the names. It happened before Lonny could hold himself. Lonny also swung his head so his eyes met Meyer's.

"Gave yourself away there," Blancanales said.

"Mistake," Meyer said sharply. "We don't know anyone with those names."

"He tells lies, as well," Blancanales said.

"Doesn't that come under federal offenses?" Schwarz asked.

"Right here, right now, Meyer," Lyons said, "you are done. No more hiding behind your friends."

Meyer smiled. "Whatever little department you represent, this is way above you. I'm covered. You have no jurisdiction over me or my associates." He reached for the phone. "One call and you people will disappear."

"Touch the phone and I might just have to shoot your hand off," Lyons said tightly.

"He does that," Schwarz said. "I'd listen."

"It's going to be okay," Liv said. "Mr. Meyer, it's okay."

The way she looked across the office at Meyer aroused suspicion in Lyons. He didn't like the smug expression on her face; any trace of youthful innocence had gone, replaced by a superior confidence.

"Hartz, check her pockets," he snapped.

Schwarz holstered his Beretta and crossed the office. He caught hold of one of Liv's wrists and pulled her clear of the others. He made her face a clear wall, arms raised and palms flat against it. Then he expertly frisked her. And came up with a small, black plastic device that fit in the palm of his hand. A small red light winked on and off.

"Signal device," Schwarz said.

"You've been picking up some sneaky habits," Blancanales said.

"It's the company she's keeping," Lyons said.

"Like I told you," Meyer said. "You are so out of your league."

"I love it when these lower-level assholes start telling me how much trouble I'm in," Lyons said.

"You'll see," Lonny crowed, his expression giving him a gloating look. "The sen—"

"Lonny," Meyer yelled.

"You're in the naughty corner now," Blancanales said to Lonny. "Meyer, you should keep your boys on a shorter leash."

"The hell with you," Meyer said. "Go ahead, threaten all you fuckin' want. There's not a damn thing you can do."

Lyons faced the man, his eyes fixed on Meyer's. "Don't be too sure, Meyer. We've figured your game. We know what Bergstrom and Trent are doing. Your dealings with them. Names are in my little black book and we know where to find you. I'll see to it Homeland Security and the FBI are brought up to date. If it was my decision, I'd shoot you where you sit. But rules mean I have to walk away this time. If I come back, no one will save you…any of you…"

He let the words hang. Meyer stared back for a while.

His resolve wavered and he dropped his eyes finally, almost shrinking under Lyons's fierce and uncompromising gaze.

Carl Lyons put his pistol away. He dropped the magazine from the Glock, worked out the chambered round, then very deliberately thumbed out the cartridges from the magazine and let them fall to the floor. He tossed the disarmed pistol on Meyer's desk. Blancanales cleared the magazine from the miniUzi.

"I'll leave it in reception," he said.

"I would really think about a career move, Liv," Schwarz said. "Stay with these bad boys, you're going to pay a big price."

The young woman glanced around the office, face suddenly pale. For a moment it looked as if she was going to speak. Then she looked down at the floor.

Able Team eased out of the office and walked out of the building, pausing on the sidewalk.

"Now we're in trouble," Blancanales said, a slight grin on his lips. "Mr. Meyer is mad at us."

"Really mad," Schwarz agreed. "Mad enough to sic the dogs on us."

They walked to the SUV and climbed in. Schwarz had pulled away from the curb when Lyons said, "We have a tail. A very large black SUV just showed up and it's going to follow us."

"How do you know that?" Blancanales asked.

"Meyer is at the curb, talking to someone inside it," Lyons said. "Now he's pointing at us."

"That's rude," Blancanales said.

"That signal device the girl had," Schwarz said. "Must have called in a backup team."

"And that's sneaky," Blancanales said. "But one way or another our visit has stirred the pot."

"You think so?" Lyons said, a thin smile on his lips.

Carl Lyons loved to get people worked up, because upset people often did unexpected and reckless things. And that required a reaction.

"How do we handle this?" Schwarz asked. "With tact and diplomacy, or the Lyons way?"

"Whatever we do, we need to get off the streets," Blancanales said. "We know these guys don't waste time exchanging names. Last thing we need is a pitched battle with innocent folk in the firing line."

"So, let's lead these guys on a tour through the city. See if they bite," Lyons said. "Do it, Gadgets."

With the SUV behind him, Schwarz drove through the city streets. He stayed within the speed limit. Cutting back and forth through intersections, doubling back a few times. The trail car stayed with them, always a couple of vehicles behind.

"That driver has got to be pissed off with us by now," Blancanales said. "He knows what we're doing. Can't make a move with all these witnesses."

"Let's not get too cocky," Lyons said. "With everything these guys are involved in, I wouldn't be surprised at anything they did. Let's keep driving for a while."

Schwarz's route eventually brought them to Rock Creek Park, a twelve-mile area of wooded natural beauty where Washingtonians could get clear of the city confines.

"This is nice," Blancanales muttered. "Now we're doing the scenic run."

They were on Beach Drive, cruising past the trees edging the road.

Lyons opened his coat. "If they're going to do it, this is the place," he said.

As if in answer to Lyons's comment the SUV accelerated and closed the gap. The moment it was right behind

Able Team, the vehicle swerved out and pulled level with them. The front passenger window was down and Schwarz saw the muzzle of an SMG pointing at him. His reaction was to stomp on the brake, causing Able Team's vehicle to fall back. Schwarz felt the wheels lock and heard the squeal of rubber on the blacktop. The SUV slewed to the left and there was a solid bang as the two vehicles made contact. The chase car slid across the strip, the driver losing control for a few seconds, and Schwarz, seizing the moment, slammed his vehicle into the SUV again. Harder this time, using the advantage to push the SUV all the way to the far side of the strip. The far wheels hit the grassy verge edging the road and the SUV began to bounce erratically. Schwarz kept up the pressure, preventing the other vehicle from moving back onto the road.

In the rear Blancanales lowered his window, his Beretta in his hand. He saw the SMG pushing out of the front passenger window again, aiming across the gap. Blancanales didn't hesitate. He braced the 92F in both hands and triggered a fast pair of 9 mm slugs at the shape of the SMG. The weapon jerked as one of the slugs slammed into the body of the weapon. The impact knocked it sideways and the shooter pulled back inside the vehicle.

Whatever power the other driver had been holding in reserve, he piled on. The SUV surged forward, ahead of Able Team. It bumped its way back onto the road, tires smoking as it fought for traction. It held the center of the road as the driver brought it under control.

"He's going to broadside," Lyons said. "Block us off."

From the rear Blancanales yelled, "He's right. His tires are smoking."

Yards ahead the big SUV made a tight half turn that spun it across the road, the heavy body rocking on its suspension as it leveled out.

Schwarz hit his own brakes and brought the vehicle to a stop ten feet from the other.

Lyons and Blancanales were out before the SUV was still, weapons up and watching the other SUV's crew pile out.

An SMG opened up. Schwarz threw himself across the front seat as the windshield was hit by a single shot. The slug made a loud crack as it struck, but the angle of the windshield deflected it and it failed to do more than leave a score mark. Lyons had left his door wide open. Schwarz wriggled across the seat and rolled from the SUV, dropping to a crouch. He pulled his Beretta as he landed, hearing the sudden, rapid exchange of autofire and watching the enemy crew disembarking.

On his exit from the car Lyons had flattened himself on the blacktop, his Python extended. He braced his left hand against the road and tracked in on the guy who had already opened fire. Lyons's finger stroked back the revolver's trigger and planted his shot in the shooter's chest. It was exactly on target. The big Magnum round slammed the shooter back against the SUV with enough force to empty his lungs. The guy never had the chance to refill them. Lyons's shot had struck his heart, doing irreparable damage, and the man went down without a sound.

Blancanales picked up movement at the rear of the SUV as one of the crew circled the vehicle. The guy was wielding an SMG, seeking a target. He locked eyes with Blancanales as he cleared the SUV and leveled his weapon. Blancanales had the guy in his sights and he triggered his Beretta, loosing off a trio of 9 mm slugs that hit the guy's extended right shoulder and arm. The guy stumbled away from the SUV, his right arm dropping limply. The 9 mm slugs had torn through flesh and muscle to lodge against bone. The man gave a groan as his loose arm dragged against the torn muscles. He didn't hear Blancanales's next shot but felt his left knee hit by a savage blow. He fell to the road, his SMG clattering as it slid from his grip.

Schwarz had seen movement on the far side of the SUV, through the tinted windows. A blurred shape. The third guy from the vehicle. The Able Team commando pushed up on one knee, extending his Beretta. He fired the moment he had target acquisition, his first slugs taking out window glass. Schwarz fired again, clearing his magazine in a rapid burst. There was a splash of red as the shots caught the target in the head and throat, knocking him off his feet.

The quiet after the shooting was unnerving. Overhead birds scattered by the gunfire were circling and starting to protest at being disturbed.

Schwarz stood upright, replacing his spent magazine.

Back on his feet Lyons brushed grit from his clothes as he checked out the area.

Only Blancanales moved toward the SUV and the man he had shot.

He holstered his pistol and crouched beside the guy.

"Hurts, doesn't it?"

The man stared up at Blancanales. His face was sheened with sweat, teeth chattering as reaction set in. His coat was soaked with blood, so was the leg of his pants around his shattered knee.

"Get me some help," he said.

"You talk first," Blancanales said. "Make it fast 'cause you are losing blood."

"You fucks are going to be sorry for this. You messed with the wrong people."

"I learned a long time ago not to be too concerned with threats from guys I just shot. Now, do you give me the answers I want, or do I leave you to bleed all over Rock Creek Park? Your choice."

The man bit back on the pain, his eyes staring up at Blancanales.

"You are out of the tough-guy business," Blancanales said. "All shot to hell and no use to anyone."

The man saw Blancanales was not about to let up on him. He also had the sense to realize the trouble he was in, with no one about to come and rescue him. The pain from his wound helped to convince him it was time to look after himself.

"Meyer called us in. He's working for Bergstrom."

"Now, see, that didn't hurt," Blancanales said. "Not as much as the bullets I put in you."

"Bastard."

Blancanales shook his head. "Not according to my mother."

Schwarz was on his sat phone, relaying his request for assistance through Stony Man.

"Are you all safe?" Price asked.

"Yes. And we have confirmation Meyer was the guy who set these Boy Scouts on us. Bergstrom's name was flagged up, as well."

Lyons crossed to stand behind Blancanales. He was still holding his Python in his hand.

"It would save everyone a lot of trouble if we finished this creep right now," he said.

The wounded guy stared up at Carl Lyons's angry scowl. Lyons had a way of intimidating people simply by being there, his presence threatening.

"He did answer my question," Blancanales said.

"What about the big one?" Lyons asked, cocking and uncocking the large handgun. "C'mon, I can do this before the medics show up. Save us having to do a heap of paperwork."

"He won't…will he?" the man asked.

Blancanales shrugged. "If he doesn't get what he needs, he might. Out here it comes down to you and us."

"Not even Senator Trent can pull you out of this," Lyons said.

"He'll cover himself," Schwarz added. "Guy like that doesn't worry about the hired help. The man will use his position to shut you out."

"Time like this you have to cover your own ass because no one else is going to," Blancanales said.

"You want I should fetch the first-aid kit?" Schwarz asked.

The wounded man lifted his head. Resignation showed on his face. With his gun in his hand he had been in charge. A hard son of a bitch. Down on the ground, in severe pain, and with an unsure future ahead of him, the bravado had gone.

"Jesus, help me," he said. "Please. It hurts bad. Help me and I'll tell you what I can."

A cell phone rang. It came from the man's jacket. Blancanales reached in and pulled the phone out. He handed it to Lyons.

Lyons scanned the readout. Smiled. The incoming call was from Meyer. Lyons answered.

"Is it finished?" Meyer asked. "Are we done?"

"Done is the word," Lyons said. "You should have cooperated when we were in your office. Your team is down, Meyer, and we have one guy ready to talk. Now, how do you want to play this out? Stay hardball? Or give it up and negotiate? It's down to you to make a deal. The alternative is we come calling again. Only this time we don't knock and ask if we can come in."

Meyer's silence made Lyons smile. The man was thinking.

How to get himself into the clear.

How to gain time.

"I know what you're thinking, Meyer. Do I contact Bergstrom and ask him to bail me out? No point. Bergstrom is next on our list. He believes he's untouchable. Let me correct that assumption, Meyer. The man is finished. The play is over. His black ops protection isn't going to work any longer. You guys have run out of places to hide. All you can do now is try to make a deal. Save yourself or go down with the rest. Your choice."

Lyons heard the distant wail of police sirens approaching. He held up the cell so Meyer would be able to hear.

"Cops are on their way. Your live guy is going to be in custody soon enough and he'll be making his own deal. What's it going to be?"

"We can meet? Talk this out?" Meyer said.

Lyons smiled. Meyer had been quick to capitulate. Maybe too quick. He was trying too hard.

"I'm listening."

"Give me two hours. There's a diner off Interstate 295. Next to a closed-down gas station. Old road that was bypassed when the highway was planned." He gave Lyons the exact location. "Diner is ready to shut down, too, so there shouldn't be any interruptions. Two hours. Just your team. I see anyone else, I'm gone. I'll have a couple of my people with me for witnesses. Deal? What do I call you?"

"Matthews will do," Lyons said. "Two hours."

He shut off the cell.

Local P.D. cruisers rolled to a stop, an ambulance close behind.

Lyons stepped forward and held up his ID as armed cops surrounded Able Team.

"Call home," Lyons said to Schwarz. "If these guys give us any hassle, tell base to call the Man. We need to be out of here ASAP. Meyer is going to buy us a cup of coffee."

For once Able Team extracted themselves from the scene in less than half an hour, due to Stony Man and the backup from the President. Kurtzman had sent the GPS coordinates for the location of their rendezvous with Meyer, and Schwarz put his foot down as they headed in that direction.

"Just one question," Blancanales said.

He didn't need to put it into words when the Able Team commander shook his head.

"No. I don't trust him," Lyons said. "Meyer is going to set us up. He'll walk in all eager to please, but he'll have a backup crew ready to jump us."

"I agree. This is one of those times I'm pleased you are a cynical son of a bitch."

"If I wasn't, we would have been dead a long time ago."

"Now, there's a guy who understands the meaning of life," Schwarz said.

"Always look on the bright side?" Blancanales said.

Schwarz shook his head. "Trust no one and keep your powder dry."

"I thought it was shoot first and ask the questions later."

"Runs a close second. I'd really hate to live on the difference between either of them," Schwarz said.

CHAPTER TWENTY-THREE

The diner was plainly on its last legs, not yet fully collapsed but close. Like the deserted gas station it showed its age and lack of customers. The parking lot out front was empty and so was the diner itself. The decor was worn and frayed, just like the lone guy behind the counter. He stared at Able Team when they stepped inside, surprised at their appearance.

"You want food?" he asked.

"Just coffee," Schwarz said.

"Good thing," the guy said. "Cook's gone. I could do food but you'd need to wait."

"Coffee's fine," Schwarz said.

They sat at the counter, on stools that creaked almost as much as the counterman's bones.

"This looks like something out of *The Twilight Zone*," Blancanales said.

"You got that right," the guy said as he poured coffee into three mugs. "I reckon by next month this place will be closed. Just waiting for the company to make the decision."

"So, what's stopping them?" Lyons asked.

The guy shrugged his lean shoulders. "Beats me, buddy."

Beyond the streaked window the highway lay empty. The main route had bypassed it by a few miles, leaving the spot abandoned and slowly wearing itself out.

"Wasn't that what happened to the Bates Motel in

Pyscho?" Blancanales said. "Highway bypassed it and left it deserted."

"Ah, you guys are safe," the counterman said. "There's no shower and you won't see me wearing a wig and a dress."

"Comforting to know," Lyons muttered.

"I can see why Meyer chose this place," Schwarz said.

"Too damn right," Blancanales agreed.

"Coffee's good," Lyons said.

"That's okay, then," Blancanales said.

"I don't think Meyer is going to play by the rules," Lyons said. "He agreed too fast to giving up his buddies. He'll have secondary backup. We need to stay sharp. All of us." He spotted Blancanales giving him a stern look. "And don't glare at me like that. He's not to be trusted."

Blancanales shrugged. "It wasn't that. I was just admiring the cut of your new shirt."

"The hell you were."

"It is particularly smart," Schwarz said. "Accentuates your coloring."

"You mean his eyes?" Blancanales asked.

"No," Schwarz said. "The angry red in his cheeks."

"One day you guys will take this job seriously," Lyons said.

Schwarz glanced at Blancanales. "You think?"

His partner shook his head. "Can't see that happening."

"Or me," Schwarz agreed.

He leaned forward as a black limousine rolled onto the diner frontage. Three men stepped out, crossed to the entrance and made their way inside the diner. Meyer was leading.

"I think our guy has arrived," Blancanales said. "I'm starting to agree. I don't think I'm going to trust him, either."

"Jeez," Schwarz said. "Take a look at those bodyguards. They weren't with him at his office. Where did he get those guys, rent-a-hunk?"

They were massive, solid, bullet-headed figures easily topping the six-foot mark. Buzz cuts. Deep-set eyes. They wore dark suits with white shirts and sober ties. They were also draped in long topcoats worn open, and it was obvious they were carrying.

"Oh, come on," Blancanales said. "Are they for real?"

Meyer stayed ahead of his escort. His suit was light gray and he wore an expensive topcoat thrown over his shoulders like some precocious playboy.

"What is this?" Blancanales whispered to Schwarz.

"He wants us to be intimidated by his overcoat."

Lyons turned his head slightly. "Just shut up," he said. Then he faced the newcomers. "I'm Matthews. These are my associates. Comer and Hartz."

Meyer glanced at Schwarz and Blancanales, a shadow of a smile edging his pale lips. He flicked a hand in the direction of his bodyguards, who stood no more than a few feet behind him.

"*My* associates," he said.

"We all know why we're here," Lyons said. "You ready to talk?"

"If you meet my conditions."

"Meyer, don't push it. This isn't open for conditions. It's too late to start throwing your weight around. Remember what I told you?"

Schwarz, sitting to one side, had kept his eyes on Meyer's bodyguards. Even though neither of them had made a sound or even moved, Schwarz felt uneasy. So he kept a close watch on the pair. The guy close to him, looking straight ahead, appeared to have something in his closed left hand. His thumb began to edge back, to hover over a black curve of plastic almost hidden in his large fist. When his thumb pressed down Schwarz realized what the man was concealing.

He recalled what the girl, Liv, had used to call in backup.

A signaling device. And the pressure of the thumb was activating it.

Son of a bitch.

Over the bodyguard's broad shoulder Schwarz spotted movement on the far side of the parking lot. A dark-colored SUV swung into view from behind the closed gas station. It made a wide, tire-squealing sweep that brought it to the front of the diner. Doors swung open and fast-moving figures exited the vehicle, crossing the sidewalk for the diner entrance.

"Incoming," Schwarz yelled. "And not for coffee."

He hauled his Beretta from the holster under his leather jacket as the diner door was slammed open. It hit the inner wall, the glass pane shattering.

The first guy inside had a 9 mm Uzi in his hands and he opened fire, directing his burst in the direction of Meyer's bodyguards. Slugs hit hard, driving the big men forward, and despite their massive bulk, the shots put them on their knees, weapons half-drawn. The shooter raised the Uzi and fired again, the second stream of slugs tearing into skulls and spraying bloody debris in the air.

Lyons and Blancanales dropped from their stools, pulling weapons as they crouched.

Meyer froze. His expression mirrored his thoughts, revealing that he had no idea what was happening.

In the microseconds between the opening shots and the bodyguards going down, Hermann Schwarz swung his Beretta around, finger sliding across the trigger as he tracked the lead shooter. He fired as he slid off his stool. His opening shot caught the guy in the left side of his jaw, taking out a large chunk of flesh and bone. The guy stumbled, his head twisting under the impact of the 9 mm slug, blood spurting from the ugly wound. His shattered jaw hung by flaps of skin and muscle. Schwarz's second shot took him over the heart and the guy went down on the diner floor.

Schwarz's partners were tracking their weapons even as backup shooters came through the door. Multiple Uzis opened up in a powerful crescendo. Slugs chunked into the counter where Able Team had been sitting seconds earlier. Lyons and Blancanales were already crouching at floor level, returning fire.

The big Colt Python in Carl Lyons's fist slammed out its noise, the .357 Magnum loads exploding with heavy sounds. He caught his target in the upper chest with two fast shots, the crushing impact throwing the guy backward into the third would-be assassin so that Blancanales's close-following three slugs cored through the guy's throat.

The final shooter saw his chance and opened up with his Uzi, driving a long burst into Meyer's back. The man gave a scream as he was slammed to the diner floor.

Able Team responded with a three-weapon burst, the multiple shots punching into the shooter's chest. A pair of .357 slugs from Lyons blew in and through his body, leaving a bloody mess where they emerged, shattering his spine.

"Check the SUV," Lyons yelled.

Blancanales and Schwarz moved to the diner door, stepping over the downed shooters, kicking discarded weapons aside. The SUV, doors open wide, stood empty.

"Clear," Schwarz said.

Blancanales walked by him, checking the highway beyond for any possible backup vehicles. The road was deserted.

As they went back inside the diner they saw Lyons crouched beside Meyer's bloody form. The man was propped up against the base of the counter. He was bleeding heavily from his mouth but he was still alive.

"What the hell just happened?" Blancanales asked.

"Oh, we were set up, all right," Schwarz said. "But so was Meyer." He crossed to the bodyguard he had spotted holding something in his hand. He retrieved the compact device and held it up. "One of Meyer's own bodyguards was earning a double bonus. He sold him out."

"He screwed me," Meyer said.

"Looks that way," Lyons said.

"He was with me for two years."

"Goes to show," Schwarz said, "you can't even trust the hired help. Or the guys they sell out to."

Blancanales went through the pockets of the sellout bodyguard and found a cell phone. He held it up.

"We need to have the call log checked," Lyons said.

"Like you said," Meyer whispered through bloody lips. "No conditions. Bergstrom is behind it and that greasy bastard Trent has been pulling all our strings. I worked for those guys but I made sure I had a lifeline in case anything went wrong. Bergstrom has been down and dirty for so long the guy has a hard time walking a straight line. His whole damn life runs on deceit and double-cross. Looks like I was smart taking out insurance."

The man started coughing up bright blood, hunching over in agony.

"Call an ambulance," Lyons said.

"Talk to Liv," Meyer whispered, his strength slipping away quickly. "She's holding something for me. Proof. I never go into a deal without insurance...."

"Ambulance on its way," Blancanales said.

When Lyons looked at Meyer again, the man had quietly died.

"This is going to take a hell of a lot of cleaning up," the owner of the diner said behind them.

He had dropped to the floor behind the counter when the shooting had started. His gaze took in the bullet damage and the streaked blood.

"You hurt?" Schwarz asked.

"Only in my damn pocket," the man said. "This is going to give the company the excuse they need to close the place down. Goddamn, I likely won't get any severance pay now." He glanced around the diner. "Hey, maybe I should call the cops."

Lyons showed his Justice badge. "I'm just about to do that."

"You know who would love that," Schwarz said.

Lyons managed a thin smile.

Schwarz was referring to Hal Brognola. The head of the Special Operations Group was used to receiving calls from the teams, where he was expected to deal with irate local authorities making noises. The big Fed had broad shoulders to take the flack, and his Justice Department clout came in handy when it became time to smooth over ruffled feathers in the wake of whatever mayhem one of his teams had caused. Brognola would customarily bawl out the offending team, which they expected, but he also knew they were working on the thin edge when going up against whatever incarnation the opposition presented. His teams were laying themselves open to all kinds of physical threats every time they played through a mission, and Hal Brognola was a walking, talking champion of Able Team and Phoenix Force. He battled for them day and night and had, on more than one occasion, gone face-to-face with the President.

The SOG was the last line of defense when it came to their missions. The threats and the people they were up against had no such thing as a rule book. They flouted every civilized expectation to try to achieve their twisted goals. The SOG played down and dirty, stepping over the lines to achieve a result. If they aggravated other agencies, who were left in the dark over the SOG's activities, the President was often the one who had to close down lines of inquiry. America's Commander in Chief understood the need of the SOG to be allowed to work by their own rules. He also understood the way the official agencies played. They kept secrets from each other, had their own agendas, and as much as they paid the President lip service they could shut him out if internal policies dictated they do so. Stony Man was the President's own black ops department, one he defended strongly, because he understood above everything else that every man in the combat teams was totally loyal.

This time around Brognola was not available, so Lyons was going to have to go through Barbara Price again.

"This is starting to annoy me," Lyons said when he spoke to Price, detailing what had just happened. "We're catching the dirty end of the stick here all the time."

"Tell me about it," Price said. "I'll see if I can cool things with the local P.D. If I hit a wall I can always bring the President on board. An irate cop should calm down if he gets a call from the Man."

"I need you to get Bear to run down a cell phone call list. We got it from one of Meyer's bodyguards. The guy sold his boss out and got stitched by the people he sold out to." Lyons read the cell phone number as Schwarz showed him the phone.

"Okay, I'll get Aaron on it," Price said. "I'll liaise with the local cops. Don't tell them any more than you need to. This thing is so off-the-wall even I don't know who's in on it."

Schwarz took cell phone pictures of the hit team and transmitted them through to Kurtzman at Stony Man. He added a text message asking for the men to be identified.

"Let's go talk to Liv," Lyons said. "See what's in that proof she's holding."

"So, WHERE IS EVERYONE?" Blancanales asked.

Meyer's offices were empty apart from Liv. She was sitting behind her desk in reception. Any bravado she might have exhibited earlier had vanished. She looked scared. Her face was white and she had been crying.

When Able Team stepped inside she stared at them with a lost expression on her pale face.

"I was only employed as a receptionist," she said. "What's been happening?"

"Quite a lot," Lyons said.

"Your employer had been a naughty boy," Blancanales said. "He was playing with some rough people."

Liv glanced at him, her eyes wide as she picked up on Blancanales's words.

"What do you mean *had been* and *was playing?* Has something happened to him?"

"Mr. Meyer is dead," Blancanales said gently.

Liv stared at him, uncomprehending. "I don't understand. How can he be dead? He was only here earlier."

"What happened to his boys?" Schwarz asked.

"He sent them away. Told them to disappear for a while until he sorted out some problems. Then he called in—"

"Backup?" Schwarz said.

"Yes. A couple of big guys he sometimes uses for special jobs. And they all left."

"No need to go into details," Lyons said, "but they won't be coming back."

"Liv, Meyer said you're holding something we need to see," Blancanales said. "It has to do with who had him shot. You want to get it for us?"

"He said for me to keep it safe. He called it his backup plan. Almost like he expected something to go wrong. He used to tell me this was a crazy business. Too many secrets and not enough trust. You know what he meant?"

Blancanales nodded. "I'm starting to, Liv."

She led them behind the reception desk and through a door. The room beyond was lined with filing cabinets and stored furniture. Liv went to an old-fashioned iron safe with a tumbler combination lock. She crouched and worked the dial. When she dragged open the thick door she reached inside and slid out a modern tablet. She handed it to Lyons.

"I have no idea what's on this," she said. "I'm sure you people will work it out."

"Thanks, Liv," Blancanales said.

She closed the safe and stood, looking lost suddenly.

"I guess I'm out of a job, too," she said. A smile crossed her face. "I guess I gave you guys a hard time when you were here before. All that stuff with the alarm device. Sorry."

"You were just doing your job," Blancanales said.

"At least I had a job then."

"You'll find something, Liv," Blancanales said. "Smart girl like you."

"I'd choose something a little less hazardous next time," Lyons said.

"You could try Starbucks," Schwarz said. "A barista is a pretty steady occupation."

They left her to close up the office and returned to their vehicle.

"Busy day," Blancanales said as they drove away.

"Not over yet," Lyons said.

AARON KURTZMAN inspected the tablet, turning it over in his big hands.

"Not going to explode?"

Blancanales shook his head. "We're just expecting it to have information that might come in handy," he said.

"Based on what's happened to you guys over the last few days nothing would surprise me anymore."

"Take your word for it."

Kurtzman connected the tablet to a power lead, then turned it on. He added a link cable that threw the screen image onto one of the wall monitors.

"Lots of folders," he said. "Company files. Personnel information. Accounts. Usual stuff. Disappointing. No secret porn stash. Only thing that sometimes adds a little spice to these searches."

"You're a funny guy, Aaron," Schwarz said.

"You don't know the half of it," Carmen Delahunt joked.

Kurtzman had thrown the tablet's icons on the team's screen so they could all trawl through Meyer's lists.

"This was a very organized guy. He's got a file for everything," Huntington Wethers said.

"So, where is the special one?" Blancanales asked.

"Maybe he's got it tucked away out of sight," Delahunt said. "If it has data he doesn't want being seen…"

"He'd keep it somewhere special," Akira Tokaido said.

His fingers flashed across his keyboard, bringing up a long, flowing list of key directories, files within files showing the inner workings of key applications.

"You lost me," Lyons said. "What is all that stuff?"

"Program codes," Kurtzman said. "The computer language that makes all the normal applications work."

"Without all these codes your computer programs wouldn't exist," Wethers noted. "These are what the programmers work with when they create the images and texts you see on your screen."

Tokaido scanned the black-and-white lists. To the uninitiated it meant nothing. Just endless lines of letters and numbers. He hit more keys and began to add some text of his own.

"How can you figure out which one doesn't belong?" Blancanales asked.

"By adding a little program of our own," Kurtzman said. "Akira is doing that now. Writing a subroutine that will scan all that text and pull out the one section that shouldn't be there."

Schwarz, who understood computer science, asked, "If there's a false line of text in there that isn't supposed to be, how come it doesn't throw everything else off?"

"Because whoever put it in there was savvy enough to create it as a benign string. In the list but without any kind of activity."

"Clever."

Tokaido highlighted the text and initiated an opening.

A new folder appeared, opened, and a substantial amount of data flooded the screen.

They all stood back to view what was on-screen.

"Meyer had himself a box of goodies," Price said.

"The guy was really planning for a rainy day," Delahunt agreed.

"This is going to take some working through," Kurtzman said. "Give us some time and we'll give you a rundown on what we find."

"Go take five, guys," Price said. "Get some food. Coffee. This could take a while."

Two HOURS LATER they were in the War Room, with the findings being displayed on the wall monitors.

Able Team was there, along with Price, Kurtzman and Delahunt. Hal Brognola was back in his own seat, there in the flesh if not entirely up to speed.

"Barb, would you take the lead?" Brognola said.

Price nodded.

"Meyer had been gathering information for some time. The way we see it, he didn't entirely trust his partners in crime. Bergstrom especially. With the number of people involved there was the chance of complications and individuals covering their backs. So, Meyer decided to put it all down in case everything went belly-up. Whatever else, he looked like the kind of guy who valued his own skin over everybody else."

"Nothing like a good crook deciding to protect himself from his business partners," Kurtzman added.

"With all this going on, I can't really blame him," Price said. "From Senator Trent on down we've got a run of dubious individuals here. Trent. Bergstrom. Callow. Then Raul Inigo. All the way to the Russian guy who handled the purchase of the nuke. Mikhail Koretski. Meyer has pulled in information from every source involved. The man could have made a career out of holding all this over their heads."

"Hell of a mix," Kurtzman said. "I'm surprised it was all holding up with so many involved."

"I'm guessing that was why Meyer decided to pull it all together," Schwarz said. "His protection if any one of them wanted to screw things up."

"Just out of interest," Delahunt said. "Aside from this. I used my FBI know-how to get this. Kris Huttner. FBI pinned him down as the guy who built the bomb in Chuck Baker's car. They located bomb fragments that had his signature. Found it in their database. Not the first time he's been hired to build a device. There's a BOLO out on him now. But the guy is slippery."

"Let's hope they catch him this time," Lyons said forcefully. "If anyone gets him in their sights they need to drop the trigger."

"That's against the law," Blancanales suggested.

"Sure. Tell that to the ones planning to detonate a nuke on Israeli soil," Lyons said.

"So, anything in Meyer's files we can use?" Schwarz asked.

"Names, of course," Kurtzman said. "And we just extracted this." He transferred text to the screen. "I'd guess location and date. Map coordinates."

"I'll run it and see what we have," Akira said.

Minutes later the unscrambled data was there for them all to read.

"Is that what I think it is?" Price asked.

"I have a feeling the answer's yes," Kurtzman said.

"The location for the exchange of the nuke package," Schwarz said.

"Between Inigo and Bergstrom's team," Carmen Delahunt confirmed.

"But no exact time or place."

"That may not be true," Kurtzman interjected. "We've had the *Boa Vista* under surveillance since it left Somalia." He worked his keyboard and an image filled one of the large monitor screens. "There she is," he said. "Moving through the Arabian Sea, on a course that seems to be taking her in the general direction of Pakistan. All we need now is to figure out her final destination."

CHAPTER TWENTY-FOUR

Trent was waiting when Bergstrom showed up. By the expression on Trent's face he was less than pleased at being summoned. Hayden Trent was not a man to be summoned. *He* did the calling and expected the rest of the world to come running. It had been like that for so long the man took it for granted. So, to have someone like Bergstrom making the play was annoying. After a little think about it, Trent had decided Bergstrom's breaking of the rule meant there had to be something important in the wind.

It was late enough in the day for the park to be quiet. Almost deserted save for a few dedicated joggers. They ran past, eyes fixed on some distant horizon, sucking on plastic bottles of water, pounding their way to physical fulfillment.

Trent ignored them. They had nothing to do with his empowered world, so they didn't exist in his universe. He stepped out of his Lincoln Executive, the door held by his dark-clad bodyguard.

"Do you want me with you, sir?" the man asked.

Trent pulled his topcoat collar close to his neck. "Just keep your eyes on me, Rick. I think I'm safe enough talking to Bergstrom."

He crossed to where Bergstrom's dark-colored SUV was parked. Bergstrom was waiting. He looked nervous. Trent enjoyed seeing that. Payback for bringing him out here.

Bergstrom gave a nod. "Glad you could make it," he said, watching for Trent's response.

"This had better be important."

"I think it is."

"Go ahead."

"We're having problems. Raul Inigo has experienced interference with some covert unit. Taking down his people and following a trail that's getting them closer to him. They pulled a Mossad agent out of Inigo's Yemen camp. Possible he may have given them leads. They showed up at Inigo's base in Somalia and burned it to the ground. Luckily, Inigo had just moved the device to his boat."

"Who were they?"

Bergstrom shrugged. "No idea. My sources tell me they were gone before any identification could be made. I've tried, but I can't get a handle on who they are. Someone is running them off the grid."

"Someone? *Someone?* Jesus, Edgar, you're CIA. Shadow ops. Are we listening?"

"Senator, maybe this team was from some blacker-than-black unit even the Agency doesn't know about. Working a different agenda."

"And there I was believing you people had a direct line to the Almighty."

"No, Senator, God isn't on our payroll."

Trent turned and stared out across the placid surface of the lake. The thought occurred he might try walking on water just to check if he could. It was as close as he was going to get to reality at this moment.

"Edgar," he said, keeping his emotions under control, "leave us not forget what is under way at the moment. We have a situation needing to be brought together. If that fucking French agent, Alexis, passed on any information to Jerome that even suggests what we're planning, the shit could hit the fan at any moment. I don't care how you do it. I don't care what it costs. Just shut this mess down and keep names out of it. Especially mine. Remind yourself that if everything comes out, you and your little Langley circus are going to look like a bunch of fucking idiots. We could all end up in a federal pen. Think about that. A concrete cell. No visitors. Nothing but four gray walls. They lock you up in one of those places, it's for the duration." Trent smiled without humor. "I think I'd prefer a quick injection."

"We'll deal with this," Bergstrom said. "We're too far along the line to walk away."

"Walk, run or hide, Edgar. We don't have the options. Make it happen. If you need additional backup, call me. Christ, Edgar, I'm having a meeting with my people in three days. I need to be able to tell them we're on track."

Trent walked back to his car and got in the rear. His man slid in behind the wheel. He started the engine, part turning his head to speak to Trent.

"I couldn't help noticing, sir. Your meeting didn't seem to go too well?"

"I begin to worry our CIA man can handle things as well as expected, Rick."

"Just say the word, sir, and I'll put together a team to scare the pants off Bergstrom's cream puffs."

"The way things are going, Rick, I might take you up on your offer." He patted the man on the shoulder. "Now let's go home. I just realized I missed lunch because of Mr. Bergstrom's panic attack."

ON THE RIDE BACK to his office, Edgar Bergstrom activated his sat phone and made a secure call.

"It's me," he said on pickup. "How are we doing tracking those bastards who took down our team at Baker's apartment?"

"Nothing."

"That isn't what I want to hear, Jay. Those people didn't just vanish into thin air. And they had to come from somewhere. I don't give a fuck how many rules you need to break, or how many fire walls you have to crack. Just find the sons of bitches so I can have them terminated. Call me when you get something."

Bergstrom's mood hadn't improved when he reached his office, slamming the door behind him. He sat behind his desk, palms flat on the surface. He was replaying his talk with Trent. He didn't fool himself into believing he could ignore the man. Hayden Trent was a powerful individual, with endless connections and more money than the Federal Reserve. His ambitions were high—Bergstrom figured they would reach the stratosphere if stacked end to end—and his relationships with people at home were downright scary.

He had got involved with Trent because the man's offer had been the kind you couldn't pass over. He knew the senator was using him because of his CIA connections and his black ops independence. Then there was the overall plan Trent was backing. Setting off a nuke on Israeli soil was going to create all kinds of trouble. It would shake up the region and drag in a whole shit storm of hostility. The main intention being the involvement of the U.S., siding with Israel once the retaliation against Iran was under way.

Okay, maybe Trent's plan was extreme, but Bergstrom had to hand it to the man. He believed he was right and unlike many politicians, the guy was prepared to stand up and be counted. Kick-starting a local brawl, as Trent likened it, was going to force the U.S. to make a stand against the Iranians. Force the country to stop talking and do something about the extremists in Iran who were determined to build up the country's nuclear capability. With the kinds of crazies running that country, once they got nuclear missiles in their arsenal the Middle East would become even more dangerous than it already was.

Trent wanted America to step up and throw its weight behind Israel. Show the region who was top dog. He didn't give a damn about China rattling its swords. Russia was a spent force with enough problems at home not to get itself in some kind of shooting war over the Iranian sandbox.

As much as he admired Trent's politics, Edgar Bergstrom wanted his share of the gold. He'd spent too many years running around the world on America's behalf. Doing its dirty work and getting nothing in return. Let someone else carry out the trash.

Bergstrom wanted his share.

And he was going to get it.

CHAPTER TWENTY-FIVE

For Commander Valentine Seminov night stakeouts had long since become less a bore than a waking nightmare. Sitting in a chilly department car, drinking lukewarm tea and having to make conversation with his sergeant. It wasn't that he did not like Nikolai Dimitri. The younger cop was actually a good companion—on a daily basis—but after so many long hours even Dimitri's conversation started to dry up. As it was close on 2:00 a.m., Dimitri was ready to call it a day. Or night, to be correct.

But they had their assignment and both were determined to see it through.

Information had reached Seminov that Mikhail Koretski was back in Moscow. It was known he had a girlfriend he couldn't stay away from for too long. Koretski was the jealous type and when he had heard she had been showing interest in another man he'd come back to the city to find her. For the past few days and nights Seminov had been running a number of stakeouts, covering a couple of places the man was known to frequent and also his apartment in one of the up-and-coming fashionable parts of the city. To date there had been no sign of Koretski. His girlfriend had been seen. She was driving around in a new car. A shiny dark SUV. The car belonged to Koretski. It was only allowed out on the streets when Koretski was in town.

On this particular early morning, with a bitter cold rain misting down, Seminov was reaching the end of his endurance. He felt guilty keeping young Dimitri out for so long on what seemed to be turning into a fruitless wait.

He leaned forward and tried to crank out a little more warm air from the heater when something caught his eye.

It was Koretski's SUV pulling up outside his apartment building. Seminov tapped Dimitri on the arm.

"Wake up, sleeping beauty. Time to go to work. Our pigeon has just come home."

Dimitri followed his boss's pointing finger. The dark-clad figure, hunched over in a long leather overcoat, was none other than Mikhail Koretski. He was easily recognizable under the streetlamp next to his SUV.

"It is him, Commander," Dimitri said. He thrust his hand under his thick topcoat to pull his autopistol. "We need to move."

"If he sees us trying to get to him across the street," Seminov said, "he'll run and we might lose him. Better to let him get inside the building and take him there when he's relaxed."

Dimitri regarded him for a moment.

"Easy to see why you made commander," he said.

"So young and eager and so full of crap," Seminov said. "Fine, he's inside now. Drive up behind his SUV and all we have is a few feet to walk in the rain."

When Dimitri had parked behind the SUV they stepped out into the rain. Seminov walked to the SUV, took a slim pen from his coat and crouched beside the car. He used the pen to depress the valve on the front tire of the SUV, letting all the air out of it.

"If he eludes us and makes a run, he isn't going to get very far with a flat tire," Seminov explained.

They made their way inside the lobby. At least in here they were out of the rain. There was a large board on the wall. On it were cards naming the building's occupants and the apartment numbers.

"Very good of them to tell us where Koretski is," Dimitri said.

The elevator was out of service, according to the card stuck to the door. They each took out their Beretta handguns, holding them down by their sides as they climbed the stairs to the next floor.

The building's interior was neat and freshly painted, with thick carpet on the corridor floor. Seminov pointed to the wall indicator that guided them in the correct direction. When they reached Koretski's door, Seminov made Dimitri stand to one side and he moved to the other. Then Seminov leaned in and knocked on the door.

"What?" Koretski said abruptly.

"I need to talk with you, Koretski. OCD. And do not try to jump from your window. It's too long a drop and I have officers around the building with orders to shoot."

Seminov tapped on the door with his Beretta.

"Don't take all night, Koretski. I have little patience left."

The door clicked. Seminov pushed it wide with his foot and let it swing clear to show inside the apartment.

Even from the doorway it was possible to see the expensive layout of the apartment. Seminov was impressed, though less enamored at the thought of how Koretski had financed the place.

The man himself was standing near the door, a dark scowl on his face. He still held his leather coat in one hand. Beyond him, dressed in black ski pants and a cream turtleneck sweater, was his young companion. Blond hair and, even from a distance, startling blue eyes and a pouting mouth.

"Move from the door, Mikhail," Dimitri said as he followed his boss into the apartment. The OCD sergeant closed the door, leaning against it.

"What do you need the guns for?" Koretski asked. He was smiling, but not with overall confidence. "Do you think we are going to shoot you?"

"I never underestimate the criminal mind," Seminov said. "It is a very unstable thing."

"Criminal? I am a businessman. Import and export, that is all."

"Please, no childish games, Mikhail. We both know what your business entails," Seminov said. "The little trinket deals you make are simply cover for your real enterprises."

"Weapons," Dimitri said. "Buying and selling weapons. Don't insult us by pretending otherwise."

"I do not understand what you are talking about," Koretski said. He threw his coat onto a nearby chair. "Perhaps we should sit down and sort this out."

"If we do sit down, it will be at OCD headquarters. In one of our interrogation rooms," Seminov told him.

Koretski reacted to that suggestion. "Margretta, I think maybe you should call my lawyer."

The blonde moved in the direction of the telephone.

Dimitri crossed the room and blocked it off. "No phone. No lawyer. It would be bad manners to wake him at such an hour."

"No. You can't do this," Koretski protested.

Seminov looked around the room. "But we are doing it, and you are going to cooperate. I will tell you why. You made a deal with Raul Inigo. He purchased a SADM nuclear device from you. You bought that device from the late Major Kiril Vertikov. Late because you reneged on that deal and had him silenced shortly after. Run down on the street near his home. The car that hit him was driven by one of your employees, Stanislaus Borodin. How do we know? Because a witness saw it happen and wrote down the registration of the car. Local cops traced it. That car belongs to you, Koretski. Borodin was brought in and he has talked."

"The cops couldn't stop him talking," Dimitri said. "He's given you up for a lighter sentence. He's still going to end up in the gulag, but for less years than you."

"I suspect you will be able to discuss the merits of your sentences on the long cold nights," Seminov said. "Unless you get the death penalty for selling nuclear weapons."

Koretski's face had turned considerably paler as he contemplated what lay ahead.

"How do I know you are not bluffing me?"

"Commander Seminov doesn't bluff," Dimitri said. "Especially over such serious matters."

"Selling a few AK-47s is bad enough," Seminov said. "But trading in nuclear weaponry is going a step too far. Supplying it as part of a terror campaign is even worse."

"I know nothing."

"Now you are treating us like idiots. Selling a nuclear bomb means a potential disaster. Thousands dead. More from lingering radiation, and the possibility of escalation. Poison clouds drifting who knows where."

Seminov put away his pistol. He rubbed his big hands together. Only a split second before it happened did Dimitri understand.

Seminov's closed fist swept around in a brutal arc. It connected with Koretski's jaw. The blow was heavy, driving the arms dealer to the floor in a blur of arms and legs.

"That was for what you have done, you bastard. And for what might happen if that device is set off. Just think of it as a down payment."

Seminov signaled to Dimitri. The younger OCD officer took out a pair of handcuffs.

"Now I want my lawyer," Koretski yelled. He pawed at the blood streaming from his mouth. "You cannot do this."

Seminov smiled as he massaged his knuckles. "I already have," he said. "You might get a lawyer after we have you back at OCD headquarters. I'll think about it. Sergeant, make sure those handcuffs are good and tight."

Seminov crossed the room and took out his sat phone. He tapped in the sequence that would eventually connect him to Sarah. The news he had for her would not be the most cheerful, but it would at least confirm what they had talked about earlier. It would definitely pin down the existence of the nuclear device and that it was in the hands of Raul Inigo. This was no imaginary threat. It was real and it was on its way to a final destination.

Stony Man Farm

AKIRA TOKAIDO HAD BEEN hard at work for a good couple of hours. The usually vibrant young man, known for his denim dress style and the earphones constantly secured in place while he listened to loud music, was almost subdued. Kurtzman had noticed his current attitude and, sensing Tokaido was into something that needed his full attention, he left him to it, making sure the rest of the cyber team was aware.

"Check this," Tokaido said after his long silence.

"What have you got?" Kurtzman asked.

"The location of a drop Inigo is going to make on the Pakistan-Iran border. Coordinates and date-time."

Every head in the room turned as the statement sank home. Kurtzman wheeled his chair alongside Tokaido's.

"Run me through it," he said. "Carmen, get Barb up here and make a connection with Phoenix."

"Since we've been tracking Inigo's boat I figured I'd try to get a fix on his communications. I tried all sat phone signals, but he wasn't giving anything away through those. Then I happened to latch onto his on-board ship's radio phone. A lucky break when I locked on to his settings. He made a call to Bergstrom. Nothing to shout home about until he sent some kind of encrypted message at the end. Said something to Bergstrom about this being what they were both waiting for and he could go ahead and close the deal."

"Tell me you managed to open that encryption?" Huntington Wethers said.

Tokaido nodded. "That was what took the time. It was a hard code. I used every encryption breaker we have and then some. There were two parts. First was in Russian. Had to send it to Erika to translate."

Erika Dukas was Stony Man's top linguist. A smart young woman who could handle a great many languages. Though he would never admit it, Akira Tokaido carried a torch for her, usually becoming tongue-tied and bashful in her presence.

"What did it tell us?" Delahunt asked.

"Short version was the setup and arming process for the nuke. It had been sent from Mikhail Koretski for Inigo's attention," Tokaido said. "The second part of the message was simply time and place for handing over the device from Inigo to Bergstrom's team in Pakistan."

Kurtzman slapped the younger man on his shoulder. "Great stuff. Akira. We need to send that location detail to Phoenix Force."

"I'll do that," Price said. She had been quietly listening to the conversation. "Print it out, Akira."

"On its way," Tokaido said.

He handed Price the sheet. She already had a call going through to McCarter on board the U.S. Navy carrier in the Arabian Sea. She could also tell him Valentine Seminov had made contact to confirm their fears.

The nuclear device was en route and all the information was simply confirming it.

CHAPTER TWENTY-SIX

Arabian Sea

The call from Stony Man had laid out the current situation for Phoenix Force. They now had the time and location of the nuclear device exchange. McCarter had relayed it to the team and they were preparing their strategy.

"We need to go for the *Boa Vista* and the rendezvous. So, we need to split the team," McCarter said.

"Am I to be included?" Chaka asked.

"He's earned the right," James said. "You take him with you, Jack. The rest of us will go after the device."

"You all happy with that?" McCarter asked. He received solid affirmatives from the rest of the team. "Any doubts, voice them now."

Manning shook his head. "My vote doesn't count seeing as I'm sitting this one out. But we need to shut these crazy mothers down before they set off something we're all going to regret."

"The man might have had a kick or two in the head," Hawkins said, "but he talks some sense."

"Chaka and I will take the boat," McCarter confirmed. "Make sure if Inigo gets away he isn't going to sail off into the sunset this time."

"You get the chance," Encizo said, "pull the damn plug and sink it."

"Not until Inigo is in my sights. I don't want that slippery bugger going anywhere."

"Just one question," Encizo noted.

McCarter grinned at him. "How are we all going to get in place?"

"Needs to be asked."

"Agreed. That's why I asked Chief Cochrane to help out." McCarter opened the briefing room door and the carrier's flight chief, a tall, lean man in his late thirties, stepped inside. He had boyish looks, his blond hair buzz-cut, and the expression on his face told Phoenix Force he was enjoying the challenge McCarter had placed on his shoulders.

"Mr. Coyle has outlined your needs," he said. "I think we can oblige. It's going to mean some precise timing and risky actions, but he tells me this is nothing you haven't done before."

"Doesn't mean we're going to enjoy it, Chief," Hawkins said.

"Can't have fun every day, son."

"Just one day would make a change," Encizo said.

"Way I see it," Cochrane said, "we need to make a flight that's going to get you fellers in place way before first light. One team to be dropped onto the water to access this *Boa Vista*. The other taken and put on dry land so they can intercept whatever it is the opposition is bringing to the party. Is that a fair assessment, gentlemen?"

"I'd say that covers it pretty well," McCarter said.

"We can outfit you with whatever ordnance you need from the Marine locker," Cochrane said. "For the team going in by water, we can supply a rubber craft. You'll need to paddle in for a silent approach. Give me a list and I'll see it's filled."

"Thanks for your help, Chief," McCarter said.

"I'll be going in with you as flight chief," Cochrane said. "Word coming down from the XO is you guys are A1 important. You get what you need, no questions asked. XO said the skipper got his orders from the guy in the White House. We're on a need-to-know basis, so this has to be urgent."

"It is, Chief," McCarter said. "Hate to land this on you, but that's the way it plays out."

Chaka was watching the team smear on the dark-colored camou cream, a smile on his black face.

"Hey, I'm ready," he said. "Natural camouflage."

"Landis always gets a laugh out of this blacking-up routine, as well," McCarter said, nodding in James's direction.

"You must get your own back if you ever get Arctic assignments," Chaka said.

"Never thought of that. I'll have to set him up sometime."

Chaka worked on his SMG. "I get the feeling you're all pretty close."

"We've worked together a long time. In some bloody tight spots, too, and that tends to make for a strong bond."

"That's worth hanging on to," Chaka said.

Chief Cochrane appeared. "We're set. Rest of your guys are already on board. Gear is all stowed."

McCarter and Chaka followed Cochrane across the wide deck. There were no other scheduled flights at this time. The carrier was on stand-down. The comparative quiet was deceiving. If an alert was called and aircraft readied for launching, the peace would be shattered and the near-deserted flight deck would be a busy place.

McCarter picked up the sounds of the HH-60H Seahawk's twin turboshaft engines powering up. The massive rotors began to turn, creating their own air currents, and the air reeked of aviation fuel and exhaust smoke.

"All aboard the night flight," McCarter said. "No in-flight movies and no shots of whiskey. Hell of way to run an airline."

"Just had a call from the bridge," Cochrane shouted. "The skipper and the XO send their best."

"Not too late if they want to join us," McCarter said.

"Once they knew I was riding with you, it gave them a way out." The chief grinned.

At the open hatch of the Seahawk, Cochrane slapped a hand on McCarter's shoulder.

"Remember we're here when you need a lift back," he said.

"You'll hear me yell without a sat phone." McCarter grinned.

"Let's do this, gentlemen," the chief yelled above the rising beat of the Seahawk's engines.

The helicopter vibrated as the power was poured on. The deck moved under their feet, tilting slightly as the Seahawk began to lift. It gained height, turning away from the huge bulk of the carrier, already lost beneath them in the darkness. The HH-60H swung until the correct course had been achieved. Phoenix Force and Chaka settled back for the two-hour flight, and there wasn't a man among them who didn't wonder what lay ahead once they reached their respective destinations. The only certainty was the fact that they were flying into a hostile environment.

THERE WAS LITTLE TO DO during the flight. Weapons were re-checked. Equipment secured. They synchronized watches, made sure their sat phones were fully charged. The com sets were tested. Finally Phoenix Force sat back, taking time out to simply rest.

When a light flashed on the bulkhead, Chief Cochrane signaled to McCarter.

"Time to go, mate," McCarter said to Chaka.

The Kenyan nodded.

McCarter and Chaka were to be lowered from the helicopter along with the F470 rubber boat at least three miles out from where the *Boa Vista* was anchored. They would paddle in and maintain a position under the vessel's stern until dawn. The *Boa Vista* had remained at its location according to the GPS signal McCarter had on his sat phone.

The CRRC was attached to a line and pushed out of the open hatch. It was lowered from the hovering chopper, then inflated. McCarter and Chaka clipped on their own harness rigs and positioned themselves in the hatch.

"Watch your backs," Chief Cochrane said.

"Try and manage without me," McCarter said over his shoulder.

"Get out of here," James said.

"Go hijack a boat," Encizo said.

The cable drum whined softly as McCarter and Chaka were lowered to the rubber boat. They made contact. The cables were detached and the Seahawk rose out of sight. McCarter and Chaka were left alone on the ocean swell. They broke out the oars, taking opposite sides of the craft.

McCarter checked the GPS readout. He pointed across the empty sea. "That way, mate."

They dipped the oars and set up a strong rhythm.

The moon was up, allowing them a degree of illumination.

"You suffer from seasickness?" McCarter asked.

"I'll let you know," Chaka said.

The air was cool, but it didn't take long before they began to feel the effects of their actions. A light film of sweat coated their arms. McCarter called a halt after a half hour, allowing them a ten-minute rest. He made another GPS check. They were still on course.

"Let's go," he said.

Neither of them spoke much after that until in the distance the eastern horizon began to show light. Pale streaks broke the darkness.

"We going to make it?" Chaka asked.

They took a break from rowing and McCarter checked the GPS screen. Their steady pace had pushed them through the calm water and had closed the distance. He glanced at the horizon.

"We'll make it," he said.

"Man, you sound certain."

McCarter grinned. "No sweat, Chaka. Look."

The African followed McCarter's pointing hand.

The configuration of the *Boa Vista* could be seen, emerging from the darkness. A few lights gleamed. There were more around the stern, shining on the Bell helicopter on the landing pad.

"That is a welcome sight," Chaka said.

They took up their oars and started rowing, swinging in the direction of the boat's overhanging stern. McCarter guided them in close. As they slid into position they heard the low murmur of voices. There was a metal inspection ladder bolted to the stern and Chaka took a line fixed to the F470's hull and looped it around the lower rung. He pulled it taut, pulling them in even closer. Unless someone actually climbed down the ladder, the rubber boat could not be seen from the deck.

"Now we wait," McCarter said.

THEY WAITED UNTIL full light. Activity ceased on the *Boa Vista*. When McCarter took a look at his watch, it read twenty minutes after seven.

The whine of the helicopter broke the silence. The power plant sparked into life, crackled and coughed, then settled into a healthy beat. The rotors turned with a solid whup-whup.

Chaka looked across at McCarter, a gentle smile on his lips. He adjusted his SMG across his chest. If he was nervous he didn't show it.

"We let the chopper go," McCarter said. "Then give the crew time to settle into their routine."

He glanced in a northerly direction. He could see the hazy outline of the Pakistani coastline. McCarter realized that Phoenix Force would be down by now, hopefully moving toward the rendezvous point.

CHAPTER TWENTY-SEVEN

Pakistan

Phoenix Force waited until the chopper had lifted and turned back for its return flight.

It was still dark. Night-vision goggles gave them a green-tinged view of the terrain. The uneven, rocky landscape had a desolate look to it.

They squatted for cover in a crescent-shaped spread of rocks. It gave them a little cover against the predawn chill.

They were into the waiting game now.

When daylight flooded the landscape Phoenix Force checked their position. The terrain spread out empty and dusty. Pale clumps of grass. The odd scrubby tree. In the far distance a straggle of low, rocky hills. No roads. No signs of habitation.

"Not exactly paradise," Hawkins said.

"Not really anything," Encizo agreed.

"Which would suggest this is why it's the ideal spot to complete a dodgy deal," Hawkins said.

"Check the GPS," James said. "I'll update with David."

James took out his sat phone and called McCarter. Their phones were set on vibrate to avoid potentially risky ringing. McCarter picked up after a few seconds.

"We're on the ground," James said. "Can you update us?"

"Helicopter took off ten minutes ago. Set course for

the coast. We're giving the crew time to settle down before we move."

McCarter's voice, delivered at a low whisper, sounded odd to James.

"Roger that." The call ended. "David and Chaka are in position. The chopper left the *Boa Vista* a short time ago, so we assume it's on its way here."

"GPS puts the meeting place west," Encizo said. "About three klicks."

"Let's move," James said. "Just keep your eyes open. We don't need to run into any locals."

They cleared the rock formation and settled into a line. James took point, Encizo behind and Hawkins taking up the rear. They moved steadily, aware of their exposed position, and also knowing there was nothing they could do about it. They were responding to information received via Stony Man. The existing terrain offered them no help so they accepted the restrictions. Having the offer to choose a possible battleground was a rare thing. The scenarios appeared and that was an end to it.

The sun climbed quickly and the temperature rose with it. This was Pakistan-Iran border country. Not known for its gentle climate. A hard and irregular land with weather to match. Dusty and hot about summed it up.

Hawkins's main responsibility was to keep an eye on their back trail. He concentrated on this task, leaving the others to monitor ahead and to the sides. They had packed their night-vision goggles and replaced them with sunglasses. With the glare of the sun, reflected from the pale land, it might have been easy to miss any signs. Hawkins maintained his watch. In any event, there was nothing to report to his partners. If there were any watchers around they were keeping themselves well hidden.

Stony Man had cautioned them about local insurgents.

Baluchi rebels were engaged in an ongoing struggle against the Pakistani government. They stated the government was trying to push them off traditional Baluchi land. The government said otherwise. So, the argument went on, and in time-honored fashion the war of words became a physical and bloody struggle.

There was, Hawkins decided, nothing new under the sun.

Power.

Religion.

Wealth.

All the old mantras.

"Hold." James's voice came through the com sets.

"You see something?" Encizo said.

"I see a guy perched on a rock. He's armed. And right now he's looking the other way."

They crouched, staying low, and scanned the area James was indicating.

"I see him," Encizo said.

"Why's he looking the other way?"

The pulse of an approaching helicopter reached their ears. Then the growing image of a civilian aircraft came into view. It was moving in from the coast, sweeping down for a landing.

"That's why," James said.

"Lock and load," Hawkins said.

They broke cover, angling in the direction of the seated guard. He had left his rock and was fully concentrating on the chopper as it descended, partly obscured by a dip in the landscape. Dust swirled into the shimmering air.

"Second chopper coming in," Encizo said.

A dark shape had appeared and was heading for the same coordinates as the first machine.

"Must be transferring the device," James said, more to reassure himself than his partners.

"This is going to be quick," Encizo said. "We don't have time to make this too fancy."

Hawkins put on a sudden spurt, bringing him up close behind the guard. He let his SMG hang from its strap, unsheathing his knife. His final steps brought him up behind the man. Hawkins's left hand closed over the guy's mouth. His right arced up and buried the blade in the back of the guard's neck, the thrust pushing it in to the hilt. The guard stiffened in a single spasm as the keen steel pierced flesh and muscle to sever the spinal cord. The guard simply collapsed, falling forward as Hawkins pulled his knife from the wound.

Seconds later James and Encizo were alongside. Hawkins put his knife away and brought his SMG into play as they took in the scene below them.

Raul Inigo had already stepped from his helicopter, ordering two waiting men to slide open the hatch.

The second machine had touched down thirty feet away. Five armed figures jumped from the open hatch and started for Inigo's position.

The open hatch of Inigo's chopper exposed a four-foot-square crate. The waiting men reached inside to slide it out, grasping it by the corners as they lifted it.

"That other chopper doesn't leave with that nuke on board," James said. "That's priority."

"Let me cut around and get in closer," Encizo said. "Get a shot at it."

"We'll make noise," James said.

The Cuban slipped away. James and Hawkins watched him sprinting across the open ground, his SMG ready in his hands.

The four men were moving the crate in the direction of the waiting helicopter.

James set his SMG for single shots. "This is where I wish Gary was on board," he said.

He shouldered the SMG and settled on his target. He stroked the trigger and could have yelled when he saw his slug hit one of the carriers in the leg. The slug slammed into the guy's leg, inches below his knee. The guy went down as his leg was kicked from beneath him. The other carriers struggled to hold the crate in place and failed. It sank to the ground as their grip faltered.

Heads turned in the direction of the shot.

"Now you've done it," Hawkins said as he followed James to the ground.

An opening round of shots struck the slope. Dirt geysered into the air.

The armed men rushed forward, ignoring the fact they were in a more vulnerable position. That was pointed out when James and Hawkins opened fire. They dropped two of the men with their first volley. The others fell back, firing as they moved, the shots wild and uncoordinated.

RAFAEL ENCIZO HEARD the first shot and the following bursts that came seconds later. The hostilities had started. He ignored the sounds, concentrating on his part of the mission.

He had moved fast, before any of the armed men were aware of his existence. It gave him the advantage. He closed in on the helicopter.

Two figures were seated in the front of the chopper. The pilot and his copilot. One of them spotted Encizo's presence and yelled over his shoulder.

A dark-clad figure leaned out of the open hatch, SMG rising in his hands. Encizo leveled his own weapon and fired. The burst of slugs punched ragged holes in the fuselage of the aircraft close to the hatch. A flying fragment hit the man in the cheek. He lost his concentration as the pain flared. Encizo took that moment to settle his aim and fired again. His second burst took the guy in the side, pushing him sideways. He lost his balance and fell from the hatch, hitting the ground on his knees. The next burst from Encizo slammed into the side of his head and burst his skull open.

With the bulk of the helicopter directly in front of him, Encizo angled the muzzle of his SMG and raked the cockpit canopy. The 9 mm burst punched through the Plexiglas bubble and sent showers of hard splinters into the exposed face of the pilot.

Moving on, Encizo emptied his magazine into the engine compartment. The slugs penetrated the thin aluminum and the idling power plant faltered and died. Oily smoke began to curl from beneath the cowling. The rotor blades slowed.

Encizo ejected his spent magazine and replaced it with a fresh one.

The firing that had started intensified.

Encizo turned and fired on the men facing James and Hawkins.

The confusion held the opposition back for a short time. They recovered quickly enough, but Encizo had joined the fray and his deadly autofire was helping his partners gain the advantage.

INIGO REALIZED the exchange was ended. The men who had come to take the device off his hands were struggling to defend themselves against the trio who had appeared out of nowhere. Inigo didn't have to be told who they were. These were the unknown commandos who had been hounding him recently.

Once more they had seemingly appeared out of no-where. Showing up at an opportune moment for them.

But not for Inigo.

His mind froze as he tried to take in the ability of these men to strike at his carefully orchestrated plans yet again.

And the most frustrating thing was, he still had no idea who they were. Or how they managed to step in and wreck his arrangements.

Smoke had started to rise from the engine compartment of the other helicopter. Inigo had seen the bullet-shattered canopy. There was not going to be an airlift for the device.

The deal had been broken.

Without hesitation Inigo scrambled into his own helicopter through the open hatch. His pilot was already boosting the power. He had kept the aircraft on a fast turnover in case there was need for a fast getaway. Hernandez was an expert at handling his machine and he achieved his fastest-ever takeoff. The chopper lurched sideways as the pilot sped it away from the landing site. Inigo was thrown across the compartment.

The screaming power of the rotors sucked up dust from the ground, sending it swirling across the area. It became a churning fog that obliterated vision and enveloped the men on the ground in its gritty coils.

The gunfire slackened. No one could see what they were shooting at and the chance at hitting one of their own made them all cautious.

As THE DUST CLOUD thinned, Phoenix Force, now back as a group, hit their stride again.

Encizo and Hawkins took down one of the remaining shooters, firing from opposite sides of the guy, leaving him torn and bloody in the churned-up dust.

"That son of a bitch Inigo is getting away again," Hawkins yelled.

"Never mind about him," James said. "Let's just make sure we keep our hands on that nuke."

Autofire broke out again as Phoenix Force pushed forward, hitting the opposition with everything they had.

The fact they had lost Inigo became secondary.

Possession of the nuclear device was Phoenix Force's ultimate responsibility.

Bodies fell and resistance wavered. Strengthened by the need to protect the bomb, Phoenix Force completed their task as the last of the enemy was put down.

In control of the site, they were finally able to stand back and relax after reloading their weapons.

"Let's check these guys out," James said.

"They're Americans," Hawkins said, turning one body over.

He searched for any identification but the bodies were clean. No labels on clothing. Nothing in their pockets except extra magazines for their weapons.

"Who are these guys?" Encizo asked.

"Mercenaries. Guns for hire. Could belong to Inigo."

"Or Bergstrom's off-the-books black ops," Hawkins said.

"One here could be Iranian," James said. He stepped back and surveyed the bodies. "Brought in to take the bomb the rest of the way to Israel. Chopper. Truck along the back roads. Camel train. These guys work this kind of operation all the time. The Russian brings it to Inigo, he ships it here and hands it to the end users."

"Hell of a long route," Encizo said.

"Long way around is sometimes best," James conceded. "Move the goods into areas no one expects. Different modes of transport. Some modern, others traditional,"

James said. "Used for decades to move illegal goods across regions. Not hard to bribe people when most of them are starving. Officials can be bought. Eyes look the other way when someone is counting a thick wad of banknotes. We've seen it before. And until we recently figured out what was at the back of all this, no one was on the lookout for what's in that box."

Encizo was taking a look around the bomb package. He spotted a leather satchel strapped to the side. He found it contained documents and USB information disks. There were also documents written in an Arabic language he couldn't understand. That would have to be something for Erika Dukas to decipher.

James took out his sat phone and called home. It was time to let them know they had their package and needed a lift off Pakistani soil before the situation changed.

The sooner, the better.

His thoughts were back to McCarter and Chaka. He wondered how his partners had fared since the Navy Seahawk had lowered them into the predawn darkness....

CHAPTER TWENTY-EIGHT

McCarter checked his watch. A half hour had passed since Inigo's helicopter had lifted off, enough time for the *Boa Vista* crew to settle into whatever routine they had. He nodded at Chaka. The Kenyan looked so relaxed he might have been asleep, but he responded instantly to the Briton's signal.

Grasping the lower rungs of the stern ladder, McCarter pulled himself up, moving steadily. Now they were committed, there was no point in delaying. He paused as he reached the point where the ladder curved in over the stern deck. The helicopter pad obstructed most of the view. There were no sounds, no sight of any movement.

McCarter made it off the ladder onto the deck. He crouched and moved to the rear section of the landing pad, using it as cover. He brought his SMG into position and spoke quietly into his com set. Moments later Chaka's head appeared. He scrambled over the rail and slipped into cover beside McCarter.

"And that was the easy part," McCarter said.

"For our next trick?"

"We get the bad guys," McCarter said.

From farther along the deck a man called out. There was no alarm in his voice. A deck hatch banged shut.

"You have any preference?" McCarter asked. "Port or starboard side?"

"Now tell me in English," Chaka said. "My nautical knowledge is very limited."

"Left is port. Right starboard."

"I'll take the right." Then he asked, "We taking prisoners?"

"These boys are not going to be pleased we invaded their territory, Chaka. I don't expect anything but the worst reception, so let's not waste time."

Chaka worked his way to the far side of the pad. He caught McCarter's eye, nodded briefly, then slid from view.

McCarter clicked his selector on full auto. He glanced around the edge of the landing pad and along the deck to where the boat's superstructure beckoned.

"What the hell," he muttered, and moved off.

The soles of his combat boots made no sound on the smooth timber deck. He reached the first bulkhead and flattened against it. About to edge around the corner, he picked up the sound of someone close by. McCarter risked a quick look and saw a dark-haired man in light pants and a flowered shirt moving toward the stern. The barrel of an autopistol was jammed down the front of the guy's pants. He looked relaxed, which was in McCarter's favor.

When McCarter stepped into full view the guy stared at him, surprise etched across his face. As the shock faded the man reached for the pistol. McCarter's SMG slammed him across his face, tearing his lips open. The man gasped, the sound cut off as McCarter rammed the SMG into his midsection. As he doubled over, McCarter launched his right knee and caught the guy full in the face. The guy backpedaled, his face blossoming with streams of blood from his crushed nose. Dazed from the impact, he wasn't even aware of the deck rail until he hit it and went over. Arms and legs flailed as he dropped and struck the water.

"Nothing like making a silent entrance," McCarter berated himself.

And then he heard the stuttering crackle of an SMG on full auto....

CHAKA WAS HALFWAY along the deck, SMG probing ahead. He hadn't encountered anyone so far. If there was a crew on board the boat it was either small or gathered belowdecks. Where the superstructure gave way to the bow section, Chaka paused, remaining within the cover of the bulkhead.

"Hey, ¿Qué pasa?"

Chaka swiveled his gaze and caught the image of a man in the glass of a bulkhead window. The man was three feet back, an SMG cradled in his hands. He saw the man's finger was alongside the trigger. Maybe the guy figured Chaka was one of his crewmates.

That illusion wasn't going to last for long.

Chaka let his knees go, slipping into a crouch, and turned fast.

The guy realized his mistake and went for a shot.

Chaka shot him. A tri-burst that punched into the target's chest, angling up into his heart. The guy staggered back. His finger curled around the trigger of his weapon too late. The burst of fire from the SMG hit the bulkhead, shattering the thick fiberglass shell.

There was no time left for caution. Like it or not, the fight was on.

Inigo's crew was going to be on the defensive, ready to resist whoever had come aboard.

Ahead Chaka caught movement on the deck. An SMG was turned toward him. Chaka ducked as a stream of slugs hit the corner of the superstructure. A shower of fiberglass chips peppered the side of his face. Chaka returned fire and saw the distant shooter fall, weapon slipping from his fingers as he struck the deck.

Now there were more shouts. Chaka saw movement inside one of the enclosed passages. A weapon chattered and the window glass blew out ahead of him. He brought his SMG around, clearing the edge of the shattered window, and caught the shooter as the man was changing position. Chaka's burst hit the guy in the chest, then rose to tear at his throat. The guy stumbled, went down hard.

Chaka saw the companionway to the upper deck. He went up fast, saw a shadow fall across the head of the flight. A brown figure in tattered denim shorts, barefoot, came into sight. He was in the act of hefting a short-barreled shotgun when Chaka fired. His burst stitched the guy from crotch to ribs, turning him aside. Chaka's second burst cored in between his shoulders and the guy fell out of sight, bare feet drumming on the deck.

"On the upper deck," Chaka said into his com set, and heard McCarter's brief response.

Chaka could hear firing from below.

He reached the upper deck, muzzle swinging back and forth as he looked for targets.

He only sensed the attack from behind. There was no time to turn around and Chaka knew a feeling of regret.

There was the sound of a shot. Something smashed into his shoulder. Chaka tumbled forward, a heavy numbness engulfing his upper body. Shoulder burning with pain, he hit the hard deck, his face slamming against the wood. He felt his SMG being kicked from his fingers and heard a muffled voice that faded as quickly as his senses, and then it all went away.

McCARTER SWIVELED AROUND a ventilator housing, hearing the slap of sandals on the deck, and dropped to a crouch as he registered movement ahead. A dark-clad figure swept into view, the guy wielding an SMG that began to pick up on McCarter. The Briton twisted aside as the other guy's weapon opened up. The ragged chatter of autofire followed McCarter as he slammed against the closest bulkhead and dropped low. Glass shattered above his head. McCarter braced himself against the bulkhead, saw the opposition slide into view. The guy kept his line of sight at a high elevation so he lost precious seconds picking up his target. McCarter didn't waste the moment. His SMG angled up and he triggered a burst that hammered the hostile center mass. The guy tumbled aside, grunting under the impact of McCarter's burst. He slammed to the deck, his weapon flying from nerveless fingers.

One overboard.

A second gone down under his gun.

McCarter forged ahead, his ears ringing to the additional sound of autofire. He received the garbled message from Chaka, then a screaming figure launched itself at him, a wooden club in the guy's hand, swinging wildly. The club slammed against McCarter's SMG, the blow hard enough to loosen it in his grasp. The clubber moved fast, face taut with rage as he lashed out again. The solid wood cracked down across the back of McCarter's right hand and the Briton felt something crack. The flesh split and blood welled out of the deep gash. The pain enraged the Phoenix Force leader. He swung his weapon in his left hand, catching the guy across the side of his face, sending him stumbling sideways. The man recovered quickly, throwing himself at McCarter. They grappled, losing their balance, and McCarter felt the deck vanish under his feet as he and his attacker went headlong down one of the companionways leading to the lower deck.

They hit bottom with a bone-jarring crash, still entwined and each fighting to gain the upper hand. In the fall they had both lost their hand weapons. McCarter bellowed against the surging pain in his right hand when he tried to use it. He seemed to have lost most of his strength there but he managed to jam his palm under the other guy's chin, forcing the man's head back and lifting his solid weight from McCarter's chest. They were reduced to a kicking, scrambling struggle. Blood was streaming down the other guy's face from where McCarter had hit him with the SMG, and McCarter's right hand was bleeding heavily. The Briton's opponent had his hands wrapped around McCarter's throat, trying to dig his fingers into the flesh.

They lurched to their feet, each still hanging on to the other, bodies swaying with the effort. They slammed off the bulkheads on each side of the passage. McCarter freed his left hand and drove his bunched fist into the other's jaw. He managed to put a great deal of force into the blow and it landed with a heavy thud. The guy's head snapped to one side, and McCarter hit him again and again. The guy sagged against a cabin door, spitting blood. McCarter pushed hard and the door swung inward, throwing them both across the cabin floor. As they landed, McCarter managed to break free. He rolled away from the guy, reaching across his body for the Hi-Power holstered on his right side. It was awkward using his left hand, but McCarter got his fingers around the Browning's butt, dragging it free and reversing his hold on the pistol. He thrust the weapon up in front of him and, as the other guy lurched to his feet, McCarter put a pair of 9 mm slugs in his head. The range was close and the shots went in and through and out the back. The guy went down without a murmur.

Behind McCarter there was a rush of sound, voices breaking through his dazed thoughts. He felt hands snatching at his clothing. Heavy blows rained down on him. A hard blow struck the side of McCarter's head. The Browning fell from his hand and clattered against the deck. His feet were kicked from under him. He lay on the deck, heard angry words. Someone stepped forward, hovering over him. A boot slammed down on his already bloody right hand. Sweat beaded on McCarter's face as the pain grew.

He stared up at the man who had stomped on his hand. The guy was grinning down at him.

"We will save you for Inigo. He very much wants to meet you."

McCarter sensed someone stepping into view, placing a hand on the man's shoulder.

"Remo. It is Inigo. On the radio. He must speak with you. It is urgent."

The one called Remo nodded, then turned away, and the thump of boots on the deck told McCarter he was being left alone for the moment. Alone except for one armed guard who was turning to retrieve the Browning McCarter had dropped.

McCarter counted off the seconds he would have while the guard was distracted.

He could almost hear them dropping away in his mind.

Move yourself, you lazy sod.

McCarter shook his right hand, shedding blood from his fingers. The dull, aching pain engulfed his hand. He tried to push it to the back of his mind and reached out with his good left hand to slide out the sheathed knife he was carrying.

The guard had completed his bend forward, fingers stretched out to take hold of the Hi-Power.

McCarter gathered his legs under him, braced his left hand against the floor and levered himself to his knees. He pushed up and forward, a nauseous sensation rising from the pit of his stomach.

Do this, he told himself, before he looks up.

The guard had the Browning in his hand and was starting to straighten when something warned him.

Too late.

McCarter slammed into him, knocking the off-balance guard to the deck and hammering the blade of his combat knife into the back of the guy's neck. He squealed in pain and terror as the brutal force of the blow buried the knife in to the hilt. He struggled, trying to dislodge the blade, but the sheer force of McCarter's strike had wedged it in bone. McCarter leaned over and snatched up the Browning. He jammed the muzzle against the back of the man's skull and fired a single shot. The guy arched up off the deck for a few seconds then collapsed.

McCarter realized there was something warm and wet running down the left side of his face. Flowing freely. He touched the area with his fingers and traced it to where a ragged gash on his forehead was bleeding profusely.

The thump of running feet beyond the open door caught his attention. As McCarter fixed his gaze on the opening, he saw an armed figure block it.

He recognized the man called Remo. The sound of McCarter's shot had brought him back.

The Colombian carried a black SMG, the weapon angled toward the deck. When he saw McCarter, the man exposed his teeth in an angry scowl.

"I should not have left you," he said.

"I'm always disappointing people," McCarter said, and he leveled the Browning he had been holding partially hidden against his thigh.

Remo's eyes widened as he realized his error.

The Hi-Power fired twice, the 9 mm slugs hitting Remo in the chest and pushing him across the passage. He was brought up short by the bulkhead and hung there. He made a supreme effort to stay on his feet. As McCarter reached the doorway, he moved the Browning again and put a third slug directly between Remo's eyes. The back of the man's head rapped against the bulkhead, a mushroom of blood and bone spattering the wall.

McCarter pushed the Browning behind his belt and bent to pick up the SMG. He checked the transparent magazine. It was full. He made sure it was set to fire, then made his way along the passage. He could hear shouting. His gunshots had alerted Inigo's crew. That meant they would be sourcing where the shots had come from.

He picked up on scuffling feet ahead, where the passage divided into left and right branches. McCarter raised the SMG as the sounds got closer.

He kept his ears tuned for any sound behind in case the crew moved in from that direction.

Shadows on the bulkhead warned him of the opposition approaching from ahead. A pair of shooters rushed around the left-hand passage, loosing bursts as they spotted the Briton. McCarter heard the slugs strike the bulkhead close by, above his head. He had already dropped to a half crouch. Before the pair could adjust their aim, McCarter angled the SMG and triggered a solid burst that caught them center mass. They twisted away, one giving a shrill scream, and became tangled as they stumbled. McCarter was not in a forgiving mood and hit them a second time, seeing fragments of cloth fly from the holes punched in their shirts. His hearing picked up on movement behind him and he dropped to the deck, turning his body as he did. The shooter faced McCarter from yards away, triggering his SMG, the spray clearing the Briton by inches. McCarter returned fire, cutting the guy's legs out from beneath him. The man collapsed, his limbs bloody and chewed by McCarter's long burst. As he fell face-forward, the SMG in McCarter's hands fired again and the top of the guy's skull was blown apart in a surge of bloody debris.

Back on his unsteady feet, McCarter moved to the first shooters he had dropped. He leaned over and took the magazines from each weapon and pushed them into the pockets of his combat pants.

McCarter took the left passage. It ended in a companionway that offered him access to the upper deck. With his SMG tracking ahead, McCarter went up the steps. He could see bright sunlight beyond the open hatch.

Someone called out. McCarter ignored the challenge and waited. A shadow fell across the opening. The outline of an armed figure. The man called again, this time angrily because no one had replied. The shadow grew larger, the shape of a weapon in the man's hands. Then the bulk of the body. A bright yellow shirt. Above it the dark face of one of Inigo's men. He spotted McCarter and made an aggressive move forward. McCarter's SMG crackled and sent a volley at the yellow shirt. The guy grunted under the impact and fell out of sight. McCarter hurried up the steps, then took a cautious scan of the open deck. The man he had just shot lay in a crumpled pose, arms thrown wide. The front of the yellow shirt was sodden with blood.

How many more of them were scattered around the Boa Vista?

Even as he was considering the question, McCarter's hands were automatically exchanging his nearly exhausted magazine for one of the fresh ones. With his weapon again fully charged and ready, the Briton hauled himself up out of the hatchway and rolled across the opening into cover behind a vent shaft rising from the deck.

He felt the full heat of the high sun on him. The boat's engines were idling, sending a vibration through the structure. The slap of water against the sleek hull added what might have been a peaceful distraction at any other time.

McCarter let go of the SMG with his right hand and wiped the blood against his shirt. The back of his hand was still bleeding from the ugly tear in the flesh, but at least there was a return of feeling there.

"Inigo, I owe you for that," McCarter muttered.

The close-up sound of metal against metal broke the comparative silence. Behind him. McCarter spun, the SMG moving with him. He saw a figure no more than five feet away, gripping an autopistol that was aimed at him. McCarter didn't hesitate. He was convinced he could see the guy's finger already easing back on the trigger. The SMG fired first because the guy had delayed, wanting to get his target in full sight. As McCarter fired he squirmed his body to the side, knowing that if the guy did fire he wouldn't avoid the bullet, but might take it in a lesser part of his body.

The shooter fell back, bloody eruptions showing where McCarter's burst had caught him in the lower torso.

McCarter felt a searing flash of pain across his left side, just under his ribs. The pain was instant and hard, and McCarter swore violently.

He saw a second man rise up from behind a hatch cover, pistol raised, and triggered a long sweeping burst from the SMG. The target was shirtless and McCarter saw bloody chunks of flesh detach from the guy's left upper arm and shoulder. He sagged back against the hatch, staring at his badly torn flesh. He still had hold of his pistol. McCarter fired again, this time settling on-target, and put the guy down with shots to his chest.

McCarter scoped the deck, a full 360 degrees. He saw no one, heard nothing. He leaned against the vent shaft and peeled his shirt away from the wound in his side. The slug had left a nasty furrow, oozing blood. The edges of the wound were ragged and showed the flesh under the outer skin.

Cal, where are you when I need you?

The silence stretched.

Then his mind registered his missing partner.

Chaka.

McCarter spoke into his com set. No response. He called again. Chaka's last call had informed McCarter the man was going to the upper deck. McCarter searched for the closest companionway. He headed for it, hauled his aching, weary body up to the deck, eyes searching.

Chaka was on the far side of the wide deck, facedown, left shoulder sodden with blood. There was a body on the deck a few feet away. McCarter crossed and knelt beside the Kenyan. He reached out his left hand and checked the man's pulse. It was there. There was more blood spreading out from beneath Chaka's shoulder. Exit wound. But the man was still alive.

McCarter sat back, leaning against the rail and figuring his next move. He stayed where he was for a while. His body ached. The various wounds, though not life-threatening, were taking their toll. McCarter decided he might as well go and find the boat's communication center. If he could, he might be able to raise a friendly contact. Maybe even get someone to come and find him. He also needed to do what he could to make Chaka comfortable before he did much else.

Trying to avoid disturbing Chaka's damaged shoulder, McCarter raised the man and hoisted him over his shoulder. It was no easy task with his right hand being virtually useless, but the Briton eventually had Chaka in position. With his Browning in his left hand, McCarter made his way to the *Boa Vista*'s bridge. He lowered Chaka into the captain's chair, hearing the Kenyan's low moan as he started to regain consciousness.

There was a first-aid station fixed to a bulkhead and McCarter opened the cabinet. He cleaned himself up as best as he could using medicated wipes, then strapped up his side and placed adhesive strips over his forehead and hand. This would only provide temporary protection but McCarter had no other choice in the short term.

Then he turned his attention to Chaka. The man was awake now, staring around the bridge.

"What...happened?"

McCarter peeled off Chaka's bloody shirt. The exit wound in his shoulder was a mess. His body was slick with blood.

"It's called getting shot, mate, and you were. Now sit bloody still and I'll try and tidy you up."

The Briton was no medic. He understood enough about bullet wounds to judge that Chaka had a broken shoulder bone. He could see white bone below the torn flesh. Blood had started to clot so he didn't think any major blood vessels had been ruptured. The best he could do was to treat the wound and cover it until Chaka could be evacuated. He pulled on latex gloves and used sterilized swabs to clean the torn flesh. Sweat beaded on Chaka's face as McCarter gently probed. It was obvious he was in considerable pain but he made no sound throughout the procedure. McCarter covered the wound, back and front, with medicated pads and bandaged the shoulder, then fashioned a sling to keep the arm immobile against Chaka's chest.

He found a built-in chiller cabinet at the rear of the bridge and pulled out a couple of bottles of cold water. He opened one for Chaka and handed it to him.

"That is good," Chaka said after taking a swallow. "So, now what do we do?"

"Give me a minute and I'll tell you. Just keep your eyes on the outside. If you spot that chopper heading this way, just yell."

Chaka slipped his handgun from its holster and laid it across his lap.

"You got it."

McCarter went on a search. He located the radio room situated behind the spacious bridge. In keeping with the rest of the *Boa Vista,* it was well equipped. McCarter found the installed radio phone link and punched in the Stony Man number. He sat in the comfortable leather swivel chair while the call connected. He identified himself, then heard an acknowledgment he hadn't been expecting.

"So, what have you guys been up to in my absence?" Hal Brognola asked. His voice was weak but there was no mistaking his gravelly tones.

"I thought they had you under 24/7 watch."

"That was never going to happen."

"Nice to hear you're back on your feet."

Barbara Price's voice came on over the conference line.

"Not exactly," she said. "He's sitting down and not allowed to move around. So, where are you? What's with you guys this mission? You keep losing each other."

"Let's say I'm keeping things afloat," McCarter said, unable to resist the remark.

Price picked up quickly. "The *Boa Vista?*"

"Yo-ho-ho, me hearties, you are speaking to the new captain."

"But what about the crew? Raul Inigo?"

"He left. To conclude his negotiations. The small crew he left behind…" McCarter paused. "Well, let's say they've had a change of heart."

"Barb has brought me up to speed on the situation,"

Brognola cut in. "What about this nuclear device? You any closer to getting your hands on it?"

"Rest of the team are on land waiting for Inigo and his collection party to show up."

"You sure about this?"

"As we are anchored off the Pakistan coast, I'm guessing Inigo is making his delivery. He took off from the *Boa Vista* and headed inland."

"I hope you guys have this right."

"Well, boss, seeing as how you're giving me a hard time, I'll hold up my hands and admit we're working on it. But what the hell, it's nice to have you back."

McCarter heard Brognola's distant grumbling. Despite the situation he couldn't stop himself smiling.

Price came back on the line. "Aaron still has the boat tracked. Do you need a pickup?"

"Be obliged, luv. Give the Navy a call and have them head back for us."

"Any injuries?"

"Nothing a soothing hand won't cure for me. But Chaka took a hit to the shoulder and he'll need the Navy's help."

"I've been keeping an open line with them. They should be able to get a chopper out to you in a couple of hours."

"While I'm waiting I'll have a look around. Maybe I can pick up some useful information. Or maybe not."

"David, what if Inigo comes back first?"

"Then we will have us a bloody party. Don't worry. He's in a helicopter. I've got firepower available. If it comes to anything, I'll shoot the bugger down."

"I'm sure you will," Price said.

"Watch yourself," Brognola said. "Make sure that bastard doesn't walk away free and clear."

McCarter made sure Price had the number of the radio phone before he shut off the call.

Taking one of the SMGs, he took a slow walk through the *Boa Vista*. In the main cabin he found the expansive wet bar. It carried a wide selection of drinks. As tempted as he was, McCarter resisted. He needed his wits about him in case of trouble. Losing his edge through downing alcohol was not an option. The smell of brewing coffee attracted him to a simmering percolator at the other end of the cabin. McCarter helped himself to a mug of the steaming liquid. He stood gazing out of the panoramic window while he drank. The coastline was too far away to be clearly seen.

He was tempted to call the rest of his team via his sat phone. He resisted. If they were involved with Inigo and company, they didn't need any distracting phone calls. He was going to have to wait until they called him.

He emptied his mug and went for a refill, pouring a mug for Chaka, then took the drinks with him when he returned to the bridge. The control structure had TV cameras installed that projected views of the boat fore and aft onto wide-screen monitors. McCarter could see the image of the helicopter landing pad at the stern of the *Boa Vista*.

The radio phone buzzed loudly and McCarter moved back into the radio room. It was Price.

"Navy chopper should be dispatched once the Navy gets back to us."

"Any news from the team?"

"Nothing since they landed. If it all goes to plan, the device should be intercepted and the buyers caught red-handed."

"Young lady, I wish I lived in your little happy-ending world," McCarter said.

"Since this whole thing kicked off, I've been hoping for a happy ending."

"You're not the only one. Talking of happy endings, how is the boss man? Not quite himself when I spoke earlier."

"He had to give in when his meds started to wear off. I sent for the in-house doctor and he made Hal take a break. He's over in the rest area, flaked out on a bed."

"I won't even ask how he got back to the Farm. Just keep him there," McCarter said. "Give him a double dose of sedatives."

Price laughed. "That's a thought." She sobered then. "David, they *have* to intercept that nuke."

McCarter almost told her Phoenix Force would do the job or die trying, but he instantly reconsidered. Dry humor was one thing. Taking it to extremes could have been considered bad taste.

"They'll make it," he said. The lame remark felt as bad as his near joke.

"And you stay safe, mister."

"That an order?"

"Damn right it is."

CHAPTER TWENTY-NINE

Inigo didn't take a calm breath until the helicopter was back over the water. Since ordering his pilot to fly him to safety, he had remained silent, staring out of the aircraft's side window. The pilot, Hernandez, who knew the way Inigo's moods could swing at moments like this, wisely held his tongue. He concentrated on flying the chopper.

Thoughts struggled for space in Inigo's disturbed mind. How could it all have gone so wrong?

In all the time he had been masterminding operations for his group they had never had so many problems. He was the first to deny his record was totally unblemished. But this operation had started to fall apart with the appearance of the unknown commando group. They deployed with a speed even Inigo was envious of, and their fighting skills were second to none.

He'd thought they would have a chance to learn something about them when his men had snatched one of them during the skirmish at the Somalian village. Yet even that had gone wrong. The captive had made a break for freedom, killing as he went, and then the rest of his team had showed up. Inigo had barely evaded capture himself.

And now they had successfully struck at the nuclear device exchange. It should have been a simple matter of Inigo's turning the device over to Bergstrom's people. From there they would have transported it to the point of detonation. Now even that had been prevented.

And for the second time in his life Inigo had been forced to run for his life.

The shame he could live with. As long as he was still alive, he had the opportunity to carry on.

It was going to be difficult facing Bergstrom and having to admit defeat. The thing that would hurt Inigo more would be the return of the money. His overwhelming obsession with money made it hard to even contemplate giving it back. Added to that were the expenses Inigo had paid out of his own pocket. Bergstrom was not going to stand up and agree to reimburse Inigo for those. Inigo was going to have to start building fences to restore confidence in his organization's future viability.

Repercussions might well follow. Though Bergstrom had his own failures to live up to. His people in America, supposedly dedicated and anonymous operatives, had also been handled by the people they came up against. So, his anger at Inigo's failure would have to be gauged against his own foul-ups. Regardless of those failures, Bergstrom was going to be in a rage when he learned what had happened.

Inigo was going to have to let the man know.

He felt the helicopter bank as the pilot eased onto the approach that would bring them to the *Boa Vista*. When he saw the gleaming shape of his boat Inigo experienced a little comfort. Back on board, safe in the comfort of his floating headquarters, he would feel less agitated. With the helicopter on the landing pad they could raise the anchor and sail to safer waters, giving Inigo a chance to recharge his batteries before he made his call to Edgar Bergstrom.

"Boss," the pilot said over his headset. "It doesn't look right down there."

"What are you saying?"

"No one moving around. She looks deserted."

Inigo searched for the powerful binoculars he kept in

the cabin. He brought them to his eyes and focused in on the boat. He scoped her from stern to bow.

There was no sign of anyone.

"Make a low-level pass," he ordered.

The pilot took the chopper down and Inigo took a closer look. The magnified image still showed no crew members. But when the aircraft swung across the bow, he picked up dark streaks on the deck.

Inigo felt his insides churn.

He knew what he was looking at.

Blood.

As they turned across the spread of the deck, Inigo made out two figures watching him from the bridge. A rangy white man in combat dress and a black man in the captain's chair, a bloody mass of bandage covering one shoulder.

"Hijo de la gran puta."

The curse burst from Inigo's lips unchecked and delivered with vented rage.

They were on his ship.

On the *Boa Vista*.

Of all the insults he had been forced to suffer, this was the worst by far.

His beloved boat had been violated by these foreigners. The presence of blood on the deck and now the bullet damage to the bulkhead he could see told him the boarding had not been without violence.

How many of his crew had been hurt?

How many killed?

Inigo thought of Remo, his second in command who had been with him ever since they had quit Colombia.

Was he hurt?

Dead?

Inigo reached for the secure locker fitted on the cabin

floor. He snapped open the top and reached inside for an H&K MP5. He clicked in a 30-round magazine and activated the bolt, loading the weapon.

"Hernandez, fly by the bridge."

The pilot had caught a glimpse of his employer's machine pistol and understood what he wanted. He circled the helicopter, coming in lower and holding the chopper steady as it approached the boat.

Inigo moved to the rear and slid open the side hatch, snapping a safety harness around his body as he positioned himself in the opening.

He saw the tall white man step out of the bridge and stand near the rail. The man was watching the approaching helicopter. It was as if he was defying the odds. Deliberately taunting Inigo.

Unable to control his anger, something he normally kept in check, Inigo opened fire too soon. The H&K crackled. The burst of 9 mm slugs hit the bridge bulkhead, splintering the thick fiberglass and shattering one of the side windows.

The man on the bridge raised his SMG, following the flight of the chopper, and when he fired he hit the target. Inigo heard the slugs strike the fuselage. Felt the impact as they punched through.

He heard the pilot yell in panic and the helicopter yawed violently. Inigo was thrown sideways, only his harness preventing him from falling out of the open hatch.

"Back. Go back," Inigo screamed.

"If we get within range he could hit us hard," Hernandez replied. "If he forces us down, we're finished."

"He has the *Boa Vista,*" Inigo howled, losing all control. "He has my ship."

"And it will be no use to us if we die."

Hernandez eased the helicopter away from the *Boa Vista*. He turned back in the direction of the coastline.

"We have enough fuel to get us back into Pakistan," he said. "I can put us down well away from where the exchange took place. Then we'll have to go on foot until we can call for help."

There was no answer from Inigo. He was slumped by the open hatch, staring back at the dwindling *Boa Vista*, the MP5 forgotten in his hands.

Hernandez stayed silent. There was nothing he could say to ease the moment. The loss of the boat would be hard for Inigo to accept. He had no choice. The boat was gone and most likely the crew left on board. The pilot had no doubt Inigo would recover. He was not a man who let setbacks defeat him for long. Given time, he would reorganize and fight back. It was not in his makeup to quit.

The first priority was to make land. Put down away from any highly populated area and arrange to get out of the country. Inigo would establish a new HQ, gather his forces and move on. One of the man's favorite sayings was "business goes on."

It would.

And so would Raul Inigo.

Inigo suddenly unclipped the safety harness and made his way back to the passenger seat. He snatched his sat phone from the charging cradle and keyed in a number from memory. While he waited for it to connect he glanced at Hernandez and there was a smile on his face.

"No," he stated. "We are not finished, Hernandez." He gave a harsh laugh.

Hernandez had no idea what Inigo was talking about.

"Bijarani," Inigo said. "Abdul Bijarani. The Balochi rebel commander. He has a base on the coast. I was so full of the nuke delivery it never crossed my mind. The man owes me big-time. More than big-time."

"And?"

"He has boats, Hernandez. Boats he uses to make raids on local shipping." Inigo slapped the pilot on the shoulder. "He can help get the *Boa Vista* back. The Somalis aren't the only ones who like to capture boats." Inigo's call was answered. He listened to the agitated voice on the end of the line. "I called because I have your number, Abdul. No, this is not a joke, my friend. Raul Inigo. Yes. Never mind that. I want you to listen to me. And then I want you to do something for me...."

TWO HOURS LATER Inigo's helicopter was on the ground, being refueled while Inigo sat in Abdul Bijarani's hut, discussing tactics with his longtime client and friend.

Bijarani was a man of impressive presence. A tall, powerfully built individual dressed in military khaki, a dark, full beard covering the lower half of his face. He was a man who existed to fight, a seasoned warrior who held his men in the palms of his large hands. His presence encouraged his followers and Inigo knew they would follow Bijarani anywhere he ordered them to go.

"So, these commandos, whoever they are, have destroyed your deal and have now commandeered the *Boa Vista?*"

Inigo nodded. "I cannot fault their skills as fighters. Each time we have clashed they have bested my people. But this final insult cannot be accepted."

"And you do not know who they are?"

Inigo said, "We have not been able to discover their origins, but I feel there could be a connection with the CIA. My people clashed with a CIA man in Sofia and another agent was dealt with in Washington."

"CIA? Americans?" Bijarani asked, his anger showing now. "They are scum. Parasites to be wiped off the face of the earth. Raul, you are a good friend. We have traded for many years and in all that time you have never tried to cheat me on a deal. You are an honorable man. Today, we help you."

Outside Inigo led the way across to his helicopter. Hernandez showed the rebel commander the *Boa Vista*'s position on his GPS. Bijarani studied it and entered the coordinates into his own handheld unit.

"The boats will be ready in half an hour," he said. "Then we can go and get your boat back."

"I will not forget this, Abdul."

Bijarani roared with laughter. "I will not let you forget," he said. "Especially when we are negotiating our next deal."

THERE WERE THREE high-powered launches available. Each held a pilot and six men. Bijarani and Inigo were together in the lead boat. Hernandez took his refueled helicopter aloft and acted as point man. He was in contact with Inigo via radio.

As they sped away from the wooden jetty, Inigo checked his autopistol. He leaned against the side rail, feeling the breeze against his skin. If he could at least get his boat back then the day would not have been a complete disaster.

He still had to face Edgar Bergstrom. There would be business to settle. Only right now none of that mattered to Inigo.

"Raul, did you work out how many might be on board?"

Inigo glanced around at Bijarani and shook his head.

"When we flew over all I saw were two men on the bridge. Two only, and I could not see any of my crew."

"We will work this out when we get there." Bijarani

placed a big hand on Inigo's shoulder. "You worry too much, my friend. Have faith in the day. By evening you will have your boat back."

SOMETHING HAD UNSETTLED McCarter. He paced the bridge, going outside, then returning. From his perch in the captain's chair, Chaka watched him until his patience ran out.

"Enough," he said. "If you don't stop you will wear a hole in the deck. Tell me what is troubling you."

"Bloody Inigo."

"I suspected that. Tell me why. Hasn't he flown away?"

McCarter nodded. "But he flew toward the coast. Pakistan. That chopper has a limited range so he can't have gone far."

"I feel a *but* coming next."

"Inigo is a dealer. A negotiator. And I'm bloody sure he has clients around this area. People he does business with."

"You think he may have contacted someone and asked for help? To come back and retake his boat?"

McCarter let the Kenyan answer his own question.

"Then let us hope your U.S. Navy reaches us before Inigo's possible return."

McCarter used the sat phone to call Stony Man and get some kind of update. This time it was Brognola manning the call.

"I thought you were taking it easy, boss," McCarter said.

"Just relieving Barb. That young lady has worked herself off her feet monitoring the situation. So, I sent her to get some rest."

"The way she's been operating, she deserves a bloody big raise," the Briton said.

"She tells me you guys have been a little busy out there."

"No walk in the park, but we have the situation under control. Well, near enough."

"Come on, what is it?"

"My suspicious nature tells me Raul Inigo might be coming back to snatch his ship away from us. So, the sooner the Navy drops by to lift us off, the better."

"It's going to happen," Brognola said, "but time-wise we're in a bind here."

"What?"

"There's an alert in the Straits of Hormuz. Ironically the Iranians have decided to send ships to mount a blockade."

"No Navy taxi available just now?"

Brognola cleared his throat. "Until the Iranians back off. Navy intel believes this could happen anytime. This is just a show of defiance. U.S. Navy carrier group is already facing them down so it's a who-quits-first scenario."

"Bloody great," McCarter said. "A chicken run at sea."

"I just spoke with the President. He understands you guys are at the sharp end and he's made it clear he wants you all pulled clear the moment a window opens. I wish I could give you better odds right now."

"Make sure when they do come for us the Navy extracts the rest of the team first. They're stuck in hostile territory. Whatever we have to handle here, get them out first."

"I hear you. If Inigo does show up, what the hell are you going to do?"

"Bloody hell, boss, I'm a limey. We have a tradition for these situations. Me and Chaka are going to repel boarders."

McCARTER CHECKED the Kenyan's wound. The bleeding seemed to have quit. McCarter knew the man needed some intensive medical attention but until it arrived Chaka was going to have to stay in the game. If—and more likely when—Inigo showed up there would be no sitting on the bleachers. The Kenyan would be in a fight for his life alongside David McCarter.

"Tell me how you want to do this," Chaka said. "Your call might have been one-sided from my perspective, but I got the idea. We're on our own."

"That serves you right for listening to another bloke's conversation."

"Don't try to wriggle out of it," Chaka said, smiling. "Tell me what I can do."

McCarter passed him one of the SMGs and spare magazines.

"If they don't have a boarding pass, shoot them."

"You going somewhere?"

"This is no Red Cross boat. Inigo has got to have a stash of weapons. I need to find it. Give us some additional firepower. You see anything that shouldn't be out there, use the intercom system."

McCarter shoulder-hung an SMG and left the bridge. He made a circuit of the boat, collecting all the abandoned ordnance from the earlier firefight. He carried it back to the main cabin and laid it out on the dining table. SMGs and handguns, all the extra magazines he had located on the bodies. Then he conducted a careful search of the *Boa Vista,* checking cabins and storerooms until he unearthed what he was looking for. Belowdecks, in a row of lockers in the stores section, McCarter found additional weapons. A dozen P-90s. Automatic shotguns. Handguns. In a separate locker were boxes of ammunition for the various weapons and spare magazines.

"Come to daddy," McCarter said.

He began to transport the weaponry and ammunition up to the bridge. When he had the full armory spread out McCarter set to loading magazines and arming the weapons. Chaka helped, his pace a lot slower than McCarter's, but they finally had the task complete.

McCarter placed the loaded weapons around the bridge and stood back to survey his handiwork.

"You think if Inigo sees all this he'll turn around and quit?" Chaka asked.

"I wish."

"You haven't spoken of it in so many words, but I believe you are expecting Inigo to come at us in boats."

"That way he can hit us with a larger number of men. Even surround the *Boa Vista*."

Chaka made an exaggerated show of looking around the bridge.

"What?" McCarter asked.

"I was trying to see where you have the rest of our squad hidden."

"Okay, Chaka, I get your point. It's just the two of us."

McCarter was checking out the monitors that showed pictures from around the boat. He leaned forward and muttered to himself before tapping Chaka on the shoulder.

"Bridge is yours again, mate. Something I need to check."

McCARTER STUDIED the layout of the stern, concentrating on the helicopter landing platform and the equipment around it. He was interested in the half dozen steel drums stenciled with the words Aviation Fuel—Highly Flammable stored there to refuel Inigo's helicopter. A flexible hose and filler nozzle with a long plastic insert tube hung from a chain attached to a bracket. Below the hand nozzle was a further tube that was connected to a compact pump assembly. This in turn was fixed to a small compressor that would deliver a stream of air direct to the pump assembly. When the feed tube was placed in a drum of fuel, the compressor would create the power to spin the impellor needed to suck up the fuel to be delivered to the helicopter's tanks. The six fuel drums sat on the starboard side of the deck, on a metal base plate. There was a safety mechanism designed to flip the drums off the boat in case of an emergency. That part of the arrangement didn't concern McCarter. He was more interested in the placement of the fuel. He checked the compressor, making certain it was ready to be turned on, then pressed the button. The compressor chugged into life. McCarter opened the feed valve and heard the sound of the air as it coursed along the pipe. He lifted the nozzle assembly and held the mechanism over the side. When he pressed the trigger lever, a stream of aviation fuel spouted from the nozzle.

"And that answers one question," McCarter said.

He switched off the fuel and cut the compressor and made his way back to the bridge.

"I been watching you," Chaka said. "What are you up to, *bwana?*"

McCarter smiled. "Might be we can offer our visitors a warm welcome," was all he said.

He looked around the bridge and located the bulkhead cabinet that held a couple of flare guns and a number of cartridges. He loaded one of the guns and set it down where it was easily accessible.

His sat phone buzzed. McCarter picked up and recognized Rafael Encizo's voice.

"They patched me through from home," Encizo said, "and told me what you've been up to. Sounds like you painted yourself into a corner."

"What can I say, mate. How are you guys doing?"

"Waiting. Hoping we don't get a visit from the local rebels or the Pakistani military. Going to need some fast talking to explain why we have a nuke sitting next to us."

"And you think I got into a mess?"

"You get the message about the Navy delay?"

"We picked the wrong day to drop in for a visit. How about you?"

"Ready to defend the Alamo, as they say down in Texas."

"Incoming," Chaka called out. "Three launches heading right at us."

McCarter stared out the bridge window and saw the trio of power launches cutting through the calm water. White wakes trailed behind the crafts.

"Call you later," McCarter said.

"Good luck," Encizo said.

McCarter put down the phone.

He saw Chaka ease himself out of the captain's chair, his SMG in his right hand, braced against his hip. He crossed the bridge and made his slow way out onto the walkway, leaning against the rail.

McCarter tucked one of the flare guns behind his belt and stuffed a number of cartridges in a pocket. He took one of the SMGs and some extra mags and joined Chaka.

"This, my old buddy, is where it could get hairy."

CHAPTER THIRTY

McCarter watched as the three launches circled off the starboard side of the *Boa Vista*. In the lead vessel he could make out two figures in deep discussion. He guessed they were arguing tactics, how to approach the boat. They were close enough for the Briton to recognize Inigo's tall figure. The man he was conversing with was equally tall, but that much broader than Inigo. His darker skin and heavy beard marked him as Pakistani. The discussion was lively from what McCarter could make out. Not angry. Simply full-on and after a couple of minutes the bearded man nodded to Inigo and began to call out to his men.

"I believe they've made up their minds," Chaka said.

"That they have," McCarter said. "And here they bloody well come."

The three launches powered up, each moving in a different direction. The crafts began their main approach, one circling around the *Boa Vista*. It took little guessing the launch was going to make its strike from the port side of Inigo's boat. One of the remaining launches sped forward and curved in toward the starboard side. The third launch hung back and McCarter saw it was the one carrying Inigo and his bearded partner.

"Inigo doesn't want to get in too close until he sees what we have set up for him," Chaka said. "You want me to move to the other side of the bridge?"

"We need to cover both sides," McCarter agreed.

The Kenyan used the rail section to support himself as he edged around the wheelhouse, then braced himself in position. He saw the launch appear around the bow, then ease in close to the sleek hull. Chaka heard the launch bump against the side of the *Boa Vista,* scraping along the smooth surface.

"Inigo is going to love that," he said, grinning.

The launch heading in McCarter's direction turned sharply, sending up a spume of white foam in its wake. McCarter saw an armed figure rise up, directing the muzzle of an AK-47 at his position. The weapon crackled harshly and a burst of 7.62 mm slugs pounded the bridge bulkhead over McCarter's head. He had ducked briefly before returning fire, his slugs raking the hull of the launch. McCarter adjusted his aim as the launch sped by and this time a couple of his shots caught the shooter in the right shoulder before he could pull back out of sight.

The Briton followed the launch as it curved away, then swung around and made another run. As it sped directly at the *Boa Vista* McCarter dropped flat and heard multiple shots as the launch crew opened fire. The shots, angling up from the lower position of the powerboat, hammered at the bridge bulkhead, gouging and tearing into the fiberglass formation. The image of Inigo's face as watched his beloved boat taking a pounding rose in McCarter's mind. It almost made being shot at acceptable.

From his prone position McCarter pushed his P-90 under the lower rail and fired off a long volley. His burst hit water, then found the bow of the launch, tearing holes in the molded foredeck. The guy at the wheel, face taut with a mix of sheer fright and anger, hauled on the wheel and almost capsized the launch in his haste to move out of range.

ON THE FAR SIDE of the bridge Chaka heard the sound of firing from McCarter's position. With his attention focused on the now hidden launch on his section of the boat, the gunfire faded from his conscious thoughts.

He saw a hand reach up and grip the gunwale. Chaka waited and saw a second hand appear. He picked up a murmur of voices. One hand lifted and vanished. When it reappeared seconds later it was gripping an AK-47. The guy, being boosted up from the launch, made an effort to hoist himself up onto the deck. Chaka let his turbaned head clear the gunwale before he settled his P-90 and eased back on the trigger. The weapon on full-auto blasted a stream of slugs that shredded the boarder's head, his face vanishing in an explosion of flesh and bone.

The guy uttered a shrill scream and fell back out of sight. Chaka heard the heavy slam as the body dropped into the launch. A screaming outburst reached Chaka as the man's companions yelled and cursed at the unseen shooter.

Though he had drawn first blood, the Kenyan knew it was far from over.

He prepared himself for another attempt. His gaze was drawn to the blood spatter on the deck where the man had been hit. The guy's AK-47 lay where it had dropped from his fingers. Unfired and abandoned.

When it came, the move almost caught Chaka off guard. He was watching the side of the boat and had let the presence of the stern ladder slip from his mind. The same ladder he and McCarter had used to board the *Boa Vista*. That was where the crew of the launch made their second attempt to board.

It was Chaka's elevated position on the bridge that allowed him to see over the raised helicopter pad. Out the corner of his eye he spotted a flicker of movement at the far end of the boat and realized what had happened. One, then a second armed figure appeared, swiftly clearing the stern and moving along the aft deck.

"Coming aboard at the stern," Chaka yelled.

He swiveled, his SMG following, and he opened fire on the closest of the boarders. The P-90 spit fire. Shell casings hit the deck plating at Chaka's feet. He fought back the pain from his shoulder as his hand gripped the SMG.

His unrestrained fire pushed the boarders back, slugs ricocheting off metalwork and tearing slivers of fiberglass from the structure.

One of them braved the heavy fire, crouching and skirting the rear of the landing pad to emerge on the opposite side of the deck. He shouldered his AK-47 and triggered short bursts that slammed into the bridge structure. A deflected slug sliced across Chaka's left cheek, opening a bloody furrow. The Kenyan warrior ignored the burning sensation as he kept up his intense barrage of shots.

The Pakistani who had taken the chance and moved across the deck was suddenly confronted by the tall figure of McCarter. The Briton had left his position on the bridge, dropping down the companionway to the lower deck and had raced to the stern.

The boarder sensed the presence of McCarter and swung around to confront him. His move ended as McCarter opened up with his SMG and stitched him from waist to chest. The guy was knocked back, his khaki T-shirt riddled with holes that started to leak blood. He tumbled and fell and as he dropped, McCarter hit the second boarder with a hot burst that chewed at his torso and kicked him back over the stern of the boat. The guy dropped, hit the edge of the launch and catapulted into the water. Without pause McCarter stepped to the stern rail and aimed his P-90 down into the bobbing launch, where the three remaining crew were already reaching for the

Boa Vista's stern ladder. When they looked up all they had a chance to see was the muzzle of McCarter's SMG a second before he opened fire and raked the launch with concentrated fire. The three men were torn and bloodied by the nonstop burst, bodies flopping limply as they dropped back into the bottom of the launch.

McCarter turned and moved back across the deck, snapping a fresh magazine into the top of the P-90. He looked out across the water and saw the second launch commencing another run. Armed figures knelt ready to fire. Men from Inigo's launch had transferred so the launch was a veritable gunboat. More than McCarter, even with the aid of Chaka, could take on.

He backed away and leaned his P-90 against the edge of the landing platform. McCarter fired up the compressor and checked that it was set for full delivery. As the pressure mounted he picked up the pump nozzle and trailed it across the deck.

This, he readily admitted, was a last-ditch defensive move.

He took out the flare gun and eased back the hammer. Glancing up, he caught Chaka's eye. The Kenyan was back on the starboard side of the bridge. McCarter signaled with his hand, making a sweeping gesture toward the stern of the *Boa Vista*.

Get them to the stern.

He wanted the launch closer to his end of the boat.

Chaka stared at him, then gave a nod. He leaned over the rail and began to send short bursts at the launch. The rear of the vessel. Return fire from the launch sent loose shots at the bridge, but Chaka stayed below the trajectory of the shots.

McCarter peered over the line of fuel barrels. The

launch had powered forward to get clear of Chaka's fire. It was closer to the boat's stern.

"This might not be a good idea, David my boy," McCarter said. "But it's all we've got."

He leaned over the fuel drums and raised the flare gun. He targeted the bow of the launch and pulled the trigger. The gun made a soft whoosh as it launched the flare. McCarter saw it curve across the water and slam into the launch, the flare bursting and creating a ball of heat. He dropped the flare gun and swung the nozzle of the fuel pump over the side, pulling back on the release trigger. A stream of aviation fuel spurted from the nozzle. It arced across the gap between the *Boa Vista* and the launch.

For a moment McCarter didn't think it would reach. Then the fuel splashed against the launch and McCarter guided it to sluice across the deck until it reached the burning flare. Fumes ignited and spread, and the launch was soon alight with the hungry flames as McCarter hosed down more fuel. He depressed the trigger fully, increasing the pressure and the stream of fuel reached along the launch. The armed figures abandoned their weapons as fuel splashed their clothing, setting them on fire as the inferno spread. Human torches slapped at their bodies as clothing burned and so did flesh, bubbling and sloughing off bones. Screaming figures toppled from the launch into the water, thrashing around to try to douse the flames. McCarter kept it going until the launch was a floating pyre, flames rising feet above the craft and the men manning it engulfed in the fiery mass.

McCarter shut off the fuel and dropped the nozzle to the deck. He retrieved his SMG and made his way up to the bridge. Chaka had dropped to his knees, favoring his shoulder where fresh blood was seeping through his bandage. He glanced up as McCarter approached.

"Jack, when you are hot, you are hot, brother."

McCarter was watching the burning launch drift away from the *Boa Vista*. The engine was still turning over and it was pushing the launch on a slow course toward the distant shoreline. Smoke rose from the vessel. It had a sickly sweet smell.

"You see Inigo's helicopter up there?" Chaka said.

McCarter had seen the chopper hovering at a safe distance. He didn't think the aircraft presented any threat.

He hadn't made up his mind about Inigo yet. The surviving launch was remaining well clear of the *Boa Vista*. McCarter could see Inigo standing, watching. It was a repeat of the scene back in Somalia when Phoenix Force had overrun the base and destroyed Inigo's cache of weapons, drugs and money.

Inigo had lost out again.

And he had failed to regain possession of his prize boat.

That, McCarter decided, had to hurt.

The launch circled the *Boa Vista,* giving it a wide berth. It stayed out of weapon range.

"That guy has got to be wishing all kinds of hell would rain down on you," Chaka said.

"He's just one in a bloody long line," McCarter said. "Come on, chum, let's get you back inside and comfortable."

McCarter helped the Kenyan back under cover. He guided him into the main cabin and eased him down onto one of the luxury leather couches.

"Whatever Inigo's business," Chaka said, "it pays well."

McCarter poured him a tumbler of whiskey.

"Try that. You'll believe it even more. Best money can buy."

CHAPTER THIRTY-ONE

"Are you sure about this?" Abdul Bijarani asked. He was torn between his friendship with Inigo and a desire for blood vengeance against those who had killed his men.

"You saw what they did. How they slaughtered your men. I feel responsible because you agreed to help me."

"In war there are casualties. It is to be accepted. But the *Boa Vista*."

"I will not get it back now," Inigo said. "That is something I must accept. So, if I cannot have her, then no one can."

"We could return and bring back more men."

"I won't allow you to sacrifice any more of your soldiers to satisfy my need."

"Very well," Bijarani said. He flicked a hand at one of his remaining men. "Bring them."

The man opened a wooden locker and pulled out an RPG-7 rocket launcher. The Soviet standby weapon was a much-used instrument in the global terror wars. A simple yet effective weapon that was still in use, alongside the ubiquitous AK-47 rifle. Long after the fall of communism, their weapons carried out deadly retribution.

Inigo took the launcher and inserted one of the rockets. It was not the first time he had handled the RPG-7. He experienced a pang of regret as he shouldered the weapon, sighting in on the *Boa Vista*'s hull, just below the waterline. He took a breath and held it, settled his aim and squeezed the trigger.

The launcher spit out its missile, a flash of exhaust emitted from the rear of the weapon. The rocket stabilized as it flicked out its fins. It streaked over the surface of the water and impacted against the gleaming hull. The detonation was surprisingly loud as the rocket exploded, the impact rocking the *Boa Vista*. A three-foot hole appeared in the fiberglass hull, water immediately starting to flood the interior.

Inigo accepted a second rocket from Bijarani's man. He loaded and prepped, this time aiming for the stern of the boat where the fuel drums stood.

"This one is for you, Abdul," he breathed, and fired.

The missile struck the fuel drums. The fuel ignited as the blast blew the drums apart, sending blazing fuel across the stern of the *Boa Vista*. The flames coiled in a fiery ball, smoke reaching up into the clear sky over the stricken boat.

MCCARTER WAS in the radio room, speaking to Stony Man when the first missile struck. He had to cling on to the desk as the *Boa Vista* rocked violently.

"What was that?" Price asked, her voice rising.

"I think we upset the neighbors," McCarter said.

Smoke had drifted across the window, hiding Inigo's launch. As it cleared, McCarter saw the man targeting the boat with a second load in his RPG-7.

"David? Talk to me."

"We're having a bit of a problem," McCarter said.

The second missile exploded, taking the fuel drums with it and engulfing the stern section of the *Boa Vista* in raging flames.

"Was that an explosion? David…"

"Got to go, luv. Getting a bit dire around here."

McCarter cut the connection.

He barely acknowledged Price's final words as he dropped the sat phone.

"Navy...chopper...your way..."

McCarter snatched up a pair of P-90s as he headed for the main cabin. He handed one to Chaka, then hustled the man out of the cabin and along the port side of the boat.

"Stupid question, Jack, but where are we going?"

"Remember where we came aboard?"

"Yeah."

"We left our rubber dinghy tied to that steel ladder. I'm hoping it's still there."

Chaka stared at the heavy flames spreading across the stern section.

"I'm hoping it hasn't already melted."

"Keep the faith, brother," McCarter said.

"I'm more concerned about not getting my arse cooked like a kebab," Chaka said.

Smoke swirled across the deck as they pushed forward, feeling the savage heat from the burning fuel. They had no choice but to keep moving. McCarter felt his clothing start to smolder. Chaka was just ahead of him, his tall figure moving surprisingly fast despite his wound. He stumbled once and McCarter made a grab for him, physically holding the man upright.

The only good thing about the fire and smoke was that it shielded them from Inigo's launch. McCarter hoped it stayed that way until they got to the rubber boat.

Chaka grabbed at the upper section of the steel ladder and stared down through the drifting smoke.

"It still there?" McCarter asked.

"Yes," Chaka yelled above the roar of the fire.

The overhang of the *Boa Vista*'s stern had protected the rubber craft.

They both felt the *Boa Vista* tilt as the water gushing in through the shattered hull began to affect the boat.

"Go," McCarter yelled.

He took Chaka's SMG as the man swung his legs over the ladder and climbed down into the F470. McCarter passed down the weapons, then hauled himself over the side and slid down the ladder. He yanked at the tether rope and freed the rubber boat, pushing off. Chaka was unable to row, so McCarter locked both oars in place and started to stroke, taking the rubber boat around the tilted stern so they were on the far side, out of Inigo's sight.

There was a secondary reason McCarter wanted to be away from the *Boa Vista.* As the boat sank it would create a powerful sucking motion that might drag the rubber boat in. They could be pulled under by the whirlpool action if they didn't get clear enough.

My day keeps getting better and better, McCarter decided.

The rowing put a great strain on McCarter. His body was still sore from the rough treatment he'd received from Inigo's crew. And his right hand, burning with pain, had started to bleed again.

He glanced across at Chaka, his face glistening with sweat, bruised and bloody, and found himself grinning wildly.

"Chaka, what a bloody sight we must look."

Chaka didn't reply. He was slumped back in the boat, eyes almost closed. The bandage over his shoulder was heavily soaked with fresh blood. His wound was draining his strength to resist.

McCarter dug in with the oars, feeling the boat edge sluggishly clear of the *Boa Vista.* The bigger vessel was sliding down now, foaming surges of water spurting up as air was expelled from the hull. A sudden explosion sent one of the fuel drums into the air, trailing a fiery tail in its wake. It hit the water feet away from the rubber boat, hurling a mass of seawater over it. McCarter felt the rubber craft rock crazily and it almost turned over.

He waited until the boat settled, then started rowing again, muscles protesting. The *Boa Vista* gave up its final hold on staying afloat and went under. A great, surging boil of water rose, bubbling and steaming, and then the boat was gone. And so was the obscuring mix of fire and smoke. As it cleared McCarter found he could see Inigo's launch.

Which meant Inigo could see him and Chaka.

The launch moved ahead. Cautious but heading in their direction.

McCarter picked up one of the P-90s and waited. There was no use rowing any longer. He couldn't outdistance Inigo's launch.

This is a real mess you've got yourself in this time.

He wasn't going to just sit there and hand it to them on a plate. The moment they were in range he would start firing. He had a pair of P-90 SMGs, each holding a full magazine, which gave him a combined total of one hundred 5.7 mm bullets. A nice amount of firepower. Not to be wasted. The problem was Inigo and his crew would be similarly armed.

Chaka stirred restlessly, a soft groan bubbling from his lips.

Though he wanted to check the man out, McCarter refused to take his eyes off the launch that was closing in slowly.

A multitude of thoughts raced through his mind, each one discarded even as it was created. The Briton, survivor of countless standoffs, couldn't imagine how he was about to pull this off.

One man against a launch full of armed shooters. Each and every one of them ready to drop the hammer on him.

And none more determined than Raul Inigo.

McCarter and the rest of Phoenix Force had been responsible for Inigo losing his most important deal. Having the nuclear device snatched away at the last moment.

And then having to lose his precious *Boa Vista*.

The hardest loss of all.

McCarter pushed to his feet, bracing himself against the sway of the rubber boat. He brought his P-90 to his shoulder.

Maybe, he thought, I can get off enough shots to make them turn aside. If I'm lucky I might hit that bugger Inigo.

McCarter stroked the P-90's trigger, felt the weapon jerk in his grip, heard the crackle of autofire.

He saw the launch yaw to one side and knew he had missed. It was simply lining up to offer its shooters a better target.

But the enemy were raising their weapons over his head. Firing blindly.

McCarter had no idea what was happening.

Until a huge dark shadow covered the rubber boat and a powerful downdraft almost knocked him off his feet.

When he looked up he could have screamed with joy as he saw the descending bulk of a Navy Seahawk helicopter. It hovered over him, the massive bulk blotting out the sun. The pounding roar of its turboshaft engines silenced everything in the immediate area.

The HH-60H Seahawk swung around, side-on, and McCarter saw the hatch had been slid open. He saw Rafael Encizo and Calvin James framed in the opening.

McCarter raised his left hand and waved.

The Seahawk made a sudden swing to the right. McCarter saw bullet hits bouncing off the underside of the helicopter's fuselage. The HH-60H was constructed with defense against small-arms fire, but Inigo and his people had made the mistake of attacking a U.S. Navy aircraft. The Seahawk positioned itself sideways-on again.

McCarter saw the configuration of the chopper's door-mounted GAU-17A multibarrel rotary machine gun swivel into position on its pintle, Chief Cochrane on the trigger. The 7.62 mm barrels loosed off a relentless stream of fire. With a muzzle velocity of 2,800 feet per second, the powerful explosions of the gunfire drowned out even the roar of the Seahawk's GE-401C power plants.

McCarter saw the launch vanish in a haze of splintered wood and fiberglass. The terrible destructive power from the hail of 7.62 mm slugs took the launch apart and turned Inigo and the crew into red mist. Their shredded bodies were reduced to bleeding, steaming lumps of flesh and bone. The water around the launch was littered with debris—human and material.

The minigun ceased firing. Only the hot barrel assembly winding down made any sound. The launch began to take on water and started to slowly sink. The torn remains of its crew floated on the bloody surface.

McCarter let the P-90 drop over the side into the water. He disposed of Chaka's weapon, as well. He pressed his damaged right hand against his chest, feeling the warm blood soaking through his shirt.

The Seahawk's line was winched down. It had a canvas cradle on the end. McCarter looped it around Chaka's body, trying to avoid catching his damaged shoulder. He sat and watched as the Kenyan was hoisted on board the helicopter. Then the cable came down for him and he slipped the cradle over his head and under his arms.

"Looking good, man." James grinned as McCarter was helped inside the cabin.

"Hundred percent," McCarter croaked, suddenly feeling every year of his age.

He saw the square box strapped down in the center of the cabin.

"That our bad boy?" he asked.

"The very same," Encizo said.

"Might not have been detonated," Hawkins said, "but that mother has caused some upset."

"And cost some lives," James added.

McCarter felt the Seahawk swing around and power up as it headed out to sea.

"Anybody got a fag?" he asked.

He heard somebody laugh.

"No smoking once the aircraft is in flight," Chief Cochrane said.

"Bloody spoilsports," McCarter grumbled. "You blokes are no fun anymore."

He slid down beside Chaka. The Kenyan glanced at him.

"It is very dangerous to be anywhere near you and your people, Mr. Coyle," he whispered. "But it has been one hell of a ride."

"Anytime you feel bored, just give me a call."

"Cochrane, you're a hell of a chief. That was some shooting. Now can we go home? I think we've all had enough for one day."

"You got it," Cochrane said.

CHAPTER THIRTY-TWO

Israel

Isaac Tauber waited until his office door had closed behind the young agent before he opened the diplomatic pouch received from the President of the United States. He had taken a call from the President, informing him the package was on its way and he was half expecting what the contents would comprise. Even so, he was both surprised and not a little shocked when he did study the enclosed material.

It comprised a number of photographs showing the ex-Russian SADM nuclear device. There was a file holding the documents that had been prepared to be released to the press and the sound bites to be issued on radio. All created to bolster the representation of a preemptive strike against the State of Israel by Iran. A calculated scenario intended to ensure a response from the Israeli military.

Tauber read through the documents and listened to the sound bites. Authenticity screamed at him from the material. He checked the documents over again. They would have fooled him if he hadn't already been assured they were high-quality fakes, even down to the grade and type of paper. When his experts investigated them, they would be unable to recognize them as manufactured documents.

Later Tauber called the telephone number he had been furnished with and spoke to the American President.

"I am still finding it hard to believe," he said. "But seeing the evidence you have provided, Mr. President, what else can I do. This elaborate scheme was created in order to upset the balance here in the region. To bring us to a state of war against Iran, which I have no doubt could have happened. I am trying to see the bigger picture here. And it begs the question—why? And by who?"

"When I have complete answers, Isaac, you will be the first to know."

"Thank you for that, Mr. President. I take it the nuclear device has been rendered harmless?"

"Yes. It is in our possession and will be disarmed. How is your agent?"

"Sharon? He is recovering and being looked after. He asked me to send his thanks and good wishes to your people. I trust they all returned safely?"

"With the minimum of injuries."

"Good. This damned man Inigo? Has he been dealt with?"

"He paid the price for his meddling. We will not be seeing that man again."

"A great deal to be dealt with over the next weeks, Mr. President. Our main threat has, thanks to the United States, been removed in this instance. Without the help of your people, Israel, apart from suffering from the nuclear blast, could easily have been duped into reacting against Iran. That would have been a sad day. The status quo is unlikely to change in the foreseeable future, but a great tragedy has been avoided. But we should learn there will be others who desire to cause such mischief. All of our defenses must be maintained. We are in this for the duration. No weakness must be shown."

"Agreed. I believe we will be talking again over this matter. Be assured, Mr. Tauber, that my administration will pursue those ultimately responsible."

War Room, Stony Man Farm

"Right now," the President said, "I have no answer for Tauber. We may have stopped what Bergstrom and Trent were planning, but coming up with an answer the Israelis are going to be happy with is not going to be easy."

The conference table was seating a full complement. Phoenix Force and Able Team, Barbara Price and Aaron Kurtzman.

And Hal Brognola.

The President was speaking over the telephone conference unit again.

"We know Senator Trent was involved," Price said, "but from what I see and hear the man is still walking around. Isn't this picture wrong, Mr. President?"

The Commander in Chief chuckled softly.

"Hal, I have to say your Ms. Price has a unique way of hitting the spot. In answer to your question, Ms. Price, as of now Trent is starting to feel the pressure. Now that Edgar Bergstrom is no longer at his beck and call and the infrastructure surrounding his scheme has all but fallen away, our esteemed senator is out on a limb. He'll be finding support from his *friends* is disappearing and life will become distinctly chilly. It's surprising how a few well-chosen words and closing doors can isolate someone like Hayden Trent."

"I hope," Lyons said, "it's going to be more than just a slap on the wrist."

"Oh, I'm not finished with Trent yet. The man is responsible for a number of deaths, as well as the machinations of his plan. That will not be forgotten. Nor will it go unpunished. I can promise you that. What Trent doesn't understand yet is the amount of evidence we have against him. The day is not far off when he will feel the weight of responsibility come crashing down on him. I am looking forward to him sitting across from my desk when I deliver it."

"I'm glad to hear that, sir," Price said.

"I had a feeling you would, Ms. Price."

Brognola cleared his throat. "I'd like to offer all our thanks for the personal input during this crisis, Mr. President. Your intervention on our behalf smoothed the way on a couple of occasions."

"Hal, all I did was wave my Presidential stick and push matters along. I'm just happy you all came home safe and sound."

Price was unable to hold back a chuckle as she stared around the table at the various bandages and adhesive patches in evidence, the bruises and grazes showing.

"Sorry, Mr. President," she said, "but it does resemble a Band-Aid convention at the moment."

"I have to say she's correct, sir," Brognola admitted. "I'm taped up pretty good myself."

"Hell," McCarter said, "keeping the peace is a risky business."

"What about our allies?" the President asked. "Ben Sharon and your Kenyan friend?"

"Chaka is recovering," Price said. "He's going to be out of action for some time but last we heard he's making slow progress."

"He will need to be recompensed for his trouble," the President said. "And Sharon?"

"When I last spoke to him," McCarter said, "he sounded happy enough. Lying in the sun, being looked after by pretty nurses."

"We can't forget the ones who didn't make it through," Schwarz said. "Alexis, the guy who started the operation. Or the two CIA agents, Harry Jerome and Chuck Baker."

"Be some time before I forget Baker," Brognola said. "You stand talking to the guy one minute, the next he's gone. Fast as that."

"It's fragile. Life," the President said. "That's why we keep fighting to stay holding on. And do what we can to deal with the threats that keep trying to tear it apart." He cleared his throat. "My thanks again for everything you people have done. This began on uncertain ground and you had little to really go on, but the way you pulled this all together has been an eye-opener."

"You pitched in pretty good yourself, Mr. President," Price said. "If you ever get tired of being stuck behind that desk, I'm sure we could find a spot for you here."

"I may keep you to that, Ms. Price. I just might."

CHAPTER THIRTY-THREE

Bergstrom sat in his office, staring out the shaded window. For the past hour he had been sorting his thoughts and feelings into some kind of order. The whole goddamn house of cards had come tumbling down and the way things were going he would be left with nothing.

Meyer was dead. He had received the news from one of the man's employees. The call had been garbled, the man having difficulty getting a clear picture across. When Bergstrom finally managed to coax a straight explanation out of the man he was shocked at what he heard.

Meyer had received a visit from the mysterious group at his place of business. They had handled his crew and had left him with a warning. If Meyer hadn't panicked and agreed to a meet with those men, they could have settled the matter with a better outcome. Meyer had taken the wrong path, trying to talk his way out of trouble. Luckily, Bergstrom had a man in Meyer's organization acting as a backstop. The guy had put out a signal as Meyer's meeting had got under way, calling in Bergstrom's hitters. The meeting had ended bloodily.

With Meyer dead, one of the connections to Bergstrom had been eliminated. It didn't clear him entirely. He knew there were people trying to make his name fit the frame. They wouldn't give up.

That wasn't the end of it. The harder news didn't reach

Bergstrom until later in the day, and when it did he took some minutes to absorb it.

The nuclear device exchange had been compromised. Inigo's people had been taken down, and so had Bergstrom's own team, there to take possession of the bomb.

The deal was off. Hayden Trent's plan to create chaos had been stopped.

The weeks of planning and organization all for nothing.

Time and money expended.

People dead.

And an ending in sight.

Not a pleasant one.

There was panic initially. Bergstrom sat in his office looking at possible outcomes. Even expecting his door to crash open and finding himself under arrest.

Then reasoning had filtered in through the panic. Maybe he could move out of this without harm.

Meyer was dead.

So was Laker, the man who had created the false documents.

The French agent, Alexis, Jerome and even Chuck Baker were dead.

A long list, but with each of them removed, the connection to himself became thinner.

Bergstrom had been thinking about how the rumors had even started. The plan had been kept fairly close in-house. Apart from himself and Trent there had been no leaks he could put his finger on. He was certain the first whispers had come from abroad. Somewhere in the Middle East itself, where his off-the-books black ops people had been in place. Security. Secrets. Call it whatever. Those things were talked about among the people involved. It was part of the human condition. It only took a lapse in protocol for words to be overheard, then picked over and passed on.

Conversation in a street café by a couple of his own men.

Pillow talk with some girl. Innocent at the time. Passed on in conversation. Casual.

But once picked up by an interested party. Perhaps a scrap sold on to a buyer.

Alexis the French agent.

Rashid the information peddler.

Enough to arouse interest.

Even Bergstrom's covert meeting with Inigo.

It all started to build into something substantial. Small pieces that grew into something larger.

A need to put a stop to rumors. Perhaps a heavy-handed reaction that led to the involvement of the mystery group.

The ball had been set rolling and it seemed to have gathered size as it did.

So, what happened now?

He imagined he could say goodbye to his payoff from Trent. The senator would cut all funding once he learned about the failure of the exchange. Knowing the man as he did, Bergstrom imagined Trent would be cutting off everything to do with the plan. He was going to need to explain to his backers what had happened. Bergstrom could see that ending in tears. He didn't have a great deal of background on some of Trent's cronies, but if they were like Trent himself, losing money as well as prestige would hit them harder than most.

Bergstrom would not have been at all surprised if he found his access to Trent cut off, as well. The man would make sure he distanced himself from any fallout if facts were brought into the open.

Bergstrom hoped that didn't happen on a personal basis. His career might survive if he could keep the news at a low level. It wasn't a matter of record and the only individuals concerned were within his black ops division. If he came out of this untouched he could maintain his position and with time he could bury the details.

He wasn't in the clear yet.

His mystery group was still out there. They had got as close as Meyer. That suggested they might have eyes on him now. If so, he would need to watch his own back. They didn't seem the kind to give up. So, he needed to protect himself.

That brought him to Inigo. The man had already professed he wanted the team, as well. In that case Bergstrom had a strong ally on his side.

If he could get in contact with the man.

Inigo seemed to have dropped off the map.

Bergstrom had failed to make contact with Inigo. He was not answering any of his phones. Which was usual in itself.

Bergstrom called the *Boa Vista* again.

Nothing. Even if he was not around there was always someone on board. A flickering worry rose in his mind. Bergstrom searched his call list and rang one of the alternative numbers he had for Raul Inigo. The number would get him through to Inigo's accountant. Bergstrom had used the number before when he was negotiating deals. The phone rang out for some time before it was picked up.

"Who is this?"

Bergstrom recognized the man's voice.

"Bergstrom," he said. "Is that you, Manolo?"

"Yes."

"I can't make contact with Inigo. I need to speak with him."

"Then you haven't heard? Inigo is dead. We only received the news a couple of hours ago."

"How? What happened?"

"We are still trying to get the full story. He was making a transfer on your current negotiation. The exchange was compromised and the receiving team were killed. The package was seized. Inigo barely escaped in his helicopter. The *Boa Vista* was anchored off the Pakistani coast. The only detail we received was from his helicopter pilot. There was some kind of firefight on the water. Inigo was trying to reclaim the *Boa Vista*. It had been boarded. The pilot said Inigo was losing the fight so he hit the boat with rockets and sank it. The pilot saw Inigo's launch hit by machine-gun fire from a large helicopter before he flew away. He said the launch and everyone in it was torn to pieces."

Bergstrom ended the call without another word.

Now it *was* all over. Even Inigo was dead.

It was down to him and Senator Hayden Trent.

His phone rang. Bergstrom picked it up.

"I just heard," Trent said. "A call from a friend overseas. Amazing how bad news travels so fast."

"So, what do we do now?"

"Edgar, don't be such a dismal Johnny. We need to clear the air. Meet me at the club. Seven. Go home. Put on your dinner jacket and we'll make plans."

The phone clicked.

Bergstrom picked up his briefcase and stepped out of his office.

"I'm going," he said.

Jay Callow glanced up, nodding. "See you tomorrow, sir."

BERGSTROM LIVED in a Colonial-style house standing in quiet surroundings a few miles from Falls Church. The area was peaceful, surrounded by lightly wooded acres, the houses well spaced apart. Although the house was large for someone who lived alone—Bergstrom had been married many years earlier but his work for the CIA meant he kept unsociable hours and he and his wife had parted amicably—he enjoyed the solitude. He had been planning to move but with the failure of the Trent scheme that would need to be put on hold.

He parked outside the front door and let himself in. He realized he had time for a shower before he changed. Afterward he dressed slowly, looking at himself in the full-length bedroom mirror. He admitted he did look good in an evening suit.

Finally ready, he stepped outside into the quiet dusk and climbed in the SUV. He swung the car around the drive, toward the open gates.

The explosion shattered the peaceful surroundings, the heavy blast lighting up the graying sky. Edgar Bergstrom and his SUV were blown apart. Burning debris littered his drive. Very little was found of Bergstrom himself. The bomb had been placed beneath the driver's seat. The explosive charge used was far stronger than the one that had destroyed Chuck Baker's vehicle.

When the bomb squad started to sift through the collected remnants of the bomb they were lucky enough to find part of the mechanism. One of the techs had worked on the aftermath of the Baker bombing.

He saw the piece and knew almost immediately it was the work of the same bomb maker.

Senator Hayden Trent was eliminating all ties with anyone involved in the failed plot.

He was feeling reasonably secure.

In reality he was far from being safe....

* * * * *

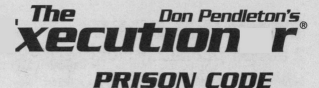

The Don Pendleton's
Executioner®

PRISON CODE

**Terror infiltrates New York's most
lethal prison....**

When a plot to unleash weapons of mass destruction on
U.S. soil is discovered in a coded message, all clues
lead to the country's most notorious prison in upstate
New York. With time running out, Mack Bolan goes in
undercover as an inmate to find out who's behind the
attack and stop it from happening.

**GOLD
EAGLE**®

Available May wherever books are sold.

GEX414

TAKE 'EM FREE
2 action-packed novels plus a mystery bonus

NO RISK
NO OBLIGATION TO BUY

Don Pendleton's Mack Bolan

Apocalypse Ark

Cult devotees unleash a crusade of terror straight at the Vatican....

It's Day of Judgment time for the Holy Church as militant members of a secret cult plot to destroy the Vatican and usher in the Apocalypse. These so-called soldiers of God arrive armed with a weapon of "divine power," which they claim is the biblical Ark of the Covenant stolen from its holy shrine in Ethiopia. As the cult's hellish agenda spills blood in cities across the globe, Mack Bolan's mandate becomes to neutralize the threat by direct means. And he demands the ultimate sacrifice from those willing to kill for their faith—death by Executioner.

Available June wherever books are sold.

GSB158